Marigold

*Also by Grace Livingston Hill
in Large Print:*

Astra
The Best Man
Bright Arrows
Cloudy Jewel
Ladybird
Partners
The Red Signal
Stranger Within the Gates
The Substitute Guest
The White Flower
The Gold Shoe

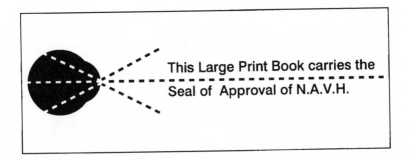

This Large Print Book carries the
Seal of Approval of N.A.V.H.

Marigold

Grace Livingston Hill

Thorndike Press • Thorndike, Maine

LP
FIC
HILL
G

Published in 2000 by arrangement with Munce Publishing.

Thorndike Press Large Print Romance Series.

The tree indicium is a trademark of Thorndike Press.

The text of this Large Print edition is unabridged.
Other aspects of the book may vary from the original edition.

Set in 16 pt. Plantin by Minnie B. Raven.

Printed in the United States on permanent paper.

Library of Congress Cataloging-in-Publication Data

Hill, Grace Livingston, 1865–1947.
    Marigold / Grace Livingston Hill.
       p.   cm.
    ISBN 0-7862-3022-3 (lg. print : hc : alk. paper)
    1. Washington (D.C.) — Fiction. 2. Kidnapping —
Fiction. 3. Large type books. I. Title.
PS3515.I486 M29   2000
  813′.52—dc21
                                                            00-047926

Marigold

1

Marigold brought the big white box into her mother's bedroom and put it on the bed. Her eyes were shining and her lovely red-gold hair caught the sunlight and flamed gloriously, lighting up her happy brown eyes with topaz glints.

"Come, Mother, and look. I brought it home with me. I couldn't wait to have it sent up. I wanted so much to have you see it at once."

The mother came and stood beside the bed smiling, with just a bit of a troubled look in the deeps of her eyes.

"It's a lovely box, anyway, satin-smooth, and looks as if it ought to hold a wedding dress at least," she said wistfully.

"Yes, isn't it!" said Marigold gaily. "And to think I have a dress in the house from that wonderful shop! I never thought that would happen to me! The best part of the box to me is that magic name on the top, 'François.' I've dreamed of having that happen!"

"Dear child!" said her mother with a sad little smile. "But, do you think it is so much better than other places that aren't so expensive? I've always thought we had some

7

lovely things made for you here at home."

"Of course you have, you dear! I never discounted them. It's only that I wanted this one to be, well, different from anything ever. I wanted it to have a big name back of it. And then there's always some little touch that can't be achieved except by those great ones. You know that, Mother. Oh, Mother dear! Don't look so grieved. The things you've always had made for me have been wonderful, and some of them much much prettier than any I ever saw from the great man dressmakers of the earth. Some of those are positively ugly, I think, and yet they do have that something about them that nobody else can quite achieve, and only the initiated recognize."

The mother smiled.

"I suppose so," she said with a sigh. "But go on and open your box. I'm curious to see the garment that is worth a whole hundred and fifty dollars. I hope it comes up to my idea of what it ought to be."

"I'm sure you'll think it does," said the girl with happy eagerness in her face. "It's wonderful!"

She lifted the cover slowly, such a happy light in her face that her mother was busy looking at her instead of watching for the first glimpse of the Paris frock.

Marigold put the cover down on the floor, and turned back the satiny folds of tissue paper. Even the tissue paper seemed to have a rare quality. Then she stood back and watched her mother's face.

"There!" she said, "isn't that gorgeous?"

The dress lay folded carefully, showing its lovely quality even at the first glance, rich, glistening, thick white taffeta, memories of yesterday woven into its texture and silvery finish. At the slender waistline was knotted a supple velvet girdle, soft as thistledown, in deep vivid crimson, with long silken fringe at the ends, and on one shoulder a dark deep velvet rose to match.

Marigold's eyes were like a child's with a new doll she was exhibiting.

Mrs. Brooke caught her breath in a soft exclamation of admiration.

"It is very lovely," she said, "it looks — almost regal!" And she gave a quick glance at her daughter and then back to the dress, as if trying to harmonize them. "You've never worn that deep shade of crimson. I'm wondering —" she studied her daughter's vivid face and then turned back to the dress.

"How will it go with my red hair?" asked the girl joyously. "Wait till you see it on me. I'm some sight!"

"Your hair is not really red, Marigold,

only reddish-gold," answered the mother. "It really goes with anything."

"Well, you ought to have heard the saleslady rave over the combination," laughed the girl. "She positively waxed eloquent."

"She probably wanted to sell the dress!" said the mother wisely. "But put it on. You can't always tell beforehand. Wait! Let me spread a sheet down on the floor! You mustn't run any risks with that lovely thing!"

When the sheet was spread Marigold slipped out of her little green knitted dress and into the rich shimmering evening frock and turned excitedly to face her mother.

The mother stood studying her daughter critically.

"Yes, it's good," she assented. "I hadn't realized that you could wear that color before, but it's rather wonderful. It does something to you, makes you look as if the light of the sunset were shining on your face."

"I thought you'd like it," said the girl in satisfaction.

"Yes, it's very beautiful, and very becoming," said Mrs. Brooke. "Turn around and let me see the back."

Half-shamedly the girl laughed.

"I'm afraid you won't like the back so well," she apologized, twisting her head to look over her shoulder at her mother. "It's a low back, of course, but I couldn't get any other. Everybody, simply *every*body wears them. I couldn't find one without. And really, Mother, this was the most conservative back they had!"

"Oh *my dear!*" said her mother sorrowfully. "I couldn't think of you wearing a back like that! Your father would have objected to it seriously. He hated such nakedness. There was a woman in our congregation who used sometimes to put on evening dress for a church social quite out of place of course, and he disliked it so. But even that wasn't like this. I can hear him now comically saying: 'Mrs. Butler had her dress trimmed with real vertebrae, didn't she?' "

Marigold laughed half-heartedly.

"Oh, but Mother, that was a long while ago. He wouldn't have felt that way now. Why you even see low sun-backs in the daytime, and on the beach, and everywhere. And nobody has evening dresses made high in the back."

"Yes, I suppose so," sighed the mother, troubled. "But couldn't we fit in a piece of my real lace, or perhaps get some of the material and do something with that back?"

"Mother! How simply *dread*ful! You would take all the style away, and ruin it! Everybody would be laughing at me behind my back. No, Mother dear, you'll have to get used to such things. Nobody thinks anything about backs today. What's a back, anyway? Just a back."

"Well, but backs are ugly!" said the mother with troubled gaze. "I don't see why they do it! And it makes me ashamed to think of my girl going around before a lot of people unclothed that way."

The color rolled up impatiently into Marigold's lovely cheeks.

"Mother, how ridiculous! You don't realize that everybody wears such things nowadays and nobody thinks a thing about it! If Father had been alive today he would have had to change some of his ideas. In those days it wasn't done, but it is now. I'm sure Father wouldn't think a thing of it if he were alive today."

"I wonder —" said Mrs. Brooke with a troubled frown.

Marigold turned to face her mother again.

"Mother, isn't that thin line of crimson just exquisite, falling down against the thick white silk? I think that fringe is adorable the way it falls down the skirt. You do like the dress, don't you Mother?"

She lifted a charming face eager for approval, and her mother's anxious face relaxed.

"Yes, it is indeed beautiful, and is surprisingly becoming."

But there was something in her mother's tone that did not quite satisfy Marigold.

"Mother! You don't quite like it! What is it that you don't like besides the low back? I knew you wouldn't like that, but any dress I could buy that would be suitable would have had that objection. But there's something else, come, own up! I know your tone of approval, and this isn't just hearty."

"Oh, my dear!" said the mother with a trembling little smile. "No, child, I find nothing else to criticize. It is very beautiful and very distinguished-looking. I'm only questioning whether a quiet little Christian girl — I suppose you still call yourself that, don't you? — has the right to spend all her substance on one dress that is so perishable, and at most can only be worn to advantage half a dozen times. You couldn't possibly get enough others of the same standard to make up a whole wardrobe."

"Mother!" said the girl, her sweet face suddenly shadowed, "you are spoiling the whole thing! I shall never want to wear it now!"

She turned abruptly towards the window,

a quick flush mounting over her fair skin to her forehead.

"My dear! I didn't mean to hurt you! But doesn't it seem too bad to spend almost everything you have in a lump sum this way? The dress is wonderful, but I'm quite sure we could have copied it, and made it just as lovely. I even know how to put fringe like that on the girdle. I've often done it. I'm afraid you'll be sorry afterwards that the money is all gone."

"No, Mother, you don't understand. I had to have something that was as good as anybody's, that is if I'm to go to this affair at all. I have to have it for sort of 'moral support,' you know; this first time among Laurie's friends. It isn't as if they were my friends whom I have always known. Those people on the north side of the city are entire strangers to me, and rather inclined to be snobbish. Laurie isn't, of course, or he wouldn't be going with me. But his mother has never called, nor recognized me in the slightest way till now, and I feel as if I want to show her that I know what is fitting for such an occasion as well as she does. I don't want to let Laurie down. His mother is not like him. She's very aristocratic and exclusive and I don't want Laurie to be ashamed of me. I don't want his family pitying me and saying what a shabby girl he goes with. I want his mother to see that I know how to dress just as well as she does."

"Oh, my dear! That's not a very good motive to own to, is it? She with her millions and you with your two hundred dollars! If Laurie's mother's admiration is worth winning I'm quite sure she would think far more of you for dressing within your means than for aping millionaires, especially since you can't keep up this style of dressing."

Marigold was silent and troubled for a moment.

"But Mother, I shan't need to," she said with a quick-drawn breath. "It isn't in the least likely there will be more invitations like this. Besides, I can put away a little money now and then for another occasion that might come up. And, too, Mother, I'm not going beyond my means getting this one dress. Aunt Carolyn told me to spend it on something I really wanted, some luxury, something frivolous if I liked, and this is the thing I wanted with all my heart. This was only a hundred and fifty dollars, and there'll be enough left for gloves and slippers and maybe an evening wrap. Oh, Mother, you're spoiling it all! You don't understand! It's a sort of an 'if-I-perish-I-perish' state of mind I'm in. I've got to go dressed so that Laurie's mother can't criticize me, or I won't go at all. If I don't pass inspection, well, she'll never be bothered with me again, that's all, but I'm going right or not at all."

The mother sighed and studied her daughter's flushed, lovely face a moment, a compassionate look in her own eyes.

"Dear! Don't look that way! In a way I do understand how you feel of course, but I'm afraid it's not right. I'm only sorry for you that you seem to be tangled up in a situation that makes you feel you must step out of your natural way of living. You know your fortune in life has not been set by God in the environment of a millionaire's daughter. Your father was a plain minister of the gospel, and when he was called away from earth suddenly, he had no millions, nor even thousands to leave behind. All this grandeur just doesn't seem consistent with your sensible life so far. But there! Don't look so sorrowful! One dress isn't going to wreck your fortune, even though it does take all you have, and perhaps the experience will be worth a good deal to you. Come, since the dress is bought we might as well enjoy it. Forget what I've said and be happy."

But Marigold stood staring out of the window at the bare brown trees unseeingly, her eyes filling with sudden tears.

"Oh, child!" said her mother in dismay. "You mustn't cry! You'll ruin that dress. Here! Wait, I have a handkerchief. Let me mop you up, and then for pity's sake take off the dress. We can't have it ruined before it's ever worn. That would be disastrous. I never meant to make you feel that way, dearest. Forgive me!"

As she talked Mrs. Brooke was dabbing Marigold's eyes softly with her own handkerchief.

"There! Take it off quickly before I start you off again! Wait! I'll help you!" Marigold began to giggle hysterically as she emerged from the enveloping silk.

When the dress was hung on the softest hanger the house afforded, swinging from the rod in the open closet, and Marigold had donned her plain little knit dress again, they stood back and looked at it.

"I so wanted to have you like it!" sighed the girl as she looked at it wistfully. "It seemed to me the prettiest evening dress I had ever seen."

"But I do like it, dear. It's a gorgeous garment, the grandest I have ever laid eyes on. It wasn't a question of like, it was a question of wisdom and suitability."

"I know," said the girl, her lips quivering just a tiny bit again, "but Mother, I thought

17

it *was* wise and suitable. There's no question about its suitability for the occasion, Mother. I've read a number of times in the society columns, the kind of clothes they wear at Mrs. Trescott's affairs."

"I didn't mean suitable for Mrs. Trescott, Marigold, I meant suitable for you, a plain little girl who has to earn her living. Won't even Mrs. Trescott question the suitability of such a dress for you?"

"Well, but Mother, if I'm going there at all, oughtn't I to go right? And if I'm going with Laurie to things I've got to be dressed the way he would want to see me."

The mother's brows drew together with a troubled frown again.

"*Why*, Marigold? Does he mean so much to you? Dear, are you planning to marry Laurie?"

"Mother!" said Marigold, her cheeks flaming suddenly into brilliant color. "Why, *Mother!* He hasn't even asked me to — yet!"

"*Yet?* Then you're expecting him to? Dear, I hate to force your confidence, but a good deal depends on your attitude toward the question. If he does ask you are you wanting to say yes?"

"Oh, Mother!" said the girl with quick panic in her eyes, "I haven't got as far as that yet. I'm only having a good time."

18

"Well, that's what I was afraid of."

"Why, Mother, you don't think a girl should go ahead and plan things like that, do you, not till she's been asked?"

"A girl ought to know whether she *could* love a man before she lets him go too far in falling in love with her. She has no right to lead him on if she knows she cannot care for him. You know, dear, you have been going pretty steadily with Laurie for several months now and people are beginning to couple your names, and to question, and to take things for granted. I only want you to know yourself. When it comes to spending a hundred fifty dollars for one dress, it seems to me you must be pretty sure of yourself."

The dear eyes were clouded again, and this time the tears really came.

"You don't like Laurie, do you, Mother?" she charged unexpectedly, whirling about and facing her mother with beseeching eyes. "He's so gay and — *dear*, I don't see how you can help liking him!" and the tears poured down with unexpected swiftness.

"I didn't say I didn't like him, dear child!" said the mother distressed. "Oh, I never meant to make you feel badly. I just wanted to warn you. Of course Laurie is likable. He certainly is gay — yes, and dear in his ways — I understand how you feel. But I scarcely know him well enough to judge whether he is suitable for my precious girl. He drops in here gaily, has a pleasant word and a smile, flashes his handsome eyes, smiles charmingly, smooths his beautiful dark hair; and he's courteous and delightful in every way for the five minutes while he is waiting for you. Then you flit off together, and hours later I hear him linger at the door a minute when he brings you back. How can I know?"

"Oh, Mother! I didn't realize! Of course you don't really know him, do you? Couldn't we ask him here to dinner some night?"

"We *could*," said the mother thoughtfully. "Are you sure he would want to come? Of course, now since his mother has invited you, it will be easier for us to invite him — *perhaps*. But dear, I want you to face the future, be sure of every step you take, and not rush into something that will bring you sorrow after the glamour has departed."

"Mother! Isn't there any real love in the world that lasts? All glamour doesn't depart, does it?"

"There certainly is a true love that lasts, and that's what I want you to have, dear. That's why I'm daring to invade the privacy of your heart and warn you."

Marigold pondered perplexedly.

"But why are you especially worried about Laurie, Mother? When Eastman Hunter, and Earle Browning used to come here a good deal, you never said anything, nor when John Potter came. You seemed to take it all perfectly naturally, and counted them my good friends. You didn't probe me to see if I was going to get married right away. I wasn't so much younger than I am now. It was only a little over a year ago. Did you like any of them better than Laurie?"

"No, not as well," said the mother frankly, "but dear, Laurie is of another class. It is always a serious question when young people of different classes try to come together. Once in a great while such a marriage is a happy one, but too often it is not. I want you to be really happy, darling!"

"Mother, I didn't think you believed in classes and aristocracy!" charged Marigold unhappily. "I thought you thought we were just as good as anybody else."

"I'm not talking about one being better than another, child. I'm thinking of the different ways of upbringing."

"Laurie has been beautifully brought up," said the girl proudly. "He has more real courtesy and culture than anybody I know."

"Yes," said the mother thoughtfully, "as far as courtesy goes he is charming! But it isn't just courtesy and culture I mean. There are other things, things of the world. Marigold, you know yourself he has been brought up by the standards of the world, and he considers worldly things first."

"Oh, but Mother, that wouldn't make any difference with us. He always wants to do what I want. That is, *almost* always," cried the girl.

The mother smiled sadly.

"That's very nice now, dear," she said, "but would it last? And have you realized, my girl, that you yourself have let down some of your own standards since you began to go with Laurie?"

Marigold dropped her glance and flushed uneasily.

"Oh, well, not in things that really matter," she said. "I don't think it's right to be too straight-laced. I found Laurie didn't understand my attitude at all, and I didn't see that a few trifles were important. He doesn't insist on much. And anyway what's that got to do with my new dress?"

The mother studied her a little sadly and then with a sigh said:

"Well, dear, let's put it all away and just enjoy your dress. I've been looking at it while we talked and the richness of it is growing on me. It is really distinguished-looking. The silk is a beautiful texture. It must have been especially woven for the house that made the dress. We don't get silk like that in the stores today. It's more like the quality of my grandmother's wedding dress. And I like that way the girdle is brought around the waist, and the line of crimson fringe falling on the heavy white. It's most unusual."

Suddenly Marigold came up behind her mother and flung her arms around her neck.

"Oh, you dear precious Mother!" she cried. "You're rare! You always did cheer me up just at the last minute when I'm ready to hate myself or something I've done. You're a good sport if there ever was one. I know you don't like that dress, not as much as you'd like to like it. You think it's all out of place for me, and perhaps you're right. At least if I had only myself to consider, I'm sure you are. But I just felt I must have it. You see, Mother, the woman who sold it to me showed me the dresses Laurie's mother and sister have ordered, and I know what I'm up against. She said this one came in after theirs were ordered, or she was sure Gwendolyn would have taken it instead of the one she got, for she had asked for white with a touch of this new red about it, and was disappointed that they didn't have it.

However, her own is lovely! It's pale apricot malines, frilled till it looks like foam. She'll be a dream in it. She has dark hair and eyes, like Laurie's."

Mrs. Brooke watched her daughter's changing vivid expression with troubled eyes. How thoroughly intrigued her dear child was with all that belonged to Lawrence Trescott! Was her warning too late? Should she have done something about it sooner? Or was she perhaps mistaken? Could it be that this was the way her child's life was planned? Could Laurie bring Marigold the best happiness? Was he worthy of her? She could not bear that there should be heartbreak in store for her wonderful little girl.

"You're not listening to me, Mother!" charged the daughter reproachfully, "your eyes are quite far away!"

"Oh, yes, I'm listening. Apricot malines would be lovely on anybody. Will she wear pearls with it, I wonder?"

"No," said Marigold eagerly, "the saleswoman said she was wearing rose quartz, a long rope of rose quartz beads, with a buckle and bracelet to match. She had the buckle there. She showed it to me. It's most unusual. Queer for her, isn't it, to chose semi-precious stones when she might have real pearls! Or diamonds! But things like that are worn now instead of the real precious gems. And I can see that there's something about the depths of rose quartz that gives just the right light and sparkle to the malines."

Her mother smiled whimsically.

"Fortunate isn't it, that diamonds are not necessary, or where would you be? We have only a small diamond pin and my engagement ring."

"Oh, Mother, you would suggest that I would demand diamonds! Well, if I wanted them I might get them at the five-and-ten!" she giggled suddenly.

"Dear child!"

The mother stooped and touched her lips to the fair young forehead, and tried to drive the shadows away from her own eyes. If her girl was making a mistake, at least she herself would try to act gallantly through the experience.

"Oh, heavenly Father, keep my child! Guide her! Save her from sorrow!" her heart prayed, even while she entered gaily into the merry talk as they prepared the evening meal.

They were just sitting down to the table when there came a ring at the door, a boy with a special delivery letter!

"A letter from Aunt Marian," announced Marigold coming back eagerly. "Special delivery, too. Open it quick and see if anything is the matter."

Aunt Marian was Mrs. Brooke's older sister, an invalid, who lived with her married daughter in Washington.

Dear Mary (she wrote),

Can't you come down and spend my birthday with me? Elinor is going with her husband on a short trip to Bermuda and she hates to leave me alone, especially on my birthday. If you and Marigold could come and make me a little visit while they are gone and stay over a few more days to see them when they get back it would be wonderful. Do you realize that I haven't seen you now for four years — though we're not so far apart? My heart is "just a wearyin' " for you. *Can't* you come? And I haven't seen Marigold since she was a wee child. It isn't right.

I'm hurrying this off because I want you to have plenty of time to plan to come, and I shall await your answer eagerly. My birthday you may remember is the fifth. Remember I'm sick and I'm getting old.

Lovingly and eagerly,
Marian

Marigold watched her mother as she read the letter aloud, and saw the wistfulness in it.

"Mother, you ought to go!" she said vehemently, when the letter was finished. "*I* can't go of course because that's the night of the Trescott party, but there's no reason in the world why you can't go, and stay a whole week or two. It isn't right you shouldn't see more of your only sister!"

Mrs. Brooke drew a deep sigh and gave a faint little smile of negation.

"I couldn't possibly afford it now, dear. It costs quite a lot to go down, even on the bus, and the rent will be due just before that. You see, having to get a new fur collar on my coat set me back a good deal this quarter, and there's no telling whether there will be any income from my few investments next month or not. Things have been terribly tied up, you know. Besides, dear, I wouldn't want to be away the day you go to that party. I want to see you dressed and ready. I want to be sure that everything is right about you, and I want to have the memory of you in your wonderful gown. Then I want to be waiting for you when you get back and hear you tell all about it. I like to see the first light in your eyes before the joy has faded and life settled down into the humdrum again."

"Oh, you dear sentimentalist!" laughed Marigold. "Those things would all keep! And as for the money, you make me ashamed. If I can afford to spend a hundred and fifty dollars for a grand gown you certainly can afford the few dollars it costs to go down to Washington for your sister's birthday, especially when she asks you in that special way."

"No, dear, it's quite impossible!" said Mrs. Brooke firmly. "I would need a lot of new things to go down there, and I'm not going now. Perhaps in the spring I'll be able to manage it. And I know your aunt will understand — your first grand party! She will know I would need to be here! She was that way about her Elinor, too!"

"But Mother, you make me feel very selfish."

"No, dear. You mustn't feel that way. It's all right. You let me manage this!"

And just then Laurie rushed in unexpectedly.

"Come on, Mara. I've got tickets for the ice carnival. Get your skates and we'll make the first number!" In almost no time Marigold was gone and her mother was left alone to read her sister's letter and shed a few quiet tears on her own account. Then she sighed and thought of her girl and wondered. Was she foolish to worry this way about Marigold? Such a good dear Marigold, always thinking of her, and wanting everything happy for everybody.

But Marigold was off skimming the ice at the ice palace, her cheeks as bright as roses, her eyes like two stars and the red gold hair flaming gaily, as she glided along. For Laurie's arm was about her, and Laurie's handsome face was looking down at her admiringly, and back at home there hung a wondrous garment from the House of François, ready for her appearance at the Trescott party. Life seemed good to Marigold. Why worry about anything? It was a mother's duty to worry, perhaps, but it would all come out right in the end. She was Laurie's girl, and that was all that she cared about now.

2 That very afternoon over in the Trescott mansion, Laurie Trescott's mother was sitting at her desk with a pile of letters and papers before her, talking to her sister-in-law, Irene Trescott, who had just run in to talk over a few plans connected with the party that was to come off the next week.

Out in the hall, Maggie, a colored woman who was sometimes called in for an extra to supplement the regular staff of servants, was washing the baseboards and wiping up the floor after some electricians had finished the work of installing some new outlets. The door stood wide open and Maggie could hear all that went on, though she hadn't been much interested to listen until she heard a name she knew.

"Well, Adele, how are you getting on with your arrangements?" asked Irene. "Everything's going as well as all your affairs do, I suppose? But say, Adele, what's all this I hear about Laurie having a little rowdy girl and you inviting her to the party? Is that true?"

"I don't know that she's a *rowdy*," said Adele facing her sister-in-law and answering in a voice that had suddenly congealed.

30

"I really don't know much about her except that she's respectable. Poor but respectable — at least they *say* so! She's the daughter of a deceased clergyman, I understand, without a penny to her name. Imagine it! Going around with my Laurie! And the foolish boy doesn't in the least realize what he's doing! He's just having a good time of course, but with quite an impossible girl. Her name is Marigold Brooke! You wouldn't know her of course. She's not in the limelight, thank goodness! Not yet, anyway, and shan't be if I can help it!"

"Then why is she invited to the party? Or isn't that so?"

"Yes, I invited her. Of course. Laurie wished it, and I didn't think it wise to argue with him. I just invited her as I would have invited any other girl he put on his list. I didn't wish to put up an opposition. Laurie is very headstrong, you know. He takes after his father in that. And if he thought I didn't want her it would be just like him to say he wouldn't come either. He never can stand being driven, you have to humor him in everything, or else you don't get anywhere."

"Well, I think you're making a very grave mistake," said Irene. "I always did think you were too easy with Laurie. However, that's not my business. But I can't understand inviting her if you don't want to foster the friendship."

"You don't know my plan, Irene. I'm doing this with a purpose. Have you never heard of the expulsive power of a new affection? They had a woman in the Club the other day who talked about that. At least, maybe it was a book by that name, or something someone had said, I'm not sure which. I was making out my list of guests and didn't listen much, but I caught that phrase and thought it was a good one. I think I can make a great deal of use of it in various ways. But it especially struck me, because it is just what I'm trying to work in Laurie's case. Irene, have you heard who I'm having as my guest of honor? Robena DeWitte! Do you know her? Did you ever see her? Well, you've something to anticipate, then. She's the most regal girl I've ever met, perfectly stunning looking, and dresses like a queen, besides being fabulously rich. She's graceful, accomplished, athletic. She flies her own plane, and is good in all sports, has the most entrancing figure, and is very clever. You've heard of her of course. Well, she's my drawing card. With Robena there, I'm not afraid any mere preacher's daughter can get any attention from my son. I shall give her just a hint of how the land lies, and I'm quite sure she's clever enough to turn the trick. When this little simple child of a preacher that Laurie has taken on, appears on the scene, she'll certainly find out where she doesn't belong! And so, I flatter myself, will my son. Laurie is very quick to see a thing when it is presented to him in the right light. Just put that poor little common child in this environment and he'll see soon enough what a mistake she is. And it will all come about in the most natural way, you see, without my having to expostulate with him at all. He'll just see he was wrong and stop going with her. There's nothing like showing up the wrong girl side by side with the right one to bring a young man to his senses!"

"Well, you're making a very grave mistake, Adele," said the sharp sister-in-law complacently. "I take it you haven't seen 'the wrong girl' as you call her. But when you do you'll be surprised. She's a raving little beauty and no mistake, and you won't work anything on Laurie that way, mark my words, for Robena isn't in it beside Marigold Brooke."

"Do you mean you've seen her, Irene?" asked the alarmed mother. "Do you mean you know her?"

"Well, I can't be said to know her, exactly," said the woman of the world, "but I've seen her plenty, and I can't say Laurie's taste in beauty is so bad. She's Betty Lou Petrie's teacher in school, and Betty Lou is perfectly crazy about her. Every time I go over to Petries' I hear it. 'Miss Marigold says this,' and 'Miss Marigold says that,' and Eva Petrie says the children just think the sun rises and sets in her. And she's got the most gorgeous hair! My word! If they wanted anybody to pose for an angel's picture I should say she would be simply stunning! Robena is no match for her in beauty."

"Oh, dear me! But Irene, not in this environment, you wouldn't think would you? She wouldn't have the clothes, would she?"

"She's clever!" said Irene dryly. "She'd get the clothes, if she had to make them, and she'd make you like them too! She'd wear them as if they came from Paris."

"But, how *could* she? A little country minister's daughter! A school teacher!"

"I tell you she's clever, and she's out to win whatever she wants! She's got whatever it is that draws!"

"Gracious, why didn't you tell me this before I invited her? I didn't have an idea it was anything like that."

"What did you think your son was, a dummy? Going with a girl who wasn't a good-looker nor a good dresser? Laurie knows the right thing when he sees it! He's nobody's dummy."

"Well, I don't think it was very kind of you not to warn me!"

"Look here, Adele, I hadn't an idea you'd do such a crazy thing as to invite Marigold to your affair. I thought your line was ignoring her, and besides you never take my advice when I give it, so why should I bother? But I will say this, if you want Laurie to walk your way, take his pocket money away. That's the only way in the world you can curb that lad. He just can't exist without money."

Maggie, out in the hall, had rubbed so hard at one spot on the baseboard that she had almost eradicated the paint, and she had knelt on her stiff rheumatic knees so long that she could hardly struggle her over-plumpness into a standing position. But she lumbered up at last, took herself reluctantly down the back stairs, and presently went her troubled way home, going over and over what she had heard, and wondering if she ought to tell Miss Marigold. Dear pretty little sweet Miss Marigold, who always had a kind word for her and a smile, and never scolded when she broke a trinket cleaning her dressing table! Mean woman, calling that pretty child a "rowdy girl." Maggie's blood boiled.

Marigold, when she got home after her pleasant evening with Laurie, glimpsed her beautiful dress hanging in the closet, with a throb of pride. How wonderful to own a dress like that! She would show them all that she knew how to enter their world in the right garb, even if she was a minister's daughter and wasn't rich! How proud Laurie would be of her!

But when she turned out her light, after a hurried prayer, and crept into her bed, a thousand little demons jumped up and hopped around her, tormenting her and driving sleep from her eyes. Why had she thought she ought to buy as expensive a dress as that, anyway? And how was she ever to enjoy the party knowing that her mother could not afford to take even a brief holiday with her only sister?

In vain did she tell herself that she had to do this for Laurie's sake. The night grew long and wearisome as she argued things out that she had never questioned before. Had it been Mother's searching questions that started her off, or the fact that Mother couldn't go to her sister for a few days? She wasn't sure. She struggled to get to sleep, trying all sorts of devices to fall unawares into a doze, but all to no effect, until almost morning. Gray streaks of light staring into the windows at her, and fevered thoughts chasing one another indistinctly through her excited brain blurred finally into a restless doze, a kind of waking consciousness climaxed in a terrible nightmare such as she had never had before.

She seemed to be standing on a narrow ledge high up in a great room like the library where Mother worked, a great vaulted room, with a frail cornice extending along above the tiled floor, at least the height of two stories up. There was no gallery below her, and she was walking close to the wall, her back to the room, so that she did not realize at first the dizzy heights on which she crept along. It seemed to be a task set her which she must accomplish, and she had at first no doubt but that she could do it, but as she went on, the ledge grew narrower, and she was obliged to put out her hands and cling to the smooth wall as she edged along, a step at a time. But suddenly the task seemed impossible. The frail ledge on which she stood would now hold only one foot at a time, toe pointed straight ahead, one foot behind the other. Inching along, she could see that just a few feet ahead the ledge became still narrower, and then vanished into smooth wall! What would happen when she got to the end? She *was* at the end now! She could go no farther, and hope to cling up there.

Then for the first time she turned her glance downward, a hundred feet or more below her, and was frozen with horror at the dizzy height. How had she ever started out on this perilous way? Why had she come? What had been her aim? She could not tell. But here she was, and her coming seemed somehow connected with Laurie.

And there Laurie was down below her, cheerfully walking along and talking with someone else.

She cried out to him and her voice sounded small and inadequate. She glued her palms to the smooth wall to keep her balance. She called several times before Laurie looked up, and then he only laughed and waved a gay hand and walked on.

What was the matter? Didn't he realize where she was standing? Didn't he know her peril? She cried again desperately to him, and he turned, laughing over his shoulder and waving again. "How do you like it up there?" he called, and walked on, disappearing through the arches into an adjoining room. Had he gone for help, and was he trying to be gay to give her courage till he could bring a ladder?

But the thought of going down a ladder all that terrible distance made her head swim, and she had to turn her face to the wall again to keep from dropping down into space.

And then she tried to turn the other way, edging her feet about. She had come out there, somehow, she ought to be able to go back the same way, she thought. But the ledge was too narrow to turn her feet, and when she tried to edge them backwards, she suddenly realized that the way she had come was narrower, too, since she had passed over it. She must hurry lest it vanish entirely, yet she could only creep! What awful situation was she in, and how was it she had got here? She was paralyzed. She could not move, and any instant she might fall down into that awful space below her. Clinging to the wall with desperate hands outspread she tried to scream, but could make no sound. Struggling with all her might to call out, suddenly something seemed to snag and send her dizzily through a dim foggy place back to herself and life again. But she found her hands and feet drenched with cold perspiration, and horror still filled her being.

At first she could not get away from the thought of her awful situation just past, and had to fancy herself back on that height, edging along toward safety. She tried to think how she got there, and why, and to plan a possible way that she might have been saved if the situation had been real.

At last she sprang from the bed and dashed cold water in her face, trying to forget the fear that had possessed her. But thoughts of it lingered with her as she dressed, and back in her mind the sting of it all seemed to be that Laurie, her Laurie, had done nothing to save her. He had just walked off with a gay wave of his hand and a mocking call! Laurie would never have done that!

She reminded herself how careful he had been of her last night on the ice, how gentle and thoughtful he always was for her. She tried to thrill again as she had then over the tone of his voice, the touch of his hand as he led her out to skate, the ecstasy of motion as they swayed together around the arena. But she had been too shocked by her dream to shake off her terror yet. Was this whole thing a symbol of what her friendship with Laurie was going to be?

Nonsense. Laurie was the soul of honor. He would never leave her in straits. He would plan some instant relief for her. He would — and she tried to think what he would have done if it had been reality.

Meantime Maggie had thought a lot about the conversation she had overheard at the Trescott house. Lying awake on her none-too-comfortable bed which she shared with her cousin, sometime in the night she arrived at a conclusion.

"Dat chile ain't gwine enjoy no pahty where folks feels dataway towards her. I guess I have ta wahn huh!"

It wasn't her day to clean at the Brookes' apartment, but on her way to her day's work she stopped there a little early, and barged into the kitchen just as Marigold was getting her mother a cup of tea for the headache that had gripped her during the night.

" 'Scuse my buttin' in, Miss Mar'gole," said Maggie, looking half frightened in what she was going do, "but is you-all gwine to dat swell pahty dey's givin' upta Trescotts' house?"

Marigold gave her a surprised look.

"Why, I'm invited," she said with a bit of pride in her voice. "Why?"

"Well, Miss Mar'gole, 'f I was you-all I wouldn't go! I really wouldn't. 'Scuse me fer buttin' in. It ain't none o' my business, but I jes' wouldn't go!"

Marigold laughed out, her clear ringing laugh.

"Why Maggie, what funny advice! Why do you say that?"

"Well, I ain't no business 'tall ta say it, but I'se jes' wahnin' yah, you-all jes' bettah not go. I allus think a lot o' you-all's mama, an' I jes' thought I'd stop by an' tell yah. I hope you-all don't get mad, Miss Mar'gole, but I hadta tell yah."

"Why of course not, Maggie. Thank you for your interest. But I can't see what difference it could possibly make to you whether I go or not."

"Well, I likes you-all a lot, Miss Mar'gole, an' it ain't no fitten place for such as you-all. I hated ta tell yah, but I hadta. Morn'n! See yah next Friday!" And Maggie was gone.

Marigold stood staring blankly at the back door for a minute.

"Well, of all things!" she said at last, and then dropped down into a chair and laughed.

Marigold told herself that of course she wouldn't let the words of an ignorant old woman affect her, and she hadn't the slightest intention of staying away from the party. What would Laurie think? What would he say?

But the truth of the matter was she was not happy about it herself. Why, she did not know. When she sifted her thoughts down to the truth she found she kept seeing her mother's eyes when she had renounced all idea of going to her only sister on her birthday. But what had that to do with the party, and why should that trouble her conscience? She couldn't help it that her mother didn't have the money, could she? Of course it did seem terrible that Mother couldn't afford to go to her sister, when her daughter had been able to pay one hundred and fifty dollars for a single frock. But Mother would never have accepted any little part of that money for herself. She was sure of that. It was Aunt Carolyn's gift, and she knew her mother. Aunt Carolyn had always been a little lofty about Mother. Mother would never use a penny of money Aunt Carolyn had given. Aunt Carolyn was Father's rich sister, and Mother liked to be independent. No, Mother wouldn't have heard of it that even a part of that precious two hundred should be spent on her.

So she tried her best to put away such thoughts, just as she had tried all night to get rid of that uneasy feeling about that expensive dress she had bought.

But she had her hands full, what with getting her mother to stay in bed until she had had some breakfast, and swallowing a few bites herself before she got away to school. She knew her mother would go to her duties in the library despite all she could say, if she could possibly drag one foot after the other, so all she could do was to see that she had something hot to drink before she went, and a hot water bag at her feet, for a little while before she left.

It was just as she was going out the door that her mother called her back.

"Dear," she said weakly, "won't you please stop at the telegraph office and send a wire to your Aunt Marian? I meant to go a little early and do it, but I guess you'll have more time than I will."

Marigold cast a furtive glance at the clock. She had meant to do a bit of shopping herself on the way to school. Slippers and gloves and a few little accessories, but the telegram must go of course.

"What do you want me to say, Mother?"

"Just tell her it is impossible for us to come just now, perhaps we can come later. Say I am writing."

Marigold kissed her mother and hurried away. If she took a taxi instead of the trolley she might get in her shopping and the telegram too.

But there were no taxis in sight, and Marigold was too excited to wait, so she walked. After all she could walk almost as fast as a taxi in traffic.

But as she went down the familiar way, trying to word that telegram in just ten words that would say all that was necessary, somehow her thoughts got tangled up with the look in her mother's eyes when she asked her to send the telegram. Such a shame she didn't feel she could go now.

But after all why shouldn't she go? Couldn't it be managed somehow? What nonsense that Mother should let anything keep her away from her sister when she so much wanted to go! Why, she, Marigold, had seventy-five dollars in the savings account, besides the two hundred Aunt Carolyn had given. If Mother was fussy about taking Aunt Carolyn's gift she would give her that. Of course she had been half planning to put that with the rest of the two hundred and get that perfectly gorgeous evening wrap of black velvet with the ermine collar, but she didn't really have to have that. A cheaper one would do. And the seventy-five would pay Mother's fare, and get her some new clothes too. Mother never bought expensive things.

Suddenly she stopped short and the color flew hotly up into her cheeks, as it all came over her how she was planning to do things in a cheap way for her mother, and splurge out herself in grand style, salving her conscience by getting her mother a couple of bargain dresses and maybe a five dollar hat. She, going to a grand party where she had no right to be, in a dress that cost a hundred and fifty dollars!

Suddenly she despised herself, and then more slowly, very thoughtfully took up her way again.

It was queer how things looked at from a new angle took on an entirely different atmosphere. It suddenly became extremely important that Mother should go to see her sister, right now, when she had been invited, and when Elinor and her husband were away and Mother could have Aunt Marian all to herself. That might not happen again in a long time. Of course Cousin Elinor and her husband were very pleasant and would be most hospitable but it wouldn't be quite like having her sister all to herself. And then, if she waited until she felt she could afford it, Aunt Marian might die. She was very frail! Or — Mother might die!

Marigold stared into the future with new panic in her eyes. She had never thought that Mother might die! And if Mother died and she had it to remember that she went to that grand party wearing the price that might have given Mother the vacation and the companionship of her only sister, how would she ever stand it afterward, no matter how much good fortune came to herself?

Her eyes blurred with sudden tears, so that she failed to see a traffic light and almost walked into a car that was coming. As she stepped back just in time she realized that she was standing in front of François' shop where she had bought her wonderful party dress, and she fairly hated the sight of it. She gave a little shiver and turned away again, but the light was still red, and she could not go on. Her eyes went back to the window where her lovely dress had hung but yesterday, and now in its place a street dress was on display, the single offering in a cream colored exclusive plate glass front.

It was a lovely dress, quiet and distinguished-looking, of a rich dark brown with a touch of sable in collar and pockets, just the kind of dress she would like to wear — well, anywhere. But of course it would be expensive too, probably. She sighed as she remembered that her mother had said she never could afford to complete a wardrobe that would go with the white evening gown. And here she was, her eyes still filled with tears for the thought of her mother, her heart still sore with compunction over having bought the white dress, and now turning her eyes toward more of the world's gorgeous goods put on display. Oh, this window of François' had been her undoing! She wished she never had passed here, never had seen the white frock, never had bought it! If she had been going to buy anything here in this ultrafashionable place she would have been so much wiser to have chosen this dark suit which she could go on wearing for months, even years. And this brown would have been most becoming, too. What a fool she had been! If she could only undo it all and begin over again, how differently she would do! It was ridiculous, as Mother had said, for a poor girl who was earning her own living to buy a dress that a girl with millions would wear. It was true they could make beautiful enough things at home. And that would have taken only a very little of her two hundred dollars. The rest could have been used for things Mother needed! How silly that she shouldn't enjoy it too! Aunt Carolyn had said she was to get what she really wanted. And what could she ever want more than to have Mother have some of the lovely things of life? Why, of course, that was what she wanted more than anything else. To have Mother have nice things. Mother who had planned and scrimped all her life to get her nice things, Mother who had seldom had anything nice, really lovely-nice.

Her heart suddenly beat high, and a new thought came to her. Perhaps, if she bought something else in place of it, for her mother, François would be willing to exchange the white dress.

She turned swiftly and went into the shop, before her courage should fail her, a sharp pang of relinquishment hitting her in the heart as she entered.

The one who waited on her yesterday came swiftly toward her, and Marigold felt a throb in her throat. Now she was here and face to face with making such a request her courage almost vanished. Also, it suddenly overwhelmed her to give up the dress. But she had to say something, and she lifted her head and smiled.

"I've come to ask if it would be possible for me to return the dress I bought yesterday, exchange it perhaps for something else. You see, my Mother isn't quite pleased with it, and I thought I could get something she would like better."

The saleswoman's face grew cold.

"We don't usually exchange," she said haughtily, "not dresses like that. They're so apt to be soiled, or mussed. Too bad your mother didn't like it. What is the matter with it? I thought it extremely smart. It seems a pity to give it up when it suits you so well. Don't you think your mother would get accustomed to it?"

Marigold's face flamed, and she wished she had not ventured. After all what a mess she was making of it.

"Well," she said firmly, "I don't want her to have to get used to something she doesn't like. I want to get what will please her. After all I only had it out of the shop for a few hours."

"And it hasn't been worn?" asked the woman suspiciously. "We can't on any account exchange garments that have been worn."

"Certainly not!" said Marigold. "And you needn't bother if you feel that way. I can go elsewhere for what I want." She lifted her young chin a bit haughtily and turned to go out.

"Well, wait a moment. I'll speak to Madame," said the woman, and sailed away to the back of the room disappearing for a moment.

Marigold was more perturbed than ever when she saw Madame herself approaching with the saleswoman. But there was a smile on her face as she came up to Marigold.

"Your maman was not please with the fwock?" she said pleasantly. "Well, you know, I thought myself, a very leetle too sophisticate for ma'm'selle. It ees not quite your type. I vould have suggest a more ingénue style, but you seem so please — !"

Marigold colored quickly and looked relieved at the same time.

"That was it," she said relieved. "Mother didn't like the low back. I was afraid of that, but I loved the dress so I hoped to win her over."

"Well, that is all right, my dear," said Madame soothingly. "We do not as usual thing exchange exclusive garments, but you so soon return, and I have but just now receive request by telephone for a gown of same type. You bring it with you?"

"No, but I can go after it." She glanced anxiously at her watch. Could she get back to the house, fold it and return it without being late to school?

"If you can have here before eleven o'clock — well, yes, I will take back. I think I have customer who will take it."

Marigold gave another frightened glance at her watch.

"I'll go right back and get it," she said breathlessly.

She hurried out of the shop and up the street, fairly flying, her contradictory heart sinking. The dress was gone, her beautiful dress! But she was rid at least of the awful burden of self-reproach for having bought it.

She would not let herself think of anything as she flew back to the house, except the dress and how to fold it safely. She would take a taxi back to the shop so that she would not have to carry the big box with such haste. And would her mother be there still to question her?

Fortunately Mrs. Brooke was already starting to her work at the library. She stood on the corner waiting for her bus as Marigold came up.

"Is anything the matter?" she asked anxiously.

"No," said Marigold, "I'm just going back for something that I had to have. Are you all right, Mother?"

"Yes, dear. You won't forget the telegram?"

Marigold smiled and shook her head. She was almost too out-of-breath to speak, and was glad that the bus drew up to the curb just then and her mother waved her hand and was gone. Now she could fold that dress without fear of her mother finding out. She wanted the deed to be irrevocably done before her mother knew, because she would surely suspect it was done for her sake and protest. She simply mustn't find out until it was all over.

She rushed upstairs and found her mother had covered the dress with the satiny tissue paper, and it hung there like a white ghost, so out of keeping with the plainness of the rest of the room.

Marigold gave one gasp of sorrow and renunciation, lifted down the papers carefully, and arranged them in the big box that still stood on the little table by her bed. She took down the dress, held it off for a second, taking one last look at it, and then began swiftly to lay it in the wrappings, as nearly as possible as it had been wrapped at the shop, touching it tenderly, like some pretty dead thing that she was folding from her sight forever. While she did it she would not let herself think of Laurie, or the party, or any of her grand aspirations of yesterday. She was intent only on one thing, to see that dress safely back in the shop and its burden off her conscience. As she laid the last folds of paper carefully over the lovely silk, tucking in the last dripping crimson thread of the sash fringe, and patting it down, it came to her that this was all like her dream of the night before. She had started out to walk a great narrow highway, far above her own natural little sphere, and had found it too far and too high for her. She sensed vaguely that she had almost got to a place where disaster might have come to her soul, and now she had to get back and start over again. If she was still going to the party, or if she was not, what would happen next she could not consider now. When she got that dress back and her hundred and fifty dollars in her purse, then she could think of the next move. She had known all the time that it wasn't right for a girl in her position to spend so much for one dress.

But now she had to move so swiftly, so carefully — oh, if anything should happen to that dress before she got it safely back! Or if Madame should profess to find a tiny spot of soil! Oh, suppose she had dropped that tear on the silk! A hundred-and-fifty-dollar tear!

She giggled as she tied the cord about the big box, slipped into her coat, caught up her purse, and went out the door. She felt as if she were a little bit crazy, but she was getting that dress taken back! It was too good to be true. And she was doing it without Mother having to worry about it either!

She was unprepared for the smiles that wreathed Madame's face when she got back to the shop.

"I t'ank you a t'ousand times," she said graciously. "My customer ees on her way, and I had nothing to show her. She ees a verray wealthy woman, and verray particular. She buys many garments from me. I like to please her, and I t'ank you for your promptness in bringing it. And now, I shall return your money — or can we serve you fuirther?"

"Why, I cannot stop now. I have an engagement to which I must not be late. Perhaps I would better take the money now, if you don't mind. But — would you just tell me the price of the suit in the window?"

"Oh, that brown? Yes, that ees lufly for you, it will just suit your type. That ees now feefty dollars. Eef you like it I give you a discount on it, for returning the evening dress so quickly."

"Oh!" gasped Marigold. "I — *could* you hold it until I can return this afternoon? I would want to try it on, you know."

"*Certainement!*" smiled Madame. "I geeve you an option. You come in about four to five? *Oui!* I shall keep. Good morning, ma'moiselle!"

Marigold found herself in the street breathless, wondering. What did it all mean? She had returned the evening dress without any trouble, and here was this wonderful street suit furred and exquisite at such a reasonable price — that is, it was reasonable for garments for François. But she must think it over and do some calculating before she even considered this, bargain though it was.

She cast one appraising eye at the window as she signaled a taxi. The dress was wonderful. It did not shout its price to the world either. Her practised eye saw at once that the material was of the best and the fur was lovely. Moreover she knew that it was her type, a dress she could wear for several years, conservative, yet nice enough for anywhere. Only of course it would not do for the party!

She winced a little as she realized that the wonderful white and crimson gown was no longer hers.

Did that mean that she was not going to the party? That perhaps she would be going with Mother down to Washington for Aunt Marian's birthday?

Her heart quivered and fairly turned over at that.

Or did it mean that she was to buy some little cheap evening frock which everyone acquainted with the stores of the city could immediately price, or that she was going to slave at night making a dress for herself — or — ? Or what?

Marigold didn't answer that question to

herself. She got into the taxi and looked at her watch. If this taxi didn't get caught in traffic she might make the school door by the time the last gong sounded! That was important.

But what about the party?

3

During the morning, in the intervals of work in the library Mrs. Brooke wrote a letter to her sister, intended to supplement the telegram which she thought she had sent.

Dearest Marian:

It almost broke my heart to send you that telegram this morning, declining your wonderful invitation. I wanted to fly to you. I'm sure you know how hard it was to say no.

But you see my little Marigold is passing through a new experience, and how much it is going to mean in her life I do not know. For the past three years she has been gay and happy with a lot of young people in her church circle, and in her school circle, and has not seemed to think farther than each day.

But for several months now, her circle has been narrowing down more and more to those who move in a group with a certain young man, named Lawrence Trescott. His people are wealthy and worldly. I have been much worried. They neither know nor care anything about our Christ. They may attend church sometimes, I don't know, but I should judge their only reason would be a wedding or funeral, or possibly a christening.

I have not mentioned this young man to you before, because I hoped the intimacy meant nothing but an occasional good time, but quite lately he has singled out my little girl for his attentions, until I have come to fear for her.

There is nothing the matter with him that I know, except that he isn't of our world, and I don't think he knows much about it either now or for eternity. But that's enough, isn't it?

Yet he's handsome, charming, seems devoted. And she? I'm afraid she's more interested than I thought.

And three days ago there came a bid to a great party at his home. My girl wants of course to go and the party is on your birthday! Do you see, Marian, why I cannot leave her now? Why I must be on hand?

For I am afraid for my girl. Afraid of the letting down of standards, afraid of the worldliness into which she seems to be hurrying.

I might oppose her going, yes, but I'm not so sure that would be wise. Perhaps I should have started before it ever grew into a problem, only of course I didn't realize. Or perhaps I too was a little flattered that a handsome, wealthy, well-mannered youth seemed interested in my child. But I didn't stop it, and now it is a problem. Or — is it? How I wish I had you here to tell me, and to advise. You have piloted your one daughter into a safe harbor with a fine husband. Oh, pray that my dear child shall not shipwreck her happiness.

You will understand, won't you, Marian, and know that it is not because I do not want to come that I am staying at home with my child?

I shall be thinking of you on your birthday, and as soon as I feel I can, I will come and see you.

But you will understand — as you always did understand.

With a heart full of love and longing to see you, and many birthday wishes.

Mary

Mrs. Brooke folded the letter and addressed it. She would mail it on her way home that night. Then she put it safely into her handbag and went about her work, trying to forget her problems, and her longing for things it seemed she could not have;

counting up the future possibilities and wondering how long it would be before she could afford to set aside a little every month in anticipation of another chance to go to Marian.

Meantime Marigold, in her classroom, air-conditioned and furnished with all modern appliances for teaching the young mind, was trying to make clear to her class of well-dressed, well-groomed adoring little girls, the difference between adjectives and adverbs, and trying to keep her mind on what she was doing. But in spite of her, white silk evening gowns with long velvet sashes would persist in parading up and down the aisles in range of her vision, and the grand party which had for the past few days been the background of her thoughts whirled nearer and nearer to her view. And now it was Laurie's smiling face that came questioning her thoughts, demanding to know why she had taken that wonderful dress back to the shop. Laurie's face as he smiled down upon her at the arena, skimming along over the crystal surface of the ice. Laurie with admiration in his eyes. How could she have so forgotten it, and her longing to please him and see the surprise in his eyes when he first viewed her in that wonderful dress? Had she actually taken the dress back? She must have been crazy! Surely there would have been some way to keep that dress and send Mother to Aunt Marian's besides! There was nothing anywhere in the city that could equal that dress! She must have it! She simply must! She could not go to the party without it! As soon as this class was over she would slip out into the hall and telephone the shop that she had changed her mind and would keep the dress! It would not do to wait until recess time. The other woman might come and buy it! She could never go to the party without that dress to give her confidence.

But when the class was over at last, a visiting mother appeared and had to be taken around on a tour of inspection. Then another class claimed her attention, and by and by with a dull thud it came over her that it was almost noon and she hadn't been able to telephone yet.

And now her common sense was asserting itself again. She must not spend so much for a dress for one evening's pleasure! She must find another less expensive! And her mother must go to her sister's birthday party.

The last period in the morning was a study period in Marigold's room. She had nothing definite that had to be done, yet she might not leave the room for it was her duty to see that the young people under her care were diligent in their work.

So she sat with pencil and paper at her desk, and began to make some plans. She wrote down a list of things her mother needed for the trip, and their probable cost. She speculated on what it would cost her to buy some other less expensive dress for the party, a wrap and accessories, also the relative cost of buying material and making a dress. She added it all up and puzzled over it until her head ached. Why, oh, why did this her first wonderful party have to be so complicated with duty, and disappointment to others?

At noon time she was frantic. She must get her lovely dress back at all costs. She would somehow manage to work a few evenings in the library or somewhere and get enough to send Mother properly provided for, too. She couldn't go to the party without that dress, and of course she must go to the party or Laurie would be offended. Although Laurie hadn't said anything about it the other night. Perhaps he didn't know yet that she had her invitation. However, she *had* to look right at that party.

So she went without her lunch and took a taxi back to the shop.

As she entered, the saleswoman who had

63

sold the dress to her yesterday, came smiling toward her.

"It's sold!" she announced cheerfully. "The customer was crazy about it the minute she saw it, and it fitted her all right, although I must say she didn't have as good a figure as yours. I thought it was a little snug. She's taller than you are, too, and the hem had to be let down a trifle for her. But she was tickled to death about it. She said it was just what she'd been looking for and she had begun to think she couldn't get it this side of Paris. And wasn't it wonderful you should have brought it back just in time for Madame to make that wonderful sale! She charged her more for it than she did you. She knew she wanted it so much. Don't tell her I told you that. But I'm sure she'll give you a good price on that brown dress if you want it. You came back to try it on, didn't you? Just go into the fitting room there and I'll bring it to you. Madame is out to lunch but she'll be back before we get it on you, she never stays long."

Marigold, with her heart drooping down heavily walked into the fitting room without a word. Her dress was gone, her beautiful dress, thrown away by her own hand. This morning it was hers, hanging in her modest closet with her plain little wardrobe. And now it was gone, to some rich arrogant stranger, and she would never likely see nor hear of it again! She wanted to sit down on the gray upholstered chair and cry! Her lovely lovely dress that she had discovered, and paid for with her own money, and rejoiced in! And now, by her own silly act she had thrown it away from her! Could she ever forgive herself?

While she unfastened her plain little school dress, and got ready to try on the brown one, she was staring at herself in the mirror and trying to remember what had worked on her to make her do this foolish thing. And as she looked at herself she caught a glimpse of her background, the gray velvet carpet, the ivory woodwork, and the delicate rosy tint of the walls, and suddenly it reminded her of the walls of her dream, and with strange whimsy she stood again on that narrow ledge, with the ivory and rose of the walls above her and below her the grayness of the tiled floor so far away, and only vast space between. Her heart contracted. Laurie had been down below there, somewhere, in her dream, and had gaily deserted her, and in the dim quiet of the room beyond the arches her mother had sat working away at her library records, while she had hung in peril on that fantastic ledge of plaster and swayed between heaven and earth!

It was all fanciful of course, yet there was something uncanny about it, like a warning of some peril that she could not see, and suddenly she was under the power of that dream again. Whatever the feeling might be, whether of peril to her dear mother, or of some danger connected with Laurie, she could not let it go unheeded. No future happiness founded on a mistake could make up for torture of soul. Well, she must be calm about it. The dress was gone, and the saleswoman was bringing the brown ensemble. She would try it on as if that was what she had come for, and then she would go her way back to her school, and perhaps this chaos of mind would finally subside. When she became normal again she would try to plan for Mother, and for another dress for herself, but now she was simply dazed with her various emotions. Was one dress and one party worth so much?

But when the brown suit was put upon her, her mood changed again. This dress was lovely and sensible, a dress she could wear for years, because the style was not extreme. And it was becoming. Yet what good would it do for the party? If she were going to Washington with Mother it would be ideal, but what would she do for the party?

"It's just your dress, you know," said the saleswoman.

"Yes," said Marigold thoughtfully. "I like it, and I'm sure Mother will like it, but I'm not sure I should pay so much for such a dress."

"You wait till Madame comes," said the woman with a knowing wink. "I'm sure she'll make the price right. You know it's getting late in the season now, and Madame always puts down the winter things. This is really your dress. You just wait! Madame ought to be here any minute."

"Well, but I can't wait," Marigold smiled. "I have to be back at once. And besides, while I'd love the dress, it's an evening dress I set out to buy and I'm not sure how much that's going to cost."

"I'll tell you what!" said the woman in a low tone. "I'll put this by for you, until you can run in this afternoon. Meantime I'll be looking up something nifty for you in an evening dress at a low price and see what we can do. Do you like green? There's one that would be wonderful with your hair. It's quite simple. I'm sure it would be better for you than that sophisticated white one with that startling red sash! It's just a little importation that was ordered in blue by a customer and it came in green by mistake. It has a high back, too, and that's what you like. I think Madame would give you a price on it. You know the season is coming to a close, and Madame never likes to carry stock over. You come in this afternoon and I'll see what I can do for you."

"Oh!" said Marigold, catching her breath and feeling more bewildered than ever. "Well, perhaps I will come in on my way home."

She got away at once and hurried back to school, buying an apple and a cake of chocolate at a corner grocery, and eating them on her way. Perhaps by afternoon her thoughts would have straightened out and she would know what she ought to do.

Back in school she suddenly remembered about the telegram she had not sent. She must attend to that the first thing when school was out. And what should she say? Obviously not the word that Mother had told her to send, for by this time she was thoroughly determined that, come what might, party or no party, Mother should go to Washington in time for her sister's birthday.

At last she succeeded in writing a message that pleased her.

"Mother thinks she can't possibly get

away now, but I am trying to plan for her to come. Will wire answer later. Love, Marigold."

She sent it off with satisfaction on her way home, and as she walked on toward the shop again she felt calmer now. She had done something, anyway. She had sent that telegram and it was up to her to plan the rest and make it a success. Mother needed some dresses. It was ages since she had had a new dress. All her things were tastefully made of course, but it would be so nice to take her something that was all ready to put on, something she hadn't slaved over herself. She ought to have at least two new dresses if she went on a journey, perhaps three. A nice suit to travel in, a pretty crepe for dress-up, a simple morning dress — perhaps her dark blue crepe would do for morning if she had fresh collars and cuffs.

By the time Marigold had reached the shop it was her mother's wardrobe she was interested in, not her own. She went in in a very businesslike way and told Madame what she wanted for her mother, and Madame smiled and brought forth dresses, just the things that pleased Marigold's beauty-loving soul. She could see her sweet quiet mother arrayed in these. And suddenly it seemed to her far more desirable that her mother should be suitably dressed than that she should have an evening dress. Why, if she gave up spending a hundred and fifty dollars she could get all three of these dresses she liked so much for her mother, and still have some left for other needs. Why should she have a grand party dress? She had always got along with very cheap little dresses and looked all right; everybody seemed to think so, anyway.

And while she hesitated Madame spoke.

"You like to take zese up and let your maman to try zem on? Or she, will she come down here?"

Marigold shook her head.

"I'm afraid she couldn't. She — is a business woman."

"I see. Zen I send zem up. Marco is driving out to deliver some dresses now. I could send zem up within ze hour, and you perhaps will return any in ze morning zat you do not keep?" She smiled, "And now, you will try on your own?"

Marigold gasped a little then.

"Oh, I don't know that I could afford — that is, if I take these for Mother. You see, she does not know yet. I want her to take a little trip. She is tired."

"Zat is quite lovely of you, my dear. But I

send zese up and you and your mother try zem, and see which you like. You can return what you do not wish to take. And now we see about zis little green fwock. It was just made for you, my child. So simple! So ingénue. And only —" she lowered her voice to a whisper and named a price that almost took Marigold's breath away, it was so reasonable. Why, even if she bought all five of these dresses she would be spending less than she would have paid for that one evening frock, which somehow in the light of this simple little green silk now seemed too stately and sophisticated for her. And suddenly her young soul which had been so tried all day seemed to have reached a quiet place, where there was a solid foundation under her feet.

She went home with a springing step and prepared supper so that it would be ready when her mother got home. She called up the bus station and got schedules and rates to Washington, and she had everything ready to convince her mother that she should go.

They had a great evening trying on dresses and making plans.

At first Mrs. Brooke was adamant. No, she could not think of going. No, she did not want to go, not the day of the party. She must be there to see her girl dressed in fine array.

But the mother was really relieved when she saw the green dress instead of the white one.

"It is much more becoming to you, dear, and I do like you to wear things that Christian people would consider decent. I cannot bear for you to go in for all the freaks of fashion, especially when they verge on indecency. You look so lovely in that green dress, and yet you look like my dear girl as well. I didn't feel as if I quite knew you in that other one last night. I felt as if you were being drawn into a world where neither you nor I belong, and that if you went there, you and I were going to be terribly separated."

"Well, but, Mother, when one goes into the world occasionally, doesn't one have to do, at least to a certain extent, as the world does?"

"You must answer that question to your own conscience, my child," said her mother with a troubled look. "I question whether a Christian has a right to go where he has to lower his standards."

"Oh, Mother — !" exclaimed Marigold wearily. And then the telephone abruptly interrupted.

It was Laurie. He couldn't come over that

evening as he had planned to take her skating again. His mother had made plans for him, some fool girl from Boston was coming on and Mother expected him to take her out. It was a beastly bore, but he couldn't get out of it. He might not be able to get over the next night either. Mother had so many plans on that seemed to require his presence, but he would see her in a day or two.

As Marigold hung up the receiver she was graver than her wont. What presage of peril was there in her thoughts? Had Laurie been less eager about getting to her than heretofore? Who was this girl from Boston? Was she staying for the party? Would there be all those days without Laurie perhaps? Would he have to divide his attentions between them? She had thought of that party in terms of being Laurie's companion, and suddenly she knew she would not be, not all the time, anyway. He was the son of the house and would have to divide his attentions. And all at once she felt terribly alone, and frightened at the thought of the party.

Her mother watched her anxiously as she went about taking off the pretty green dress, and hanging it where last night the white one had hung.

"I'm glad you found it," Mrs. Brooke said

with relief in her voice. "It is so much better for you than the other one!"

"I don't know, Mother," said Marigold in a disheartened little voice. "I'm not sure it is the right thing for such a formal affair. Madame said it was, of course, but then she wanted to sell it to me. I don't feel as if it would be a moral support like the other."

"My dear, if you were thinking to go out and conquer Laurie's family on the strength of that expensive dress, you were making a very great mistake. You would have been like David in Saul's armor."

"Oh, Mother dear!" Marigold suddenly laughed out. "You surely don't liken my going to a worldly party to anything so righteous as David going out to kill a giant, do you? Aren't you getting your metaphors mixed? I thought you didn't quite approve of my going to this party."

"Well, I don't, child, if you must know the truth. I think you are going into a world where you do not belong, and never should. I think you are getting farther and farther away every day from the things you have been taught, and more and more you are forgetting God, and your relation to Him."

Marigold was silent. It seemed there was nothing for her to say in answer.

At last she looked up.

"Well, anyway, Mother, I may as well tell you what I've done. I telegraphed Aunt Marian you would be with her on her birthday. And now you've got to begin to get things in train, for I called up your head at the library and told him I was worried about you, and wouldn't it be possible for you to get away for a few days' rest right away, and he said it would. He said he could spare you as well as not for a week, or even ten days if you wanted to stay so long, and it wouldn't affect your salary. He said you had sick leave that you had never taken, and he would be glad to let you go whatever day you wanted to start."

"Oh, my dear!"

But there was dismay rather than joy in the mother's eyes.

"Don't you *want* to go, Mother?"

"Yes, oh, yes, I want to go, but not now. Not with that party in the offing. I couldn't be easy until that is over."

"Why, how silly. Mother. Can't you trust me? You don't think I'm going to run away with anybody do you, or get into trouble?"

"I trust *you,* dear child, perfectly, but I don't trust — well — the world you are going into. I must be at home and get you ready, and be there when you come back to look into your eyes. I could not be content without that. I have written your aunt. She will not expect me."

A worn gray look settled down upon Mrs. Brooke's face and the daughter suddenly realized that she was tired out.

"There! Mother, we won't talk another word about it tonight. You are very tired. In the morning you will see things differently. Now, I'm going to put you right to bed, and you're not to think another thought about it at all tonight!"

4 When Aunt Marian Bevan got Marigold's telegram she wondered, and looked a bit disappointed. She wanted her sister to come very much indeed, but she also wanted to see her niece whom she hadn't seen since she was an adorable little child of three. But when her sister's letter came she looked troubled and spent an hour in prayer. She was a great one to take everything to the Lord in prayer.

About six o'clock that night she called up a number on the telephone and talked with a very dear nephew, the son of her dead husband's brother, who from the time of his own parent's death had been almost like a son to her.

"Ethan," she said, "what are you doing this week end? Don't tell me you have an engagement. I want you."

"If I had, dearest aunt, I'd break it for you," said Ethan Bevan heartily. "But I haven't a thing. What can I do for you? I was thinking of coming to call on you, for one thing, anyway. You have a birthday on the fifth, you know."

"Oh, dear lad! Did you remember that? Well, I want more than a call. I want you to come and stay the week end with me. I'm having a party."

"Good!" came the cheery answer. "I'm with you. Your parties are always worth while. Who's to it? Or is that a secret?"

"No, it's not a secret, but the truth is I'm not sure who will be here. You see Elinor and her husband have gone to Bermuda and I'm alone except for my nurse and the servants. There's just a little hope that my sister may be able to come. I'm not sure. Do you remember her?"

"Aunt Mary? I should say I did! She used to make maple taffy for me. That was very long ago, but I always put her in my list of beloveds, just next to you. I never saw her again after she was married, did I?"

"No, she lived here in the east and of course you and I lived mostly out west. I've never told you, have I, how glad I am that you've come east now, too?"

"Well, no, but I've hoped you were as glad as I am. I'll tell you all about it when I get there. Is that all your party? That's swell! I like parties where there aren't any inharmonious elements. I shall just bask in the light of both your countenances."

"You ridiculous boy! Remember you are talking to an old woman, and that my sister is just another old woman. It's not a very alluring party for a young man of your age. I had hoped that my niece, Aunt Mary's daughter, could come with my sister, but she has another party to keep her at home, so I'm disappointed. Her name is Marigold Brooke. I wanted her to come on so we could get acquainted with her, but she says she can't."

"Don't worry! I'm just as well satisfied. I'm fed up with girls. I just hate lipstick and red finger nails. There isn't one of them as nice as you, Aunt Marian."

"Well, but I'd hoped Marigold would turn out to be different," said the aunt. "You know she's Aunt Mary's daughter, and would be brought up differently."

"Perhaps," said the young man suspiciously, "but I doubt it. That doesn't always follow by any means these days. What a frilly name she has."

"Yes, isn't it pretty? I believe her father named her, partly for her mother whom he used to say was worth her weight in gold, or something like that — Mary-gold you know, and partly from the color of her hair when she was little."

"Well, Mary is good enough for me," said the manly voice in a superior tone. "I'm just as well pleased she's not coming. When may I arrive?"

"Just as soon as you want to come. I'll be glad to see you any time, and of course if you'd like to bring someone with you — ?"

"No! I don't want to bring anyone with me. I'm glad to get away from everything and have a little time alone with you, Aunt Marian. And besides, I have some work to do. Engineering problems. Mind if I bring them along? I really have been looking for a quiet place in which to work. Do you mind?"

"Not in the least. You may do just as you please while you are here. And if nobody else comes, well I shan't mind at all."

Aunt Marian hung up the receiver and picked up her sister's letter again, a little pang of disappointment still in her heart. How nice it would be to have Marigold meet Ethan. But then if she was touched with worldliness probably he wouldn't like her. And she might not like him, he was so quiet and big and almost shy with women he didn't know. And what was Marigold like? The little sprite with the red-gold hair and the dancing eyes. Poor little girl! Was she going to have to go through trouble? Better that than go to dwell far away from God. Poor Mary! Yes, she would pray! Of course she would!

Was the answer to those prayers already

on its way the night before they were made, while Marigold lay wide awake for the second night and tried to think her problems through?

One thing she was resolved upon, and that was that her mother should go to see her sister on the birthday. Party or no party that should be accomplished. She hoped to get Mother off Friday afternoon. The birthday was Saturday. The party was Saturday night. That was another thing that Mother didn't like about that party.

"It will run over into Sunday, dear. It can't help it, and that doesn't fit with your upbringing and traditions. Saturday night was always a quiet time in my old home, a time for resting and preparing for the day which with us was especially set apart for worship."

"Mother, times have changed!" Marigold had responded almost petulantly.

"Yes, but God hasn't changed! And people have not changed either. They are the same weak sinful creatures they have always been, and they need God, and quietness to think about Him, just as much as they ever did. And I believe God likes to have His own take time to look to Him."

She had stopped because Marigold was not listening. But Marigold had heard, and her mother's words came back to her now as she lay in the darkness and thought.

Why was it that this question of the party seemed to bother her so much these last few days? When the invitation had been received she had had no such compunctions. She was only filled with joy, that she had been included in this great event, that Laurie's mother wanted her to come, and was going to include her in her list of friends at last.

She had waited a couple of days before replying to the invitation. She wanted to get used to the great thought that she was going to be a part of the social life of the elite. She wanted time to think out what she should wear, time to get herself in hand and be sure of herself. She wanted above all to talk it over with Laurie. But Laurie had not said a word. He was likely taking it for granted as he did everything else, not realizing how strange she was going to feel going among his friends who were all unknown to her. Or didn't Laurie know that his mother had invited her? Perhaps that was it. Perhaps it was to be in the nature of a surprise for Laurie, and if that were so, it must mean that Laurie's mother had a kindly friendly feeling toward her.

All these things had influenced her in selecting that white dress. She wanted to do Laurie credit. But now that the white dress was gone, irrevocably, and it was even supposable that she would meet it on someone else at that very party, she felt a kind of unpreparedness which even the charming little green silk could not make up for. Was that green silk all right, or should she try and get some material and make another dress even yet?

Or should she stay away entirely? Stay away and go with Mother down to Washington?

She faced the disastrous thought for the first time openly, lying there in the dark defenseless, alone. It was quite possible that she might not be going to the party at all. If Mother wouldn't go without her, then she was determined to sacrifice everything for her mother. It was silly, perhaps, when there were other days coming, and birthdays, not the actual date, didn't count anyway. Mother and Aunt Marian could have just as good a time together if they came together next week, as this particular Saturday. But she had completely finished with that argument. She had settled it in her mind that Mother had to be there on the birthday, silly or sensible.

And now she had to face another issue.

Was it true as Mother said that she did not belong in a worldly place like that? She was a Christian, a member of the church, and all that. She had taught a Sunday School class for several years, she believed the Bible of course, in spite of mocking denials she had met in college. But she hadn't really been living her faith very clearly. It might even be true as Mother said that she had lowered some of her lifelong standards since she had been going with Laurie. After this party she must check up on her life and straighten out a few points with Laurie, make him understand that they didn't fit in with what she believed. But now of course it was too late till after this affair was over. It stood in the nature of an introduction to his people and it was not her place to question manners and customs of the family where she was to be a guest. Afterward she would explain a lot of things to Laurie, and turn over a new leaf as to some of his worldly amusements and ways. But now — well now, what was this new uneasiness that was prodding her very soul as she lay there trying to be complacent about her green dress, and plan how to make Mother want to go without her?

Was it, it couldn't be that she was unhappy about Laurie himself. Of course he had said he would call her up again this evening and he hadn't done it. Doubtless something had hindered. But — ah — now she was getting down to the real sharp sting that hurt her. It was not that he hadn't called as he had said he would. It was not that he had passed her in his car as she walked along on her way home late that afternoon and he had not noticed her. That might be easily explained, and she could have a lot of fun twitting him about not recognizing his friends on the street. But it was that he had been in the company of another girl, a dashing dark girl with vivid lips, and shadowed furtive eyes full of arrogant assurance, eyes that offered and dared and were never shy nor true. And the thing that cut had been that Laurie, her Laurie, as she had come to feel he was, had been looking down into those other luring eyes with exactly that same tender, melting expression that he had often worn when he looked into her eyes.

Marigold as she lay there in the dark, bared her soul for the first time to the truth. She let the vision of Laurie's look that she had seen and photographed clearly on her memory, come out in the open while she examined it, and her honest soul had to admit that Laurie had never given herself any more melting glances than he had lavished on that smart sophisticated girl he had with him. Like a knife she let it go through her soul, as if she would see the worst, press the wound, and cut out the thing that hurt.

And then a new thought came to her. Was this girl whom his mother had invited to be the guest of honor at the party? Was it this girl who would be her rival? She stared at the wall in the dark and saw as if it were her own soul, with all its unworthy motives crying out within her for vengeance and victory. Had she really been going to that party to show them all what a winner she was? To conquer his mother and sister, and his whole social set? And her only armor that fateful dress that she no longer had? What presumption! What colossal conceit! But — could she have done it even with that dress? Would it not as her mother had suggested, have become unwonted armor to her that would merely have embarrassed her with its unaccustomed elegance?

All her self-assurance, her self-sufficiency, her cocksureness had vanished now and left her in the dark alone there to face her situation. And suddenly she saw herself out again in that vast expanse of her dream, in that same impossible situation, with nothing before and no way behind, and a dizzy drop waiting to swallow her! And Laurie! Where was Laurie? Gone, waving his hand, and smiling into another girl's eyes!

In due time she got hold of herself, brushed away angry, frightened tears and tried to think what to do.

Should she go and get another dress even more regal than the first, perhaps black velvet with startling lines and a single flashing pin of rare workmanship? No matter how much it cost, she could borrow money and pay for it in time! Should she? And try to compete with that unprincipled other girl? That she was unprincipled seemed obvious, even in the brief glimpse she had had of her. But Marigold would have to be prepared for even more than lack of principle, if she really started out to compete, to have them all at her feet, and Laurie with them. Or should she just drop out of it entirely? Did she want Laurie if he had to be won by such methods? If he did not really care for her it would be better to learn it now than when it was forever too late.

Then she tried to calm herself. She told herself that she was getting all wrought up over nothing. That Laurie was only being polite to a guest, and that it was her own excited state of mind that had imagined him flirting with that other girl. Probably the mother was being very friendly, and really wanted to get to know her. Probably Laurie had asked her to invite her, and would be terribly disappointed if she didn't come. Besides, she had finally accepted the invitation two days ago. She couldn't write another note and decline it, could she?

Over and over again she thrashed out the question. Then suddenly old Maggie's warning that morning came to her. What had old Maggie meant? Was it just a crazy notion she had got into her head? Or had she heard something, seen something that made her come in love to warn her? Why hadn't she questioned her? Stay, didn't Maggie say she was sometimes called in to work at Trescotts' when they needed an extra hand?

Wearily she went on nearly all night tormenting her young soul with this and that, until the thought of the party was almost repulsive to her, and the pretty little green silk she had been so pleased about that morning, became a symbol of great mortification. A simple dress like that to appear at a party where everything was most formal! She couldn't wear it!

She slept a few moments at intervals, but awoke quite early when the first dawn was beginning to streak the sky, and somehow a great decision had been reached. She was no longer tossed about by every thought that entered her head. She knew what she was going to do, and she would lose no time in doing it. If Laurie felt hurt about it afterwards she could not help it. This surely would be a way to tell whether he really cared for her or not, or whether he was just having a good time while it lasted.

But her face had a wan white look as she hurried down in the morning and found her mother already getting breakfast.

"Now, Mother," she said firmly, as if she were the mother speaking to her child, "we've got a lot to do today. We're starting for Washington tomorrow afternoon as soon as I get out of school!"

Mrs. Brooke looked up at her daughter in bewilderment. "What do you mean, 'we'?" she asked. "Do you think that *if* I went I couldn't take care of myself, and you would have to take the double trip in order to take me there?"

Marigold laughed.

"No, Mother dear, I know you're perfectly capable of taking care of yourself, but I was thinking of going along. I was invited, wasn't I? And I'd like to be there for Aunt Marian's birthday, too."

"My dear! That would be foolish for you to take that long ride and back again just for a couple of hours there. You would be all tired out for the party, and you would look like an old rag when you got back here. You would have to rush dressing, and there would be nobody here to help you. I certainly won't hear of it."

"Party!" said Marigold calmly. "I've given up the party. I'm not going. That is, not unless Laurie makes a terrible fuss — and I don't think he will find out in time."

"What do you mean? Have you sent your regrets?" asked Mrs. Brooke with deep anxiety in her tone. What was this that Marigold was doing anyway? Giving up the party upon which she had so set her heart, giving it up just for her? Or perhaps she was disappointed about not having the dress she wanted, and would blame her mother in her heart for having disapproved the other dress.

"I'm mailing it this morning on my way to school," she said quietly. "I'm saying that Miss Brooke regrets that unforeseen circumstances will prevent her accepting the kind invitation of Mrs. Daniel Trescott on Saturday evening, February the fifth."

"But child! I can't let you do that just for me!"

"I'm not sure that I am doing it *just* for you, Mother dear. I've decided it is best. Now, don't you say another word. We haven't time. Perhaps sometime I'll tell you all about it, but now we've got too much to do to quibble over this and that. Have you got to go down to the library at all today? Couldn't you just call up and tell them you're not coming?"

"I certainly could not. If I am to be away I shall have to give instructions to whoever is to take my place. They would not understand all my records. I had to leave a number of unfinished items last night, and it is important."

"All right then, you go to the library and finish there as soon as you can, and then go to Grayson's and get yourself a new pair of shoes and some pretty slippers. Yes! Don't look that way. If you don't get them for yourself I'll go and get them for you. And mind you get good ones. It doesn't pay to buy cheap ones that aren't right. If you don't get good ones I'll make you take them back and change them, you know." She laughed and twinkled at her mother, being almost gay in spite of the hurt look deep in her eyes.

"But my dear, I cannot let things go so easily. I must understand why you are doing this. If it is for me I must positively refuse to accept so great a sacrifice."

"But Mother, I thought that was what you wanted, wasn't it? You didn't think I belonged there, and perhaps you're right."

"Yes, I thought it must be something I had said —"

"Now look here, little Mother, why can't you let well enough alone? Perhaps my conscience or something has got working. Anyway I've fully made up my mind."

"I'm afraid it is because I didn't quite like the white dress, and you feel unhappy about the green one."

"No, it's not that. I love the green one, and I guess it is the most sensible thing. But perhaps the dress or the lack of it did help me to come to my senses and see that you were right. Anyway, something did, and we haven't time to argue about it. The question is, can you meet me at Madame's shop this afternoon at half past three and try on a darling little gray wool that I know you would look perfectly spiffy in?"

"Indeed, no!" said the mother firmly. "And I'm not going to keep but one of those dresses you brought up, either. I can afford to pay for that myself. I'm not going to have you spending Aunt Carolyn's money on me. She gave that to you to spend for something you wanted most and —"

"Look here, Mother," interrupted Marigold eagerly, "that's exactly it. She said I was to spend it on what I *wanted most*, and this is it. I want most in life to have you dressed right. It was a revelation to me when I saw you in those dresses yesterday, and I don't know why I haven't seen it before. My lovely mother wearing old made-overs! I'm not going to stand it any longer. I have a good-looking mother, and I intend to keep her so. It's time you had a few stylish things instead of putting them all on your renegade daughter's back. No, there's no use in the world in your talking any more about it. I'm determined. See my lips! Aren't they nice and firm? If you think you can get out of having pretty clothes by refusing to try them on, you're mistaken. I'll buy them without trying on, and let them hang in the closet and go to waste if they don't fit well enough for you to wear! There! What do you think of having a bad wild daughter like that! I'll turn modern, so I will, and boss you around a lot!" and she caught her mother in her young arms, whirled her around, and then kissed her soundly on each cheek.

The mother laughed, and brushed a quick tear away.

"Dear child!" she said. "It's lovely of you to want to fix me up."

"Why?" demanded Marigold. "Haven't you done the same for me all my life? I think it's my turn now."

"But darling, I'm afraid you'll regret this —"

"Well, I like that!" laughed the daughter. "The first unselfish impulse I ever had in my life you think I'll regret."

"Oh, my dear! I didn't mean that! You've always been unselfish. But I meant you'll regret giving up your party!"

Marigold grew sober at once.

"I wonder, will I?" she said thoughtfully. "Perhaps I'll be glad some day, who knows? But anyway, I've given it up!"

Her mother looked at her anxiously.

"Has Laurie done something?" she asked.

"Oh, no. I think perhaps it's what he has not done."

Her mother was still a minute.

"Perhaps he's been very busy helping his mother. You know there must be a lot to do to get ready for a great affair like this, and she would need his help."

Marigold laughed a sharp little gurgle of amusement with a tang of bitterness mingled with the mirth.

"Oh, Mother mine! Do I hear you taking up for Laurie? Making excuses for him? That is too good. The idea that he would be helping his mother is also good. I don't believe it ever entered his handsome head to do that."

"Why, my dear! How could you seem to be so anxious to go around with him if you think so poorly of him as that."

"I don't think poorly of him, Mother. I just know it wouldn't be like Laurie to help his mother. It isn't his way. They don't do that! They have a lot of servants."

"But — there would be things that her own son could help in, I should think, that nobody else could do. Oh, my dear! I feel so troubled! I cannot have you give up this party that I know you counted so much on, and I know you have done it just for me."

"Now, look here, Mother! If I want to do it for you, haven't I a right? You who did so much for me? And if it gives me more pleasure to get you some new dresses than to buy — well, anything that amount of money could have bought, aren't you willing I should be pleased? And it *does* please me, truly! Besides, Mother, I thought it was best not to go. I really did. Now please don't ask any more questions. Not now anyhow. Sometime I'll tell you all about it. I'm testing something out and I don't want to talk about it."

The mother gave her a quick uneasy look, her eyes lingering, troubled, half relieved, yet not wholly satisfied.

"Can't you trust me — a few days, at

least?" said Marigold wistfully.

"Yes, I can trust you — but — ?"

"No buts, please. We haven't time. I'm sending a telegram to Aunt Marian this morning on my way to school telling her that we will be there tomorrow night on the train that reaches Washington about ten o'clock, and we'll take a taxi right up to the house. Now, will you be good and do what I want? Will you meet me at the shop? Bring the dress along that needed the hem taken up. She'll pin it for us. She offered to. Will it bother you to carry it? Perhaps I'd better take it myself. I haven't many books this morning."

"No, you run along. It's getting late. I'll bring it."

"And you will put away all your little worries and get ready to have a good time? Have a good time getting ready, I mean?"

"Yes, I will," said the mother smiling, "you dear child! I do hope this is not going to bring sorrow and disappointment to you."

"No!" said Marigold, her firm little lips shutting tight in resolve, "it won't. I'm going to have a grand time going on a bat with you. It's a long time since we've had a holiday together. I don't seem to remember any since you took me last to the zoo, and how long ago was that?"

"Child!"

"It's a fact, I don't. So much has happened since, school, and college, and then work! Now, Mother, you won't be late coming, will you? They positively told me at the library you could go exactly when you pleased. And I've put some money in your purse. You're to use it *all,* and *not to touch* your own! Positively! I won't go on any other condition! And why don't you pay the rent now and have it out of the way? Then you won't have that to look forward to when you get home, and we can have a real relaxed time with no worries."

"All right!" The mother smiled. She was beginning to catch the spirit of holiday too.

Well, it looked as if Mother was going to be all right. If she only didn't get balky about the dresses down at the shop. It really was going to be fun after all, going off this way with mother, giving her a real holiday. If she just could keep herself busy enough, and interested enough, perhaps she wouldn't feel that sick thud at the bottom of her stomach whenever she remembered the party that she wasn't going to attend. Maybe she could forget it entirely, count it a bad dream, and let it go at that.

But then, she thought, with a quick wistful catch in her breath that brought the color softly up in her cheeks, *perhaps* after all, Laurie would come over that evening and somehow straighten out the painful part of things, and fix it so that she could go to the party and yet take her mother to Washington too. She wouldn't let herself reason out the possibilities. She just liked to think that there was a little alleviating possibility in the vague uncertain way of the next few days.

It might even be that Laurie would call her up at the school during the morning, after he found out that she had sent her regrets.

So she cheered herself on her way into the day.

And her mother, watching her from the window, as she did every morning, said softly to herself:

"Dear child! Such an unselfish girl! But I wonder what has changed her mind? There is surely something back of all this. God must be answering my prayers for her in some way I do not understand."

5 But the day went by and there came no word from Laurie.

Mrs. Trescott had taken good care of that.

Her sister-in-law dropped in in the course of the morning.

"Well, Adele, are you all ready for the grand parade?" she asked sarcastically as she threw aside her wraps and helped herself to some specimens of confectionery that had been sent up for selection.

"Mercy no!" said the harassed hostess, reaching out and choosing a luscious bit of sweet. "You can't imagine what a lot of things can come up to make trouble. Here's my new butler mad as a hatter because he's got to wait on the caterer's men tomorrow night, and threatening to leave, and Daniel Trescott saying he can't have any peace in his own house with parties, and you know yourself, Irene, we haven't had but one party beside my regular bridge afternoon in three weeks. I can't see why your mother didn't bring her son up better! Men are so selfish!"

"Yes?" said Irene dryly. "I suppose you're looking out that you don't repeat the trouble with Laurie."

"Indeed I am!" said Laurie's mother. "I

told him only this morning that since I was taking all this trouble for him he ought at least to help me out a little with the guest of honor. Sometimes I wonder why I do things for other people. Sometimes I wish I hadn't been brought up to be so unselfish." She gave a heavy sigh and took another piece of candy.

"Oh yes?" said Irene lifting her brows in a way that made her look exasperatingly like Laurie. Mrs. Trescott hated to think either of her children looked like the Trescotts. She wanted them to be like her family.

"Well, I'm sure I don't know why I do so much for people when they are so ungrateful. I don't know why I took all this trouble to have this party tomorrow night. I don't believe Robena is a bit grateful either."

"Yes, you do, Adele!" said Irene. "You know perfectly well that you did it to shake Laurie free from that rowdy little Marigold. By the way, has she replied to her invitation?"

"Oh, yes, replied all right, jumped at the chance. 'Miss Brooke accepts with pleasure.' And then, what do you think came in just now from her? Regrets! Can you *imagine* it? After she had accepted! Now what do you make of that? Do you suppose she hadn't money to get the right kind of frock? I understand they're very poor."

"That's odd!" said Irene, struggling with a particularly sticky caramel. "No, I don't believe it's that. I tell you she's clever. She could make a dress you couldn't tell from Paris, if she wanted to. Doesn't she give any reason?"

"A sudden change of circumstances," quoted the mother, lifting Marigold's note with a disdainful thumb and finger as if it might contaminate. "I declare it's discouraging, after all the trouble I've taken, and now to have her drop right out of the picture — all my work for nothing."

"I'm not so sure it isn't better for your plans," said the sister-in-law thoughtfully. "She's a clever piece and very fetching. She could put it all over that selfish beast of a Robena if she tried, although I'm not so sure but she's too well bred to try."

"What do you mean, Irene?"

"Oh, nothing at all, Adele. Wait till you see her sometime and you'll understand. Does Laurie know she isn't coming?"

"No, he doesn't and I don't intend he shall. Not till it's too late for him to walk out on me. And don't you tell him either! You're the only one who knows it, and if he finds out I'll know who told him."

"What if the girl herself tells him?"

"Well, I'll take good care to keep him so busy she won't have a chance. He's out now showing Robena the sights. She hasn't ever been here before, and so there's plenty to see. She's wise to the situation too. I gave her a quiet hint, and she certainly is a good ally. She doesn't give him a minute even to call up on the telephone. We've managed so far to keep him away from it entirely, but Robena plans to follow him if the girl calls him up or anything, and be around to hear what is said."

"You surely take a lot of trouble," said Irene. "She isn't the only undesirable girl around these parts, and at that I'm not so sure she is so undesirable as she might be."

"Irene! A poor minister's daughter!"

"There are worse!" said Irene, lighting a cigarette.

"Well, of course, but you know my son wouldn't look at a girl like that!"

"Wouldn't he? How do you know?"

"Irene! And you can talk that way about your own nephew?"

"Why, Adele, I wasn't talking about him, I was talking about human nature. I haven't much faith in human nature, not in these days, anyway."

"But don't you think it makes any difference how a child is born and brought up, my dear?"

"Not much!" said the sister-in-law. "I used to believe that bunk, but when I saw the way some of my friends got bravely over their training I decided there wasn't so much to it as I had been taught."

"I do wish you wouldn't utter such sentiments, Irene. It isn't respectable to say things like that!"

"Oh, very well, I take it all back, perhaps it was the fault of the upbringing after all. It didn't go more than skin deep. But I still say if you would stop trying to manage Laurie, and simply take his pocket money away and make him go to work, you would have better results. However, I'm only an old maid and I'm not supposed to know how to bring up children, though if I didn't make a better job of it than some people I know I'd be willing to pay a fine. But what I'd like to know is, after you get Laurie pried loose from this penniless little person how are you going to prevent his falling in love with something worse?"

"Really, Irene, I don't like the way you talk. I'm sorry I mentioned it at all. I'd rather not say anything more about it."

"Well, I'm just leaving now, anyway. Give my love to Laurie-boy, and tell him to drop in and see his young aunt some day and I'll give him some good advice. But perhaps you'd rather not as I'm afraid I'd advise him to stick to his Marigold, and get out and go to work for her."

"I certainly would rather not!" said the mother severely. "If I thought you meant all you say I certainly should be grieved about it. By the way, I wish you'd run over and take a hand at bridge some evening while Robena is here. Can't you? Say Friday evening?"

"I'm afraid not, Adele. I might contaminate your child! Besides, I can't abide that double-faced Robena, and I'm afraid I'd let her know it before the evening was over. Bye-bye! I wish you well of your campaign, but I think I see disappointment of some sort lurking around the corner for you!"

Irene put on her coat and went out smiling ironically, and Mrs. Trescott looked after her deeply annoyed.

"Oh, dear me!" she sighed, "why does she always have to be so unpleasant? She wears on my spirit, I'm so susceptible to atmosphere! Now I'm all worn out. She's exactly like her brother! Always saying sarcastic things, and I'm not quite sure what she means by them! She's tired me unutterably. And in some ways Laurie is just like her. Always thinks he's entirely right. Dear me! I hope he doesn't find out his little paragon has sent regrets. If we can only get him through Saturday night I think he will come out all right. By that time he will get over his prejudice against Robena. I can see she's making good headway. I caught his glance this morning when she came over and stood in the window with him and asked him if he wasn't going to give her a good morning kiss, and I actually believe if I hadn't come into the room just then he would have done it. Once let him get to making love to Robena and he'll be safe from all the little penniless designers anywhere. Robena is one who knows how to hold her own."

As Irene Trescott walked down the street in the morning sunshine she was wondering about Laurie. Would he really be won away from his pretty little school teacher by that smart bold flirt? Well, perhaps it was just as well, for he would probably break the other girl's heart if he stuck to her long enough to marry her. He never would have the courage to do it if his mother cut off his fortune, or even threatened to. Irene loved her nephew, but she knew his limitations, and had no illusions about him. He was a chip off the old block in more ways than one.

The morning went on and Marigold at

her desk in the schoolroom was conscious of an undercurrent of excitement. Even her small pupils noticed it, and thought how pretty she looked with her cheeks so red and her eyes so bright.

For somehow Marigold had become increasingly certain that Laurie was going to call up pretty soon and make everything right, and if so all the rest would surely work out beautifully somehow. Mother would understand. Mother always did!

But the morning wore on, recess, and then noon, and no Laurie. Afternoon session closed, and no message in the office for Marigold, though she stopped and enquired on her way out.

Well perhaps he would call later. But of course with guests in the house, and his mother demanding things of him, possibly he couldn't get away. She probably ought to realize too, that since he had said he might not be able to come for a day or two that he thought he had made it plain to her not to expect him. And perhaps he hadn't been noticing the replies to the invitations. Of course, that was it. It wouldn't enter his head but that of course she was coming. Well, it was just as well that she was going away, perhaps. She ought not to let Laurie feel too sure of her.

So she coaxed herself to put away all thoughts of Laurie and the party and enter into her mother's preparations with at least a semblance of eagerness.

She found her mother waiting on the corner, the suit box in her hand, eyeing the great show window of François with hesitancy.

"Don't you think perhaps you would better just take these back, dear, and let us go to some cheaper place for what I want?" she asked in a troubled voice.

"Not a bit of it," said Marigold. "You like these dresses and you're going to have them. Come on!" and she breezed her mother into the big plate glass door and introduced her to Madame, who treated her like the lady she was, and thereby more than won the daughter's heart.

The shopping tour was a success from every point of view and they had a good time every minute, both of them. There was something about Marigold today that her mother did not quite understand, something that restrained Mrs. Brooke from protesting against the pretty little accessories that the daughter was determined to buy for her, and kept her feeling that she must play the game and give her child a good time to make up somehow for this mysterious sacrifice of the party that she still seemed so set upon. For she sensed the undertone of excitement, the firm set of the young lips, the determined sparkle in the bright eyes, and knew that underneath somewhere there was pain. Please God, it might be pain that led to something better, but yet it was pain and she must help all she could.

So they went happily through the shopping, shoes and hats and gloves, each urging some sweet little extra extravagance on the other. After all, what were a few dollars more or less if it helped her girl to go through the fire? And if it turned out that it wasn't fire after all, well, the gloves and shoes and hats would be needed sometime, and were all good buys.

A roomy suitcase of airplane luggage style, and an overnight bag to match were the final purchases, and they put their smaller parcels into them and carried them home with them.

"Now," said Marigold firmly, as they got out of the bus at the corner near their home, "we are stopping at the tearoom for dinner. No, you needn't protest. You are tired and hungry and so am I, and we have a lot to do tonight. Besides, I happen to know there isn't much in the refrigerator for dinner tonight, and I forgot to telephone the order.

This is my party and I want you to be good and enjoy it."

So Mrs. Brooke smilingly submitted again, and they had a steak and hot rolls and ice cream and coffee.

"It *is* a party!" said the mother leaning wearily back in her chair, "and we're having a lovely time!"

She noticed as they started to walk the few steps from the tearoom at the corner to their own small apartment a few doors up the block, that Marigold had suddenly quickened her step and was noticeably silent. She sensed that the child was hoping that Laurie had telephoned.

But the woman who occupied the apartment across the hall and was kind enough to answer their telephone had nothing to report, and Mrs. Brooke with a relieved sigh saw that Marigold set her lips in a determinedly pleasant smile and went straight to the business of unpacking their purchases and talking about the details of their trip, giving herself no chance for sadness. Brave little girl!

There was the hem to put in, and Marigold insisted upon doing it herself, making her mother rest awhile. After the dress had been tried on again and pressed, and pronounced perfect, Marigold insisted on getting all the little things together that they would need, and partly packing them. It was after eleven o'clock when they finally got to bed. The whole evening had gone by and still no word from Laurie. Mrs. Brooke kept longing in her heart that they might get away entirely without it. If Laurie would only keep away, and Marigold could have this outing without him, who knew how her eyes might be opened to see that he was not the only friend the world contained. But she dared not pray insistently for things to come out as she desired. She wanted only her child's happiness, and how was she to know which of all the possibilities was really in God's plan for her dear one? So she prayed quietly in her heart as she lay in her bed in the darkness, "Oh Father, have Thine own way with my child! Don't let her make any terrible mistakes. Bring about Thy will in her life."

But Marigold lay staring into the darkness and thinking of Laurie, her face burning now and again as she realized how much she had taken for granted in Laurie's friendship, and how little he had really done to actually commit himself.

And then her cheeks burned again at the thought of how she had been led along, and led along, to surrender this and that standard and opinion, and yield to every whim of Laurie's. There were not so many of these, perhaps, but in the darkness amid her heart searching, desperately facing her problems, they loomed large with her conscience, her young trained conscience that used to be so tender, and so keen to decide, before she ever met Laurie.

"Dear God," she prayed suddenly, her hands clasped tensely, her young heart beating wildly, "if You'll only let Laurie be *real*, if You'll only let him come back and be what I thought he was, I'll never go into another night club with him, never, as long as I live. I promise You!"

Then all at once it was as if God stood there and she realized what she had been doing, offering that small concession as bait to the great God to do something for her, even if it meant changing His plan for her life and Laurie's. Oh, this was a dreadful thing to do! "Please God, forgive me! Forgive me! I ought not to have prayed that way. Oh, I'm all wrong! Please help me! I'm so unhappy!"

She fell presently into an uneasy slumber that ended in that horrid dream of the high ledge again, and she woke in great distress, crying out for fear of falling down, down into space.

"Why, what is the matter, dear child!" said her mother, bending over her. "Are you in pain?"

She stared wildly at her mother standing there in the dimness of the room. Then she tried to shake off the reality of that dream, and laugh.

"I — must have had the nightmare!" she explained, rubbing her eyes. "I guess it was that piece of mince pie I didn't eat at the tearoom," she giggled. "I'm all right now, Mother, get back to bed. You'll catch cold! You haven't your blanket robe on!" She sprang up and took her mother by main force back to her bed, laughingly tucking her in, kissing her and promising not to dream any more that night. The cold of the room had somewhat dispelled the gloom of the dream, but she lay there for some time still in the power of that awful feeling that she was standing high on that ledge. If this went on she would be a nervous wreck, and that mustn't happen. She had Mother to think of. Mother mustn't be frightened. If she should get sick what would Mother do? She had to snap out of this and do it quickly, and to that end she'd got to stop thinking about Laurie. If he telephoned well and good, but if he didn't it was just going to be something she expected, that was all. She and Mother were going off on a lark to have a good time. She must forget about the party and the beautiful princess dress with its crimson sash. She must come down to living in her own world, and not go creeping after another where she didn't belong.

And of course, it wasn't as if she had been *turned* out of the other one. She had turned herself out, deliberate taken back the dress she had bought, and sent regrets to the party. She had her pride still with her anyway.

With that consolation she turned over and went to sleep again, and when the morning came was able to look fairly cheerful and even a bit excited while they ate their breakfast.

"Now, Mother, don't you get too tired," she admonished as she hurried away to school. "Everything but a few trifles is packed, and I shall be home in plenty of time to see to those. You've no dinner to get. We're getting that on the train. I'm so glad we decided to go by train instead of bus. I adore eating in the diner. And I got chairs in the Pullman, so we'll have a swell rest before we eat." She kissed her mother and hurried away, not allowing her eyes to lift and scan the road to see if a yellow roadster was hovering near, as once or twice it had done before when Laurie planned some special treat for her and wanted to make sure she would go. Laurie was out of the picture today, absolutely. She was not going to spoil her radiance by any gloom.

She was able to carry this attitude though a rather trying day, and came home excitedly with a piece of news.

"What do you think, Mother," she said bursting into the house like a child. "I have two days more holiday! Can you imagine it? And to think it should come just at this time. Isn't it wonderful? I've always wanted to have a little time to look around Washington! Isn't it grand, Mother? I don't have to be back here till Wednesday morning."

"Wonderful!" said the mother, "but how did it happen?"

"Oh, there's something the matter with the heating plant and they've got to pull it to pieces. The workmen say they can't possibly get it done before Tuesday night."

"Well," said the mother with softly shining eyes, "this whole expedition seems to have been prepared for us in detail, as if it were a gift from heaven!"

Marigold caught her breath sharply and smiled.

"Yes, doesn't it?" she said brightly, and her mother watching wondered. Was this real, or just put on for her benefit? It was hard to deceive mother-eyes.

But Mrs. Brooke noticed that Marigold was very particular about writing out the address and telephone number in Washington, for Mrs. Waterman to give to any one who might telephone during their absence, and most careful to call up little Johnny Masters, the paper boy, and ask him to save the daily papers for her till her return. It might be that Marigold had put aside her own wishes and was determined to give her mother all the happiness possible on this trip, but she wasn't forgetting entirely the party she was leaving behind, for she made all arrangements to read its account in the society columns, and the mother sighed softly, even while she rejoiced that her girl would not be present at that party after all. What would the future days bring? Would Laurie come after her again when the grand display was over? Would the interval only serve perhaps to bring things to a crisis? Well, it was all in the Lord's hands and she could do nothing but trust it there.

The next two hours were full and interesting. Putting in the last little things, seeing that the apartment was all in order to leave, the note in the milk bottle for the milkman, the note for Mrs. Waterman to give the bread man. And then the taxi was at the door, and they were off. And it was so long since the two had gone on even a short journey that they were like two children when they first started.

Lying back luxuriously in the Pullman chairs, admiring furtively each other's new garments, watching the home sights disappear, and new landscape sweep into view, was most exciting.

"I'm glad you got that lovely brown suit," said Mrs. Brooke leaning forward to speak softly to Marigold. "It is just perfect. So refined and lovely. Your father would have liked that. It seems to me the most perfect outfit a young girl could possibly have."

"I'm so glad you like it, Mother!" twinkled Marigold. "I love it myself and I'm glad I have it."

They were still a long time looking at the pearly colors in the evening sky, and then Mrs. Brooke, from out a silence in which she had been furtively watching the little sad shadows about her dear girl's eyes and mouth, suddenly spoke.

"You know, my dear, you don't have to go out gunning for a husband!"

"Mother!"

Marigold turned startled eyes toward her

parent, and sat up in shocked silence.

"That sounds rather crude, doesn't it, dear?" her mother laughed. "But I've been thinking that a good many girls have an idea that the main object of living is to get married, and that the whole thing is entirely up to them, therefore they must go out hunting and capture a man, *some* man, even if they can't get the one they want!"

"Mother! What have I ever done that has made you think I thought that?"

"Nothing, dear. I wasn't speaking of you just then. I was thinking of the scores of young things that come into the library. I hear them talking together. They seem to feel that it would be a calamity not to be married. I wish I had a chance to tell them that life is not a game of stagecoach in which the girl who cannot get a husband is hopelessly left out; that only a strong, true, tender, overwhelming, enduring love can make married life bearable for more than a few days, and love like that does not come for the running after, for the brooding over, nor for clever wiles and smiles. It is God-given!"

Marigold sat startled, looking at her mother.

"What do you think I am, Mother?" she demanded indignantly. "I know you're talking to me. I can tell by the tone of your voice. I'm not trying to fall in love! Just because I wanted to go to one party, I wasn't running after anybody."

"No," said her mother gently. "I didn't think you were. But this party was a kind of crisis in your life. You've chosen to stay away from it. You say it wasn't all on my account. Therefore there must be something else behind it all. I am saying these things, because if in the next few days or weeks you come to face any of these problems, I would like to have you think about what I have said. Don't make the mistake of lowering standards, of making cheap compromises and desperate maneuvers to win love, for it is not to be had at that price. Now, that's all. Come to me if ever you want me to say more on the subject."

Marigold studied her mother's face for a long time thoughtfully and then turned her gaze out the window to the deepening twilight on the snowy landscape. Finally she leaned over and patted her mother's hand.

"Thank you, Mother dear, I'll store that up for future use. But for the present, I've almost made up my mind that I never shall be married at all. I think I'll just stay with you, Mother, and we'll make a nice lot of money and have a ducky little house together. But now, dear, don't you think we ought to go into the diner and get our dinner? I'm starved myself. How about you?"

Yet though they both smiled and chatted as they sat in the diner and enjoyed their evening meal, watching the fast darkening landscape from the window, the brilliant cities, the quieter unlighted country flashing by like a panorama, still the mother watched her girl, trying to hide her anxiety. Why had she done this thing in the first place? Was it just an impulse to please her mother, or was it something deeper? Something about Laurie? And was she going to suffer from her rash impulse during the next few days, or would the Lord mercifully deliver her from it and give something to divert?

They had a pleasant journey, and as they neared their destination, and thickening clusters of lights announced a city near at hand, they both felt a little ripple of excitement.

Then the dome of the capitol flashed into view, like some far heavenly city painted on the sky, and the dim spectre of the Washington Monument dawned in the myriad lights. such a lovely vision! Marigold, who scarcely remembered her earlier impressions of Washington, was breathless and bright-eyed as she looked, and then rose to leave the train.

Just as they were passing through the train gate in the wake of a redcap who carried their luggage, a young man stepped up to Mrs. Brooke and spoke:

"You are Mrs. Brooke, aren't you? I thought I couldn't be mistaken. I'm Ethan Bevan. Aunt Marian sent me to meet you. Perhaps you don't remember me, but I remember you."

 **6** Marigold looked up annoyed. Who on earth was this stranger? Heavens! Did he belong to the household where they were to visit, and would he always be tagging around spoiling the good times they were planning to have with Aunt Marian? She stared at him in surprise.

"Why, of course I remember you, Ethan!" exclaimed Mrs. Brooke eagerly. "How wonderful to see you here! Though I must confess I wouldn't have recognized you. How nice of you to meet us! And this is my daughter Marigold, Ethan."

The young man gave a brief casual glance at the girl and bowed. Marigold acknowledged the greeting coolly and distantly. How annoying that there had to be a young man barging into the picture to spoil their outing. Who was he anyway? Ethan? She seemed to have heard the name before but couldn't quite place him, and she scarcely heard her mother's quick explanation:

"He isn't exactly a cousin, Marigold, but he'll make a nice substitute."

Marigold walked stiffly along on the other side of her mother and said nothing, annoyed to be interrupted this way in her first vision of the city. She had no need for a cousin, real or otherwise.

But the young man did not seem to be any more anxious to be friendly than she was. He was talking with her mother, animatedly, almost as if he considered her daughter too young to be interesting. Though he didn't look so old himself, she thought, when she got a good glimpse of his face as they passed under the bright lights of the station entrance.

He put them in the back seat of a lovely shiny car, and stowed their luggage in the front seat with himself, and then drove out into the brightness of the charmed city. Marigold was entranced with her first view and paid little heed to the young man, who was still talking with her mother.

"But I thought you lived in California," her mother was saying when she came out from her absorption enough to listen.

"I did," answered the young man. "I lived with another uncle, Uncle Norman, after Uncle Robert Bevan died and Aunt Marian came east. Then I went away to school when Uncle Norman married again, and college later of course, and then I had a couple of years abroad. But now I've got a job that brings me east for a time, and just now it's Washington."

"And are you living with your Aunt Marian?" asked Mrs. Brooke.

"Oh, no, no such luck as that! I'm boarding out in a forlorn dump near my job, worse luck! I'm only in town for a brief respite. Aunt Marian thought she was going to be by herself over Sunday and she called me up and asked if I wouldn't come out and relieve her loneliness. Then your telegram came and she commandeered my car to come after you. I don't know but she'll send me back where I came from now that you have arrived. But I'm glad to have seen you again, anyway. You loomed large in my small life the day you made that maple taffy for me, and actually let me help pull it myself. I've never forgotten it."

"You dear child!" said Mrs. Brooke feelingly. "To think you would remember that!"

Now why did Mother want to get sentimental? This was a man she was talking to, not a child. Mother always was that way, easily touched by wistfulness, sentiment! Why couldn't she see how unpleasant it would be to have this young man always around underfoot? How it would just spoil the whole lovely vacation!

Suddenly Marigold wished very much that she had kept the lovely white and crimson dress, and stayed at home and gone to her party! If this fellow was going to be around the whole time perhaps she would just go home in the morning anyway and leave Mother in Washington. Mother wouldn't mind so much after she got there, especially if this young man was so fond of her perhaps he would take her around a little and she wouldn't be missed. Then she would take her pretty green silk and go to her party after all. She had been a fool to throw all that loveliness away. Of course she had declined the invitation, but she could call up Mrs. Trescott and explain that she had been called away, but had unexpectedly been able to return, and might she come anyway? That was being a little informal, but knowing Laurie as well as she did perhaps it would be excusable.

Just in the distance of one short brilliant city block the thought came to her and left her breathless, smashing all her well-built resolves, blotting out utterly her vision of Laurie looking down into those intimate languishing eyes of that other girl, and making her heart beat wildly with the daring of it.

Well, she wouldn't say anything about it tonight of course. Let Mother enjoy her first evening to the full, and then along in the afternoon tomorrow spring it on her that she felt she must go back. Mother wouldn't stop her of course. Mother was really troubled that she had given up the party, and while she would be disappointed, still Aunt Marian would be there to make her forget about it, and she would promise to telephone her the first thing the next morning.

Then the car swept into the glitter and glow of another wonderful avenue, and she caught her breath with the beauty of the lovely lighted city.

Ethan was pointing out places of interest. Over there was the White House, here the Treasury Building, and now they were coming into the region of the embassies. He had a pleasant voice, and spoke distinctly, but it was dark and Marigold could not see his face. Anyway Marigold was not interested in his face nor in him as a person at all. She was interested in knowing about the great buildings they were passing and she sat entranced as the vistas of city widened out before her delighted eyes.

When they reached the house, the young man sprang out and opened the door for them. Then he capably possessed himself of the suitcases and escorted them into the house. Marigold didn't notice him any more than if he had been a taxi driver doing his duty.

It was a pleasant house and they had glimpses of a wide living room with a generous fireplace, a beautiful dining room beyond, and on the other side of the hall a large library whose walls were almost literally lined with books. Her cousin Elinor had married a literary man. Marigold looked about with pleased eyes on everything. She loved luxury and pretty things, and had very little of either in these days. She felt that the time spent in this house was not going to be wasted by her. She hoped she would have opportunity to curl up on that great leather couch and do some reading while she was here. Another fireplace, too! How charming!

"I think Aunt Marian is expecting you to come right upstairs," said the young man, and Marigold found herself a little jealous of the possessive way in which he said "Aunt Marian," as if she were *his* aunt and not related to them. What was he? Just an in-law by marriage!

He followed them up the stairs with the baggage, setting it down in a large room across the hall from Mrs. Bevan's room.

They found the invalid in bed, eagerly awaiting their coming.

"Take off your things and let me look at you," she said when the greetings were over.

126

"I wanted to come downstairs to meet you, but my nurse had to go away this evening, and she thought if I was going to be carried downstairs tomorrow for a while and stay up to my birthday dinner, I'd better stay in bed tonight. So here I am, flat on my back! My, but I'm happy to see you! My heart jumped up and turned over when I got your telegram. And oh, my dear! Is that your baby-girl Marigold? Grown to be a young woman! Isn't she lovely!"

Marigold's cheeks flamed as she bent and kissed her aunt, somehow terribly conscious of the young man in the background, and wishing the aunt wouldn't be quite so enthusiastic before strangers.

But when she straightened up Ethan was gone. She heard the front door closing, and wondered if that was all they were to see of him after all. Perhaps he was only on duty until he escorted them to the house. She sincerely hoped so.

But he appeared again after they had taken off their coats and hats and came back into Aunt Marian's room. He came bearing a large silver tray containing cups and a pot of hot chocolate, a bowl of whipped cream with a little silver ladle, plates of tiny chicken and lettuce sandwiches, cinnamon toast and little frosted cakes. Such a lovely little spread-out! And though they protested that they had had dinner on the train, they ate with a real relish as Ethan proved himself efficient in the art of serving them.

Marigold watched him without seeming to do so. How easy he was, how much at home, as if Aunt Marian were his own mother. He was rather good-looking, too, in a serious sort of way, had nice eyes and a pleasant smile, talked a lot of nonsense to her mother and aunt, and made himself very useful. But he looked straight through Marigold when she happened to be in his line of vision, and mostly avoided her when she wasn't. That didn't bother Marigold in the least. She wasn't interested in him, she told herself. He wasn't in the least like Laurie, who was lithe and slender of build, tall and willowy, and handsome as a picture. This man was strongly built, and seemed to have a kind of power about him.

Then suddenly she thought of Laurie. Had Laurie called her up after she left? Her heart gave a lurch and she almost contemplated calling up home tonight before she went to bed, if she could get a good chance when nobody was listening. Though it was late to hope to get Mrs. Waterman. She usually went to bed at nine o'clock and likely wouldn't hear the telephone. It would be better to wait till morning.

They sat up talking till midnight, Aunt Marian's eyes so happy, and Mother looking as if she had just arrived in heaven. Marigold couldn't help being glad that she had come. Just to look at Mother's face was enough to make her sure she had done the right thing. But surely by tomorrow Mother would be having such a good time she wouldn't mind having her go back in time for the party!

Ethan Bevan told some very amusing stories and had them all laughing, although he didn't once look at Marigold, and she had the impression he was doing that by intention. He didn't seem to be shy either. She couldn't quite understand it. It was more as if he weren't in the least interested in her, any more than if she had been a kitten that had come along. He just didn't take her into the picture at all. Well, that was all right. That suited her perfectly. She was free to think her own thoughts and not have to bother with him. Since he had to be there it was better that he didn't want her attention at all. He told them a little bit about the "camp" where he worked around the job, and gave an amusing anecdote or two of the boarding house where he stayed, eating at the same table with his men. That was interesting, and she thought more of him that he could see good in the common laborers, and be friendly with them. He must be a good sort after all. But likely he would go off to camp in the morning and she would be able to go out and see the great new city on her own. Of course her mother would want to stay with her sister, but she would slip away and look around at one or two places she had always wanted to see. The Capitol of course, and the Library of Congress, and perhaps the Smithsonian. She hadn't an idea what a proposition she had mapped out for herself for one brief morning, but she only intended to take a brief casual glance, and then telephone, and perhaps spring it on her mother at noon that she was going to take a train about three o'clock. That would give her plenty of time to dress and get to the party — !

Then suddenly her thoughts were broken by her aunt's happy voice.

"I thought you and I would take it a little easy in the morning, Mary, and have a good talk. Marigold of course will want to see the city since she hasn't been here for so long, and Ethan being here makes it nice. He will take her over to the Capitol and library and any other buildings she would like to see, and show her the really interesting points in them. He knows how to do that to perfection. Elinor's husband says he is past master at giving a quick comprehensive view of the right things without wearying one too much." She gave a swift loving smile toward Ethan. "And then," she went on, "in the afternoon Ethan is going to take us to ride. The doctor said I might go along if it was a pleasant day. I thought we would go out through the park, show you the new cathedral and a few other notable places, and then we would drive on to Mount Vernon and let the young folks hop out and look that over for a few minutes. Don't you think that would be pleasant? Of course I couldn't hope to enjoy all this with you if I hadn't been able to get hold of Ethan for the day, because there is no one else here to carry me downstairs, and help me into the car. But since he is so good as to give us his holiday I feel like a bird let loose."

Thud! Down went Marigold's plans in one blow. She looked from her aunt to her mother and back again. Their faces were radiant with anticipation. She simply couldn't dash their hopes by telling them she wouldn't be there in the afternoon. Not tonight anyway. Perhaps in the morning she could telephone and get some word calling her home and then it wouldn't be so much of a letdown for them. Not if it came in the nature of a call from Laurie. But the morning! How was she to escape a personally conducted sight-seeing tour of Washington in the company of an unwilling guide? She gave a quick glance at Ethan and it did not seem to her that he looked particularly elated at the prospect either. He must be a grouch about girls. She certainly didn't want to go with him. Well, it would be up to herself to get out of it. She could likely get an early interview with him and tell him she had always wanted to go around Washington alone and just see what she wanted to see herself, and she wouldn't bother him to escort her. He wasn't even looking at her now, and he hadn't said that he would be charmed to take her, nor any of the conventional phrases that the ordinary gentleman would use on such an occasion. Oh, he would be glad enough to get out of it, and perhaps it could be managed without either Mother or Aunt Marian knowing that he hadn't gone along. Well, she would see.

So they went to bed at last, and Marigold intended to lie there awhile thinking about Laurie and how to plan for the next day, so that she wouldn't have to go around with Ethan Bevan. But the next thing she knew it was morning and her mother was smiling down at her and telling her she would be late for breakfast if she didn't get right up and hurry with her dressing.

It was a pleasure to get up and put on the pretty little new morning dress with its gay silk print and go downstairs. Aunt Marian didn't get up to breakfast. She was saving her strength for the afternoon drive, she said. Ethan Bevan was very pleasant. He did the honors like a son of the house, talking gravely with her mother mostly, though he did turn his direct gaze to Marigold once when he first greeted her with a pleasant good morning.

Marigold had begun to hope that he would just ignore what had been said the night before about taking her around, but as they were getting up from the table he turned to her and said:

"Now, how soon can you be ready? I'm bringing the car around to the door in ten minutes. I need to get gas. Will that be too soon for you?"

Marigold had intended waiting till her mother got upstairs so that she could deal with the matter alone, but her mother hung around and she was forced to answer.

"Oh, please don't take that trouble, Mr. Bevan. I really don't need an attendant. I'm quite used to going about places by myself and shall have a lovely time. There is no need in the world for you to take time off from more important things to personally conduct me. Just forget me, please. I shall be quite all right."

Ethan turned a surprised glance at her and studied her an instant. Then he said in his pleasant decided voice:

"You know I couldn't think of letting you go around alone. I promised Aunt Marian I'd take you, and you're not hindering me in the least from anything I have to do. I'm entirely free for the morning."

He didn't say it would be a pleasure to take her. She was glad he didn't. It made her feel that it was more of a business proposition. He was doing it because Aunt Marian had asked him to. That was easier to combat than a mere feeling of politeness.

"But truly," she said lifting her firm little chin with a kind of finality, "I don't need you. I am quite capable of finding my way about alone and shall enjoy it —"

"I know," he said, lifting a chin just as firm as hers, "but it just can't be. Aunt Marian would worry like the dickens, you know, and you couldn't really see half as much nor as easily alone as if I went with you. I can see I'm not the most desirable companion you might have, but I'm capable, really, and I guess you'll have to put up with me for the time being as I'm all there is. I'll promise to be just as little trouble as possible. I'll be around in ten minutes and wait out in front for you." He finished with a nice grin that almost made her like him, and turning hurried out through the hall, catching up his coat and hat from a chair as he passed out the door.

"My dear!" said Mrs. Brooke. "That wasn't very gracious of you."

"Well, Mother, I can't see why I have to be forced into a position that neither of us wants. Can't you see he doesn't want to go? Of course he's very polite, and all that, but it must be a terrible bore to take a strange girl around sight-seeing. I know he hates it. And so do I. I shan't enjoy it at all if I have to go with him. I'd much rather go by myself. I feel as if the whole trip was spoiled, having him here, anyway!"

"Oh, my dear!" said Mrs. Brooke, a quick shadow coming over the brightness of her face. "I don't see why you should feel that way. He really is a very fine young man with splendid ideals and standards. I cannot see why you cannot be courteous and grateful even if you don't think he is just crazy to take you out. I should think just Christian courtesy would show you that you should be gracious and sweet for these few hours, and make him have as pleasant a time as you can, while he serves you as host in the place of your relatives who are absent."

Marigold stood unhappily looking down at the toes of her pretty new shoes and feeling as uncomfortable as if she were a naughty little girl being reprimanded.

"Oh, I suppose so, Mother," she said drawing a long sigh of surrender. "Don't look that way, Mother! I'll be good. Only I thought when neither of us wanted to do it there would be some way out."

"Not courteously, dear," said her mother reproachfully.

"All right, Mother, forget it, and look happy. I'll be a good child. Go on up to Aunt Marian and have a good time. I'll try to amuse the young man if that's possible, but to tell you the truth I think he prefers your company to mine." She finished with a wry smile.

"Child!" said her mother with a faint answering smile. "Run along and have a really good time. You can if you are willing!"

So Marigold hurried upstairs and put on her lovely brown ensemble, with its sable collar and cuffs, tucking a fetching little orange flame of a scarf about her neck for a spot of bright color under her chin. Then she went down to meet Ethan Bevan with her head up, and the fire of battle in her eyes.

However, Ethan Bevan scarcely seemed to see her as he helped her into the car. His own head was up too, and if Marigold had looked she might have seen an answering fire of battle in his eyes. Ethan Bevan, to tell the truth, hadn't much use for modern girls, and he took it for granted that Marigold was a modern girl.

So they started out on the pleasure trip with stark animosity between them, both determined to get the thing over as quickly and creditably as possible.

"Now," said Ethan as they drove away from the house into as beautiful a morning as had ever been born, "have you anything in mind you wanted to see, or shall I just take you the ordinary round of sights?"

"Oh," said Marigold setting herself brightly, but hating it all, "it isn't especially important, is it? I had thought of the Capitol, and perhaps the library, or Smithsonian, but any of the other buildings will be just as good if they are nearer. I want to give you the least trouble, of course. I'm really sorry to have been forced upon your hands for the morning, but, won't you please plan the trip in the way that will be pleasantest for you?"

He gave her an amused glance, and studied her haughty young profile for an instant.

"All right!" he said gravely, "only don't worry about me. I'm still new enough to the city not to be bored anywhere. There's always something of interest. Perhaps we'd better take a flying glimpse of the Capitol first, and then use the time that's left in the library, or get a glimpse of the museum. I promised Aunt Marian we would be back for lunch at one o'clock, and of course you can't see everything in that time."

"Of course not," said Marigold in a formal cold little tone.

"Here for instance is Corcoran Art Gallery," he went on. "That white marble affair on your right, and over there is the War Department. A lot of interesting matter in there, but you need time for it all. There's the South American Building, a fascinating place, with all sorts of queer plants and live birds and monkeys. And over there —" he pointed off to the right and went on describing briefly the different buildings in sight, and Marigold, eager-eyed, tried to restrain her eagerness and answer calmly.

"You are a good salesman," she said coolly. "I think I shall have to take a real vacation some week and come down and go through all these places."

"It would pay you, of course," he said, and turned a corner sweeping back to Pennsylvania Avenue. "There is the Capitol again, just ahead of us. I always enjoy this view of it. It seems so impressive, and so worthy of a great country's executive building."

Thus they discoursed stiffly, and seriously, touching on politics in a general vague way, as if neither of them cared much about it, or felt the burden of their country's policies. And then they reached the Capitol and went solemnly up the great white flight of stairs.

Marigold was filled with awe at her first approach to the beautiful marble structure and she said very little, scarcely replying to her companion's remarks. As they stepped inside the main rotunda Marigold looked up and drew a soft breath of wonder.

"I am so glad!" she said softly as if she were speaking to herself, quite off her guard.

"Glad?" said Ethan studying her face as if he saw it for the first time, and found in it what he had not caught before.

"Glad that it is just as impressive and wonderful as I had dreamed!" she explained. She was still talking as if to herself. She had for the moment forgotten her animosity, and was speaking her innermost thoughts, as she might have spoken them to her mother, or anyone she knew well.

"Yes," he said gravely, "I can understand that feeling. It is good to have great things, representative things, like buildings that stand for something real, come up to one's expectations. I remember I almost dreaded to come here and see this city about which I had heard so much, lest it would disappoint me. This is the first time you have been in Washington?"

"No, I was here when I was a child," said Marigold slowly, her eyes still studying the paintings in the dome, "but I doubt if they brought me *here*, or if they did I didn't get an idea of what I was seeing. I was probably a tired child crying to go home."

He looked at her with new interest and began to tell her what he knew of the great frescoes above them. They stood for some minutes looking up. Marigold forgot the personality of the one who was beside her and listened to what he said, her eyes wide with interest, indelibly stamping on her memory the wonderful paintings.

They roused to go on presently as groups of tourists came near with a guide and drove them from their position. They came presently to the hall of statuary and studied briefly the faces of the notables done in marble.

"I have an ancestor here somewhere

whose name I bear but he is so far back I cannot tell how he is related. Where is he? Oh, yes. Ethan Allen! Here he is. One of the famous Green Mountain boys, you know, of Revolutionary times."

"Oh, yes," said Marigold. "I know. Father had an old book called 'Green Mountain Boys.' I loved it. It was a grand story. And what a fine face he has!"

Their talk was just then interrupted by a group of men meeting near by and greeting one another intimately.

"There! There's the senator from your state," whispered Ethan, touching Marigold lightly on the shoulder. "I had him pointed out to me the other day."

They lingered for a moment watching these important personages, and then went on to visit the House of Representatives, and catch a brief glimpse of laws in the making. Then across to the Senate for a little visit, returning to the Supreme Court room in time to see those great men walk into their places and hear the highest Court opened for the day's session. It was all most fascinating to Marigold, and she would have stayed all the morning, but finally Ethan asked if she was willing to go on, and they slipped quietly out and came again to the great rotunda where they had entered.

"We have been longer than I intended at this," said Ethan glancing at his watch. "I am afraid you won't have time for much else this morning. It is almost half past twelve, and we are due back at the house again at one, you know."

"Well, I'm glad I've seen it all," said Marigold lifting a sparkling face. "I wouldn't have missed a minute of it. Is it time we started back at once? I'm quite satisfied to go."

"Well, no, we have fifteen minutes left before we need actually start. How would you like to get up nearer to those paintings above us? There is scarcely time to go to another location. But perhaps you don't like to climb stairs?"

"Oh, I'd love to go. I don't mind climbing in the least."

So they started up the narrow winding way that led nearer to the dome. And as they walked Ethan supported the girl's arm lightly and they kept step, slowly up and up, in a great circle, till they reached the narrow gallery above, quite close to the wonderful paintings.

Marigold was not tired. She had enjoyed the rhythmic climb while Ethan told her more about those pictures of which he seemed to have made quite a study. They stood for some minutes facing the outer wall studying the blended colors of the masterpiece, thinking of the master who had stood up there on a scaffold so many years before laying on the pigment and leaving behind his brush strokes the picture that had endured, and then, Ethan looking at his watch, said:

"Time's up! We must go or we'll be late. But before we go turn around and look down at the place where you were standing a few minutes ago. It is interesting to see how small the people look from here."

Marigold turned and looked down at the marble paving below her and suddenly the tormenting nightmare of her horrible dream descended upon her and took her by the throat, petrifying her with fear. There was the great empty space below her, just as she had dreamed, and she on a little ledge out there hanging over that wide awful expanse. Almost she expected to see Laurie down there somewhere waving his hand at her gaily and asking how she liked it up here. And in imagination the ledge on which she stood grew suddenly narrower beside her and vanished into nothing. She threw up her hands with a little cry of terror and covered her face, swaying backward, and everything turned black before her eyes.

7

There was no Laurie there to help her, but Ethan was there, and much more alert and ready than ever gay Laurie would have been. He sprang to catch her as her knees crumpled under her, and he lifted her in his strong arms, holding her firmly like a little child who needed comforting, holding her, turning her away from the front of the narrow gallery and hiding her face from that awful space below them. He held her so for a second or two with her face against his rough tweed coat, as if by mere contact he would compel her fright to leave her, her senses to return. Then slowly, as if she had received new life from his strength he felt her senses coming back to her and she began to tremble like a leaf.

"Oh, poor child!" he said softly, as if he were talking to himself. "I should not have brought you up here. The climb was too much for you!"

Suddenly, as if he understood better what was the matter, he turned with her still in his arms, and began slowly to go down the stairs. Step by step he went, stopping now and again to look at her, till little by little she felt the assurance of his arms about her, and slowly the color began to return to her face. When he next paused her eyes fluttered open and looked into his own, the fright still there but fading slowly, as his eyes reassured her.

"It's all right now," he murmured gently, still in that same tone, as one would speak to a little frightened child. "We're almost to the lower floor. Just a few more steps and we will be down."

Surprisingly she thrilled to the strength of the arms that were holding her and the tenseness relaxed.

She lay quite still and let the wonder of it roll over her, the relief of the end of her dream at last. Someone had saved her from that strange maddening peril, and showed her that she did not have to go on through all her life having at times to go back to the old problem of whether she would have to edge back over that ever-narrowing ledge that vanished before her feet, or take the alternative of crashing down on the pavement below at fearful speed and being blotted out in pain and darkness.

Gradually she ceased to tremble. And when he had reached the last step he stopped and smiled down at her, saying pleasantly:

"Now, it is all over. We are down! Are you feeling better?"

Her lashes trembled open and she looked up at him with relief, murmuring:

"Oh, I'm glad!"

The lashes swept down again, and suddenly a tear appeared beneath them and swelled out, making a pool in the violet shadows under her eyes.

"I'm so ashamed!" she murmured.

"You don't need to be," he said comfortingly. "I understand all about it. But there are some people coming this way. Are you able to stand if I hold you, or shall I just carry you out to the car this way?"

That brought her completely to herself.

"Oh, I can stand! Put me down please!" she said in sudden panic.

He set her upon her feet, and with his own handkerchief dried the tears from her face, and then as the footsteps came around the partition at the foot of the stairs, he drew her arm within his own, and led her out through the great doors to the outer air.

"Perhaps we should have gone down in the elevator," he said, pausing in dismay as he remembered the long white steps ahead of them. "We could have walked right out of the entrance on the ground floor."

"No, I think I'll be all right now. I feel better out here in the air," said Marigold keeping her eyes nevertheless steadily away from the long descent before her.

"Well, then, take hold of that rail, and I'll support you on this side, and only look at one step at a time. We'll soon be down, and you can't possibly fall now, because I'm holding you, you know."

And once again Marigold felt that thrill of strength come to her at his touch. It was silly of course. It was just that she was unstrung, but she was glad to her soul that he was there.

And then they were down, back in the car, and she was being borne along swiftly through the streets.

He was silent for a little as he threaded his way through the noonday traffic. At last, looking shyly up at him she spoke in low hesitant tones:

"I don't know what you must think of me," she said. "I never did a thing like that before! It was all because of a dreadful dream I had one night, a nightmare I couldn't shake off when I woke up. I thought I was walking out on a narrow ledge above a great depth like that and the ledge was getting narrower ahead of me. I couldn't go back, and no one down below would help me. A friend of mine just waved his hand and laughed and went away."

"I understand it perfectly," he said turning and looking comprehendingly into her eyes. "I had it happen to me once, when I stood high above a job I was working on and something went wrong, putting me in great peril. I lost my nerve completely, and was about to fall to my death. For days after the danger was past I could not go to my job. I dared not get to that height again. Then some One very strong came and saved me from myself, and the terror all left me. I'll tell you about it sometime, but not now. You'd better stop thinking about it at once, and get some sunshine in your face before you get home or your mother will be frightened. Aunt Marian will think I didn't take very good care of you."

She looked up at him gratefully.

"You won't need to tell Mother?"

"No, indeed, of course not. Why frighten her? It's all over, you know."

He turned and smiled down upon her, putting one hand warmly over hers, and again that thrilling sense of his strength guarding her filled her shaken young soul with peace.

The rest of the drive was taken in silence, his hand over hers to reassure her, and when they reached the house he said with a keen look into her eyes:

"Are you all right now?"

She nodded brightly.

"Only ashamed."

"Forget it!" he grinned, and with a friendly squeeze of her hand he sprang out to open the door for her.

The luncheon was a merry one. Marigold who felt shy and silent at first rallied her forces and grew talkative, telling of all she had seen and heard. Her mother, watching anxiously, decided that she needn't worry after all. Her dear child seemed to be enjoying herself hugely. Probably the two young people had managed to get better acquainted during the morning, and Marigold wouldn't be so difficult the rest of the time.

The day was gorgeous and the drive a wonderful one. Marigold, as the new interests of the trip enthralled her, entirely forgot her eagerness to return to her home in time for the party. She had thought about it as they were starting, deciding that even if they got back as late as five o'clock, she might venture to get the six o'clock train if she still felt it wise. Three hours would bring her home at nine, and she *could* change on the train if she wanted to and take a taxi straight to the party, explaining her appearance after she got there. But anyway she was going on that drive. She had always wanted to see Mount Vernon, and she might never have such a good chance again.

So the party, and even Laurie were forgotten as they glided along beside the wide silver river, getting new visions of the fairy city, that looked even more unearthly in the pearly afternoon lights than it had the evening before.

Ethan had reverted to what she judged must be his normal self. Though he had put the two sisters in the back seat and placed Marigold in front with himself, he paid little attention to her, seldom talked much to her, except to point out something of interest they were passing, and made his conversation quite general, rather ignoring her. Marigold wondered at it a little, felt even somewhat mortified. He probably thought her a little fool, emotional and silly, who couldn't keep her head. All his gentleness of the morning was quite gone. He was the same indifferent stranger that he had been the night before. It was hard to realize his kindness of the morning, to remember how he had carried her down those stairs, and held her so comfortingly as if she had been a little frightened child.

Well, perhaps it was just as well. She would be able the more easily to put the whole incident out of her mind and her life. But anyway she had somehow the feeling that a permanent cure for that dream had been wrought for her that morning, and she must always feel grateful to him for what he had done.

But the day was fine, the winter landscape a dream, the car luxurious, why not forget it all as he had suggested and just enjoy herself?

And so she tried to do, though now and then she would glance at his cool impersonal countenance and feel a trifle chagrined at his indifference, even while chiding herself that she cared. She didn't care of course, she was only trying to forget Laurie and the party, trying also to forget her mortification of the morning.

When they reached Mount Vernon they parked the car in a pleasant place, leaving the two sisters to enjoy one another's company, and went to explore the ancient landmark. Then Ethan caught her hand and said "Come," and together they ran up the frosty drive to the old house. That bit of interlude did a good deal toward making Marigold feel more comfortable. This pleasant impersonal comradeship was much better than the solemn dignity with which he had been addressing her all the afternoon. They laughed together and joked a little about the old days when knee breeches, lace ruffles, and hair ribbons were in vogue for men, and candlelight was the only illumination even in grand mansions.

After they had been over the place, hand in hand they ran down the snowy hill again, laughing like two children, and the soft color was glowing in Marigold's cheeks as they returned decorously to the car.

The two women smiled to each other as they saw them coming. It was good to them to see the young people whom they loved having a pleasant time together.

Marigold had forgotten all about going home. It was six o'clock when they reached the house and pleasant odors of dinner were abroad, Aunt Marian's birthday dinner! Of course she couldn't run away from it.

Marigold hurried up to her room and slipped on the green silk. It wasn't exactly the dress for a simple home dinner, but she felt in a gala mood, and it was bright and pretty, a dress that probably would have been much too plain for the Trescott party, but was not out of keeping for almost any simpler occasion.

"Mother, is this too much? I thought it would be fun to wear it once," she said as her mother entered the room.

"It's lovely!" said her mother, "just sweet and lovely, and your Aunt Marian will be pleased. Yes, wear it. It is very charming."

So Marigold went down to dinner looking like a flower with lovely green foliage about her, and Ethan stopped in the middle of a sentence and looked at her in wonder and a kind of awe.

"I've put on my party dress to do you honor, Aunt Marian," she said as she came into the room. "You won't think me silly, will you? I thought it would be fun."

"How dear of you, child!" said the aunt, looking at her with deep admiration. "I think that was a lovely thing to do, spend its freshness on a lonely old woman! But you know, I don't believe any party would enjoy it half as much as I shall. It is a beauty, isn't it, Mary? And so becoming, so simple and quaint in its style. It is charming. I feel as though I am selfish to have all this resplendence just for me. I *should* go to the telephone and call the neighbors in to meet my lovely guest."

"Well," said Ethan suddenly, "my opinion hasn't been asked, and of course it doesn't count, but I can enjoy a good thing when I see it too, and I should say that gown was a prize. I don't remember to have seen a prettier one anywhere. The only trouble with it is that it puts me in the shade. I had some tickets for the symphony concert tonight, and I had been daring to hope that Miss Brooke would honor me with her company, but now I'm afraid she will be ashamed to go with me. You see I don't happen to have any glad rags along."

They all laughed at that as they sat down, and the birthday supper began, but after everybody was served Marigold spoke up.

"I want to get this thing settled before I begin," she said. "I adore symphony concerts, and if my glad rag is going to keep me out of this one I'd better run right up now before I begin eating and change into the plainest thing I have."

Ethan looked at her and grinned, and almost she felt on a friendly footing with him again. She wondered why it was she cared so much whether he stayed friendly or not, and what it was that made him get solemn and indifferent every little while?

They had a pleasant supper, and escorted the invalid upstairs in a procession, Ethan carrying her lightly as if she had been a child. Marigold found herself wondering about herself in those same arms coming down the Capitol stairs earlier in the day. He probably thought no more of it then than he did of carrying his aunt now, and she must stop making so much Out of a simple little thing like that. It was ridiculous to be so self-conscious. He was nothing to her anyway. It would have been a great deal better for herself and everybody else concerned if she had stayed at home and gone to her party, and not come here and acted like a silly little fool, getting all sorts of notions in her head. She watched Ethan lay his aunt gently upon the bed, and remembered how he had stood herself upon her feet and wiped her tears away with his own handkerchief. Why on earth did she have to come down here and get her mind all tangled up thinking about a strange young man who was nothing in the world to her and never could be? Laurie was enough for her to worry about without her taking on another. She ought this very minute to be worrying over the fact that Laurie hadn't telephoned. It would have been like Laurie to get an airplane from some of his friends and come down after her, if he took the notion. What had happened to Laurie? Oughtn't she to go right into the telephone booth now while they were all busy and wouldn't notice her absence for a minute or two, and telephone Mrs. Waterman? That was an idea. She could go home even yet and get there in time for some of the party. Should she try?

But just then Aunt Marian called for a game and motioned Marigold to a chair beside her.

Well, this was Aunt Marian's birthday and she wouldn't spoil it by being absent. She would have to go to bed pretty soon. So Marigold settled down and puzzled her brains over thirty mistakes that she was supposed to find in a picture and forgot Laurie entirely.

They had a very happy hour before the nurse bustled in and shooed them all out, saying the patient really must go to bed and to sleep at once.

"Well," said Ethan turning toward Marigold as they came out of Aunt Marian's room, "what's the answer? Am I to be favored with company to the concert or are you ashamed of my informal dress?"

"Ashamed! Oh, my no!" said Marigold, her cheeks flaming bright with pleasure. "I was afraid it was too late."

"No, we have plenty of time. It's barely eight and the music doesn't begin till eight-thirty. Besides we have seats and would have no trouble getting in."

"I'll be ready in just a minute," said Marigold eagerly. "But — am I too giddy-looking in this bright dress? Will you be ashamed of *me*? I could change in just a jiffy."

"Ashamed?" he grinned. "I'll be prouder than I care to own. You look like something great! I think that is a swell dress."

Marigold's cheeks grew pinker and her eyes sparkled.

"Thank you," she said, and flew away to get her wraps.

"How about you, Aunt Mary? Wouldn't you like to go, too? I have a friend down at the office and I'm sure I can get another ticket."

"Thank you," smiled Mrs. Brooke, "I'm a little tired from the drive this afternoon. I think I'd better stay and rest. Besides I have found a lovely book I would like to read."

So the young people were off together again.

Tucked into the darkness of the car with Ethan's tall form beside her, Marigold suddenly realized that she was having a very good time indeed, and doubted if she would have had a better time if she had stayed at home and gone to the party. Somehow she felt as if she knew Ethan a little better, now that he had complimented her dress. Anyway she was resolved to have a good time this evening in spite of everything. Ethan Bevan wasn't of course anything to her, and after she went home she would likely never see him again, but at least for tonight she was resolved to enjoy everything. She loved music and if he could talk about music as well as he could talk about those paintings that morning surely she had an enjoyable evening before her.

"I'm glad you were willing to go tonight," said Ethan suddenly, guiding his car skillfully through traffic. "I took a chance buying these tickets. I didn't know whether you cared for music or not."

"I love it!" said Marigold enthusiastically, "only I don't have many chances to hear it. Mother and I don't go out very much. Mother is often tired. And most of the young people I know don't seem to be interested in music. They like wild parties and jazz and night clubs and things."

"And you? Don't you go in for those things?" He studied her face keenly in the dim light of the car.

Marigold was still in a troubled silence.

"I don't know," she said slowly at last. "I've never been but once or twice, and then I felt very uncomfortable and out of place. I don't just know why. It didn't seem real."

He was still studying her. At last he said slowly:

"You *would* be out of place. It wouldn't fit *you*. It *isn't* real."

She expected him to say more, but he didn't. Just drove on and sat quietly, now and then looking at her furtively.

"Well," said Marigold at last with a little lilt in her voice. "I know I'm going to enjoy it tonight. Though I may not feel quite at home — I think it will be something like the outside door of heaven."

He looked at her and smiled.

"I'm glad you feel that way."

When they were in the concert hall at last and the first great strains of the opening number were thrilling through the air, Marigold tried to think over their conversation on the way, and somehow she couldn't remember much that was said, but it had left a nice comfortable pleasant impression, as if they were in accord.

Occasionally when something in the program especially pleased her she glanced up at him with her eyes full of delight, and every time she found his pleasant glance upon her, evidently enjoying her pleasure. There was none of that aloofness, that disapproval, she had felt at intervals all day, and she was relieved and content.

He was enjoying the music too. She knew it by the way his glance met hers at the most exquisite climaxes. On the way home he spoke about certain phrases, the way the wood-wind instruments echoed the melody in the symphony, the technique of the solo artist, the depth of insight into the meaning of the score shown by the conductor. She listened to his comments with interest. She had never heard anyone talk about music in this way. None of Laurie's friends knew or liked any music but the weirdest jazz, and then only as an accompaniment to dancing, or as a shield for their wild hilarious conversation. She felt as if this young man regarded it almost as a holy thing, music, *real* music. The kind of music they had been hearing tonight was probably what music had been meant to be before the world turned everything upside down so crazily.

Marigold was sorry when they got back to the house and she had to go to bed. She didn't want to be by herself. She was afraid she was suddenly going to realize that the party was now going on and she was missing it. But instead when she slipped quietly in beside her sleeping mother, all the thinking she did was to wonder about the look Ethan Bevan had given her when he said good night. Did it have withdrawal again in its quality, or was it just pleasant approval? Almost he had looked as if he were sorry to have to say good night so soon. But why should she care to discuss the matter with herself? Miles away at home there was a wonderful party going on now to which she had been invited and might just as well have gone! And here she was off spending her time with a young man she had never seen before, and hadn't at all liked at first. One who had decidedly disapproved of her at first too, she was sure.

Things were queer. Why was she here? She had no one to blame for it but herself. And why did she puzzle over this young man? Let him think what he chose. He had admired her dress, anyway. Or had he? Sometimes she thought he was just poking fun at her, laughing in his sleeve at her all the time. Perhaps he thought she put on that gay dress to charm him. Why should she want to charm him? She had Laurie. Or *did* she? Was he not perhaps even at this moment dancing with that other girl, giving that long adoring look into her eyes that Marigold knew so well, and up to two days ago had considered all her own?

Oh well!

Marigold drew a deep sigh, turning softly over, and suddenly there came to her the memory of those strong arms about her that had rescued her from that terrible sense of falling, and brought her to earth so safely that her fear was lost in content! In the memory of that she drifted peacefully off to sleep.

It was late when she awoke. Her mother had dressed and gone to breakfast from a tray with her sister. Marigold dressed hurriedly and went down, wondering if Ethan

161

Bevan would be gone.

He had finished his breakfast, that was evident, for there was only one place set at the table.

As she drank her orange juice she wondered about him. Perhaps he had gone back to his boarding house. It might be that she would not see him again before he left. He had said he had important things to do.

"Mr. Ethan had his breakfast early," remarked the maid as she brought the cereal and cream. "He went out to the breakfast mission, I think he said."

Breakfast mission. What might that be? Well, she would probably not need to worry any more what he was thinking, she could go her own way now and see the city as she pleased without having to wonder whether she was pleasing his highness or not. There must be old churches. She would look some of them up and find quaint old-time landmarks, sacred historic places of worship. She might have asked Ethan yesterday about them, but she was glad she had not. He would have thought he had to attend her again, and he had certainly served his time at being host to her. She would just wander out and find them for herself. There must be churches all about, and certainly a lot of places she would like to see at her leisure.

She had just finished the last bite of her delicious breakfast and was about to go upstairs to see her mother and aunt before sallying forth on her voyage of discovery, when Ethan walked in at the front door and flung his hat on the hall table.

"Oh, you're down," he said casually. "I didn't know whether the household had waked up yet or not. I had to go out on an early quest. One of my men, my laborers at the job, has been absent for nearly a week, and I wanted to hunt him up. He has been off on a drunk, I suspect, for he left with his pay envelope last Saturday. I had a notion he must be about out of funds by this time, so I went the rounds of the usual rendezvous and found him at last at the Sunday morning breakfast mission. I thought he'd be about ready for that by this time. I gave him a lecture and fixed him with the mission for the day, arranged with another fellow to bring him to the job tonight, and he promised me he'd keep straight and be on hand bright and early tomorrow morning. I hope he will, but you are never sure."

"Oh, that was kind of you to go after him."

"Nothing kind about it," said Ethan gruffly. "It's my job, isn't it, to look after my fellow men? Especially those that are under me in my work. I only wish I could reach deeper down than just the surface and get their feet fixed on solid rock where they can't be moved. I'm always glad when that can be done!"

She looked at him in surprise. This was a new view of this young man. A man as young as he to care what became of his laborers!

But before she could make any remark about it he got up suddenly and started toward the stairs, then glancing at his watch he turned back to her and said hesitantly, almost brusquely:

"I suppose you wouldn't — care — to go to church — with me, would you?" He lifted his eyes and looked straight into hers, almost piercingly. The question was like a challenge. She had a feeling that he expected her to make some excuse and get out of it, but she lifted her eyes with sudden resolve.

"Why yes," she said gravely, "I would, very much. I was just wondering where to find a church."

He seemed almost surprised at her answer.

"But I won't be taking you to any grand church," he said with again a challenge in his glance.

"What makes you think I want to go to a

grand church?" she parried. "I'd like to go with you, that is, if I won't be in your way."

Did his eyes light up at that, or did she imagine it? And why was there something like a little song in her heart as she ran upstairs to get her hat and coat?

 **8** The church to which Ethan took Marigold that morning was a plain little structure, not even in the neighborhood of handsome buildings, but the sermon was one that she would never forget, for it seemed to be a message straight from God to her own soul. Afterwards she couldn't quite remember what the text or main theme of the sermon had been. It had only seemed to her as if God had been there and had been speaking directly to her.

She was very quiet all the way home. Ethan did not seem to notice. He was silent too, perhaps watching her furtively.

Just as they came in sight of the house she spoke, thinking aloud.

"I'm glad I heard that sermon. It made me think of things I had almost forgotten, things I can remember my father saying when I was a little girl and he was preaching."

"Was your father a minister?" asked Ethan in surprise. "I may have known it once, but I certainly had forgotten."

"Yes," said Marigold looking up with dreamy memory in her eyes. "He was a wonderful father, and he preached real things. I

166

was only a child, but I remember a lot of them, and I needed to have them brought back to my memory.

He gave her another surprised look, mixed, she felt, with something like tenderness.

At last just before they reached the house he said:

"I'm very glad you felt that way. I'm always helped when I go to hear that man preach."

But as he helped her up the steps there seemed to be somehow a bond between them that had not been there before, a kind of new sympathy. Yet he said nothing more. Just looked at her and smiled as they entered the house together.

In the afternoon they took Aunt Marian for another short drive because the day was fine and the ride to Mount Vernon had seemed to do her so much good. They wound up at a street meeting held by one of the missions in the lower part of the city. Marigold was greatly interested. She had never been to a street meeting before. She studied the faces of the young people who were conducting it, giving their simple testimonies, and reflected on the contrast between them and Laurie's crowd. Yes, she had been getting afar off from the things her dear father would have wished for her, just as her mother had hinted. She was very thoughtful after that.

They stopped for a few minutes at the breakfast mission for Ethan to look up his man and see if everything was going to be all right for him to get back to camp that night, and then they went home and had a lovely buffet supper served in Aunt Marian's room with Ethan for waiter. They all sat awhile afterward listening to Aunt Marian's favorite preacher on the radio. By common consent they lingered with the dear invalid as long as she was allowed to stay awake, feeling that their time together was not to be long, and wanting to please her as much as possible. The nurse was out, and the patient begged them to remain a little longer, saying she was not tired, but at last when they insisted that she ought to be asleep, she said:

"All right. But first let's have a bit of Bible and a prayer! Ethan, you get my Bible."

Marigold sat down again and watched Ethan in surprise as he quietly got the Bible and sat down to read. Fancy such a request being made of Laurie! How he would laugh and jeer if anybody thought of asking him to do such a thing. A pang of troubled doubt went through her soul with the thought. Had she been brought here to watch this most unusual man, and see the contrast between him and Laurie? She put the thought from her in annoyance.

Ethan opened the Bible as if it were a familiar book. He didn't ask his aunt where he should read. He turned directly to the ninety-first psalm and read in a clear voice as if he loved what he was reading:

He that dwelleth in the secret place of the most High shall abide under the shadow of the Almighty.

I will say of the Lord, He is my refuge and my fortress: my God; in Him will I trust.

Somehow as he read on Marigold felt as if he were reading these words just for her. As if, in his mind they had some special significance for her. She sat there listening, thrilled with the thought.

"Surely He shall deliver thee —"

Was he trying to remind her that when earthly friends were not by to help she was not alone?

"Thou shalt not be afraid for the terror by night —"

And now he did lift his eyes and look straight into hers, with a light in them that surely he meant her to read and understand.

He was thinking of the dream she had told him and the terror that possessed her sometimes when she wakened in the night. It could not have been plainer if he had said it in spoken words, and suddenly her own face lighted in response. Yet it was all unobserved by the two dear women who were sitting by listening, though they would dearly have loved to have caught that look that passed between the two beloved children.

And the steady voice went on:

"He shall give His angels charge over thee to keep thee —" It was like a benediction and Marigold felt she never could forget it as his voice read on to the end of the psalm.

And then he knelt and prayed, such a simple earnest petition, filled with deep thanksgiving, humble confession, heartfelt trust, and joyful praise. And this was the young man she had scorned when she came. The man she wished anywhere else but where she was to be!

She looked at him with a kind of shy awe and mingled humility as they rose from their knees, and he smiled at her again as if she were suddenly one of the elect company of intimates to which he belonged. She couldn't quite understand what made the difference in his attitude but she knew it was there and it gave her a warm feeling about her heart. That was something more than just happiness. It seemed almost as if it were something like a holy bond.

She went to sleep that night wondering about it, and not realizing that she hadn't once remembered the party nor Laurie all day long. It seemed as if somehow she was entering upon a new era in her life. She didn't question what it was to be, but she knew that she could never go back home and be the same thoughtless gay butterfly that she had been before. She found herself wishing wistfully that she might be with this wonderful young man and learn the secret of his sweetness and his strength. She hoped — and this was her last waking thought — that in the morning he would not again slam the door of his soul, leaving her outside. Not until she could ask him a few questions and perhaps get nearer to his Source of strength, anyway.

She hurried eagerly downstairs in the morning early, but he was gone. Gone without a word!

"Ethan was sorry he had to leave without farewells," said Aunt Marian to Marigold's mother, calling from her room as Mrs. Brooke went by her door. "Someone called him last night about a man, one of his laborers, and he had to go and hunt him up.

171

Some poor soul for whom he feels responsible. He slipped out without waking anybody. He called me just now on the phone and asked me to say how sorry he was not to be able to say good-bye. He had not intended to leave until after breakfast, and was hoping to get another word with you both before he left."

Marigold at the foot of the stairs heard, and her heart went down with a thud of disappointment, the light out of her eyes, and the brightness out of the new bright day! So! That was that! She would probably never see him again, and their brief contact would pass into the had-been and be forgotten!

She stared blankly about her wondering what she would do with the day. Of course she could call up Mrs. Waterman now and find out if Laurie had called, but somehow it didn't seem to matter much whether he had or not.

Then she heard her mother's footsteps coming down the stairs and she roused to a cheerfulness that she was far from feeling. What was the matter with her, anyway? Silly thing! What difference did it make whether Ethan Bevan was there or away? He was nothing whatever to her. Two days ago she would have been glad enough to get rid of him. She ought to be glad that he went away with a pleasant smile and she didn't have to remember him as a grouch before whom she had been humiliated. He had been nice to her at the last. And he was a good man. He had helped her. She must be honest about that. And it was just sheer folly for her to be disappointed that he had gone without giving her a special word. What was she to him? What could she expect? She was nothing but one of his fellow mortals upon this earth who needed help. She was no more to him than that poor laborer who had called him from his sleep to search him out and save him. She was just a weak sister who couldn't bear to stand on a height and look down, and he had carried her down and given her of his strength, for the time being, to help tide her over her dismay. She firmly believed that he had given her permanent help against that obsession, and she ought to be thankful that God had given her this brief contact with one so strong and so able to help others. And now she had to go back and meet her own world alone. But God had seen that she needed help and had sent her down here to get it. He had seen that she needed to be awakened to the fact that she was getting away from the things of her childhood's faith, the standards and customs that had been so safe and wise, and He had taken this way to show her where she was drifting. Now it was up to her to use her new knowledge. Or was it? Wasn't she just as helpless alone as if she were still standing out on that narrow ledge above a great height of peril? She couldn't get back alone, could she? She needed someone's strength to steady her till her feet were upon solid ground. Some *One,* Ethan had said! How she wished she had asked him more about that experience of his own, in some of those silences yesterday. Now, probably she would never know. But he had, at least in his reading of the psalm last night, given her a hint of where her strength was to be found. That was it. God would be her strength! She had got to find out by herself how to get back to God and the things she had been forgetting so long.

"Well," said her mother suddenly, watching her intently, "what are you going to do today, dear? You have your freedom now to go about alone as you wished. What is going to be your plan?"

Marigold looked up with sudden illumination and laughed.

"Oh, Mother! I'm sorry I was so unspeakably disagreeable the night we arrived. I ought to have been spanked. He was lovely. He really was wonderful, and I enjoyed all the places he took me and had a very good time. I don't know about today. Isn't there something I could do to make a happy time for you and Aunt Marian? It seems to me I've had enough of enjoyment to last me a good long while."

"Well, that's sweet of you, dear, but I don't see what you could do for us, this morning at least. We haven't any car, and you couldn't carry your aunt downstairs. Whatever we do for her will have to be done in her room, until Elinor and her husband get home, since she can't get downstairs."

"I could do picture puzzles with her," said Marigold brightly. "I heard her say she loves them, and you know I always did like to do them."

"Yes, well, perhaps you could part of the day, toward evening. But I'm sure she won't be happy to have you cooped up all the time this lovely day. I think she would like it better if you went out somewhere awhile. She was speaking of some of the places around here she wanted you to see, to which you could quite well walk. I think it would be nice if you were to go out a little while this morning, and perhaps again in the afternoon for a few minutes, and then come in and entertain her between whiles with what you have seen."

"All right, I'll go out for a walk. I'll bring her back a new puzzle she hasn't seen, and we'll do that some of the in-betweens. But how about yourself? You've been cooped up most of the time. Why shouldn't you go out too, or let me stay here and you go alone?"

Mrs. Brooke smiled.

"You know, my dear, the best thing I can do is stay with my dear sister. We've been hungry for each other for many long years. But I'll go out with you a few minutes for a walk if you would like it. Aunt Marian was telling me about a lovely place she wants me to see, and she says it's only a few blocks from here. She says it reminds her so much of our old home when we were children. I'll walk with you there, now, right after breakfast, if you'd like, and then you can be free until lunch time to go your own way."

So they went out together, and Mrs. Brooke studied her dear child's face, wondering if the wistful look in her eyes was for Laurie, and the party she had missed.

But Marigold never mentioned the party, nor Laurie either, and talked brightly of having her mother stay another two weeks after she herself went home. Talked blithely of little changes she meant to make in the apartment when they got back, new curtains they might have, to make things more cheery, and so they walked the lovely streets and came back to the house. Then Marigold started out on her lonely tour of investigation. But somehow there wasn't a great deal of spice in this independence after all. Where should she go?

Well, there was the art gallery. Ethan had said that was worth taking time to study. She would do that this morning. She would take a taxi and save time. And then in the afternoon she would go awhile to Smithsonian. If she ever should see Ethan again and he should ask her, which of course he wouldn't because he asked very few questions, she would hate to say she hadn't done anything with her precious time in Washington after he left.

So she spent the morning in Corcoran, and came back impressed with the fact that she knew very little indeed about pictures, and only a very few of the great ones she had seen that morning had meant very much to her. As she entered the house the thought did come to her that perhaps that was because her mind had been more or less on other things all the time.

She had stopped at a store long enough to purchase a fascinating picture puzzle, and she and Aunt Marian worked at it until her aunt hurried her off to Smithsonian, telling her that she would find the time all too short until four o'clock when everything belonging to the government closed.

So she started out again, wandering here and there, getting a glimpse of this and that, and wondering what Ethan would have said if he had been here with her.

And there she was again thinking about Ethan. How utterly ridiculous. Why not think about Laurie? How nice it would be if Laurie were like Ethan, that is, like him in some things, anyway. For instance, Laurie wouldn't have stopped a minute to look at pictures, or listen to classical music. He would have said it was too slow for him. He would have wanted something exciting. He never stopped to look into the history or the beauty or the reason of things. And Laurie, if she were frightened — well, Laurie in her dream had turned and waved his hand at her and then gone off laughing. It was so characteristic of his gay nature that she couldn't quite think of his carrying her comfortingly down those stairs, wiping her tears away. Laurie hated tears. He wanted smiles and laughter and excitement. Laurie would never have read the Bible and prayed, nor gone to church! Oh, if she started out on this new life she was vaguely planning would she have to give up Laurie? Or be continually at swords' points with him?

She began almost to dread going home. What was she going to meet when she got there? What would this strange new kind of young man she had been companioning with the last two days do if he were put into her situation?

One thing she knew, he would never give in and go the way of the world. There was something about him that showed he had distinctly given up the world as far as amusing himself was concerned. He didn't go to night clubs, nor admire girls who went to them. He hadn't said so, but somehow she knew. And by the same token she was sure he would never compromise with anything he had decided was not right.

She walked herself around and took in the main points of the great museum. Then she took a taxi back to her aunt's house, without ever really putting her mind on what she was seeing. In a vague way she recalled this and that, enough to mention a few things when she got back to the two who watched her and hoped she had had a good time, but all the time there had been that undertone of thought, gradually focusing in her mind into one overwhelming wish, that she might have one more chance to talk to Ethan Bevan and ask him a few of the questions that filled her with consternation as she contemplated meeting them all alone when she got home.

The idea followed her all day, grew deeper while she worked with the picture puzzle with her aunt, and in the evening while she sat in the lovely library and tried to read a book with only half of her mind while the other half turned over her problems. It stayed with her and kept her awake after she had retired, and met her at the break of day when she awoke. This was her last morning here. Today she must go home. If she could only talk with that young man a half hour before she went away and ask him to advise her!

And then, while she was eating an early lunch, because both mother and aunt had decreed that she must go on an earlier train than she had selected so that she would not arrive at the apartment alone late in the evening, in he walked!

 **9** Marigold's heart gave a quick little leap of gladness, and a light glowed in her eyes and flamed in pretty color in her cheeks.

"Hello, folks!" Ethan said casually, as if he had only gone out a few minutes before, but his level gaze was straight at Marigold, and an answering glow came into his eyes, as if he was pleased at what he had seen in hers. It was as if their two hearts had spoken to one another across the room in a look that neither quite realized.

Ethan held her gaze for a full second before he went on, still watching her earnestly.

"I found I had to run up to Philadelphia after some parts of a machine we need that are not to be had around here. I wondered if you might care to drive up with me, or would you prefer to go on the train as you planned? Don't feel you have to go with me if you would rather go some other way."

Marigold's cheeks flamed a sweet color now and she cried out softly in delight.

"Oh, I'd love to go with you!" she cried. "I was dreading the long car ride alone."

"How kind of you to think of her," said Mrs. Brooke in relief. "I hated to have her go home alone, it seemed so desolate, and

I've been making her start earlier than she had planned because I didn't want her to have to go into the apartment alone so late at night."

"Well, I can go in with her and help her light up," grinned Ethan. "It won't be much more than that though, because I have to start right back and drive nearly all night. We can't hold up our machine another day. I've telephoned ahead to have the parts ready so I won't lose time."

"Well, you could wait long enough for me to make a cup of coffee and scramble some eggs, couldn't you?" Marigold asked.

"Perhaps!" he said with another grin like a shy boy.

In a little while they were off into the brightness of the day, and soon had left Washington behind, the road winding ahead of them in a broad white ribbon.

But it was hard for Marigold to believe that there had been that look between them, now that they were alone in the car. He had returned to his silent aloofness, and somehow Marigold didn't seem to be able to think of anything to say that would break the spell of silence. She got to thinking that perhaps he had only asked her to ride out of a sense of duty. Perhaps he hadn't wanted her at all.

She sat there silently thinking it over, and then a sudden remembrance of that glowing look with which he had welcomed her acceptance of his invitation brought a degree of comfort. How silly she was! This was his nature, and why should she question it? If he didn't want to talk let him remain quiet. He hadn't had to ask her, and he likely was friendly enough and wanted her or he wouldn't have taken the trouble to come after her. Why be bothered by his manner? This time with him was what she had wanted, to ask him a lot of questions, why not use it? If he didn't want to answer he could say so.

So presently she summoned her courage. casting a sideways glance at his pleasant friendly face.

"There are some things I would very much like to ask you," she said in a strained young voice, almost wishing now she was started that she hadn't begun.

"Yes?" He turned a look of quick interest toward her, and all her hesitation vanished. He was again the friend who was ready and eager to help, able and understanding.

"We were speaking of worldly amusements the other day. Night clubs and dancing and movies and that sort of thing. Of course I was brought up without them, but people — sometimes Christian people — are telling me that times have changed and that everybody thinks those things are all right now. They even have dancing in some churches. They say young people can't get along without those things. I wanted to know what you think. Is it wrong for a Christian ever to go to such things? Do you think a girl or a man could be a Christian and yet do those things?"

Ethan looked at her with one of those deep searching glances as if he would find out through her eyes just what she thought herself before he answered.

"Do you mean, do I think a person can be *saved* and yet do those things? Because, yes, I suppose they can. For salvation isn't a matter of what you do yourself. It's something Christ did for you, and you have only to accept. But if you're asking about those things as the practise of a person who is saved, that's another question."

Marigold sat thoughtfully looking into the bright landscape ahead.

"I see," she said earnestly. "But if they were considering whether they would accept the Saviour as theirs, wouldn't the matter of what they had to do or not do afterward have to be considered? Wouldn't they have to be willing to renounce things if they took Christ as their Saviour?"

"It doesn't say so in the Bible. It says 'Believe on the Lord Jesus Christ and thou shalt be saved.' "

"Then you think it is all right for a Christian to be worldly sometimes, do you?" she asked with evident surprise in her tone.

"I didn't say that," he answered quickly. "I don't think those things are to be considered when one accepts the Lord Jesus as his Saviour. The question is just that Jesus Christ died for your sins, and is willing to take them and their penalty upon His own account instead of yours, and do you want Him to do that? If you say yes, if you accept what He has already done for you, and believe fully that He has done it, then you are born again. You have a new nature born of God, and that nature does not desire the things of this world. Yet you still have that old sinning nature with you, will have as long as you live on the earth, that draws you in spite of your best resolves, makes you want to do the things that you have resolved over and over again you will never do, and as long as that old nature has a chance to get on the top every little while you haven't much chance of living the steady testimony a saved soul should live. But God has provided a way of victory for you over the old nature. He has said that if you will go the whole way with Him, even to the cross, and let the old nature be crucified with Him, reckon it to have *died* with Him, that He will give you His own resurrection power in your life; that is, He will live His life in you on a different plane from ordinary living. Am I making it plain?"

"I think so," said Marigold thoughtfully. "You mean hand everything over to Him and be willing for what He wants?"

"Yes, it amounts to that. It is reckoning yourself to be dead to the things of the flesh, and alive unto God; it is asking Him to slay self in you so that you can honestly say, 'I am crucified with Christ; nevertheless I live; yet not I, but Christ liveth in me: and the life which I now live in the flesh I live by the faith of the Son of God, who loved me, and gave himself for me.' When you can honestly say that to Him, then He can come in and fill you with Himself, and it will be no more you who is living in your body, but Jesus Christ who is living your life for you. And then if He wants you to go to the night clubs, and dance and all that sort of thing He will tell you. He'll make it very plain to you. It isn't a matter of giving up things. It's a matter of whether you are willing to *die* with Him."

"Oh," said Marigold softly, a strange illumined look on her face, "that makes life all different, doesn't it?"

She was still trying to think it through, he saw.

"Yes," he said looking with a great yearning upon the sweet face as she sat thinking. "It makes life very wonderful!" and there was that in his tone that showed he knew from experience the truth of what he was saying. "It puts the power of God at your command, to conquer for you the old sinful nature that is in you. It's His resurrection power."

She looked at him perplexed.

"I don't exactly understand. What is the resurrection power?"

"It is the power of God that Jesus Christ brought with Him out of the tomb when He rose from the dead. He said 'All power is given unto me, go ye — !' meaning that they were to go forth in that power to conquer, what of themselves they never could. They were to go out to witness for Him. That was their only commission, and you know yourself, they nor we, never could do much witnessing for the Lord Jesus by the lives we live in our own power. Just our own resolves and beliefs wouldn't go very far in making others accept Christ as Saviour, nor even in showing them that He was the Son of God!"

"That is all new to me," said the girl earnestly. "You mean we can have Christ's own power instead of our own to live by?"

"Yes, if we are willing for this death-union with Him. He has promised, 'If we be planted together with Him in the likeness of His death, we shall be also in the likeness of His resurrection.' And it is just in proportion as we are willing for this death-union with Him, this daily dying with Him to the things of this world, the things of the old nature, that we shall be able to show Him to others."

They were silent for a moment while she considered that. Then Ethan spoke again.

"You know self is not easily slain. It has a habit of coming to life again, self with all its old programs and ambitions and tastes and feelings and wishes. It is a case of having to be slain continually. 'For we which live (here on this earth, you know) are *always* delivered unto death for Jesus' sake, that in our dying flesh the life whereby Jesus conquered death might be made manifest,' as one translation has it. I wonder if I have made that perfectly plain? Do you see how all this affects the question you asked me about worldly ways and amusements?"

"Oh, yes, I think I do," said Marigold

slowly. "That would be very wonderful living. I never dreamed that such living would be possible on this earth. I didn't know that — we could — get so close — to God — as that! But I can see that if one lived that way those other questions wouldn't even come up at all. They would settle themselves, wouldn't they?"

"They certainly would! They certainly do!" said the young man with a ring of triumph in his voice.

She was still a long time and then with a little sigh of troubled perplexity she said:

"That would be all right for those who wanted to have Him a Saviour like that; wanted to die with Him — were *willing* to. But what about those who are not willing?"

A shadow came over the brightness of his face. Was she then going so far and no farther? Had he been mistaken in her interest? Was she so entangled with the world that she could not surrender it?

He did not answer for a moment, and then he said with a sorrowful note in his voice:

"Does it matter? If one isn't willing to go the whole way with the Lord Jesus, just staying away from a few night clubs and movies isn't going to get you any nearer. There are plenty of people who don't do any of those things and yet are not saved."

There was such disappointment in his voice as he finished that she looked up and suddenly read what he had thought.

"I don't mean myself," she said quickly. "I mean somebody else. Suppose you had a friend who wanted to go to those things all the time, who couldn't see anything out of the way in them."

"Is he saved?" asked Ethan quickly with a sharp note of tenseness in his voice.

"I — don't — suppose he is!" she answered with down-drooping gaze and sorrowful mien.

He gave her another keen furtive glance, his lips set in stern lines.

"You mean — ?" he started, and hesitated.

"I mean do you think a Christian should try and stop him going? Or — should perhaps go with him sometimes, when he is insistent — and try to win him away from such things?"

"I should think the question would start farther back than that. I should think a Christian who was willing to have this death-union with Christ that we have been speaking of, could not possibly make a practise of companionship with one who is an acknowledged outsider, an enemy of Christ.

For you know He said: 'He that is not with me is against me!' And Christ has made it very plain that He does not want His saved ones to choose their companions from the world. A Christian lives in a different realm."

His voice was almost harsh as he said this. He would rather do almost anything than give advice to this girl on a subject like this. And she was very still considering what he had said. At last she answered in a low voice:

"Yes, I know. I was brought up to think that. And my mother has reminded me, too. But somehow I don't seem to come into contact with many believers nowadays. The church where we go is very worldly. They even have dances there sometimes. And — well — I was wondering whether there was anything I could do for some worldly people I know. It isn't a question of *beginning* to go with them. I have known them for a long time. It's a question of what I might be able to do for them now, knowing them as well as I do. Should I humor them and go with them, trying to help them to get away from such things, or should I just cut loose from them entirely?"

She waited, looking at him anxiously.

His face grew suddenly tender.

"Forgive me!" he said gently. "I'm not

your dictator. God Himself will guide you in such things if you will let Him. But I am quite sure that you could never win a person away from anything by doing it with him. If you come to know Christ and the power of His resurrection, and the fellowship of His sufferings, and share the likeness of His death, and He makes you know that these things are not for you, then surely you can see that you must be consistent in your life with what you believe. But I do not think you will have to ask me such a question. It will be something that Christ and you will settle together. And as far as you are concerned, if you know Him through dying with Him, your testimony will be such that the worldly people will drop you, and these things will likely drop away. You will no longer want to do them because you have better things to do, just as you don't want to play with dolls now as you probably used to do when you were a child. You will be as truly dead to these things as a person lying in a coffin would be dead to any temptation that used to lead him astray in his lifetime. That is, of course, you would unless you made a *practise* of doing those things constantly. You cannot hold hands with the world and expect to have this death-union with Christ and the resultant resurrection power in your life."

There was a long silence while Marigold thought that over.

Once they stopped to get gas and she watched her escort as he lifted the hood of his engine, talked a minute or two with the attendant, and then took a bit of a leaflet out and handed it to him with a smile saying, "Good-bye brother, I hope to see you sometime again." Marigold could see the young man standing where they had left him, curiously reading the little tract that had been given him. What a man this was with whom she was privileged to travel! He was trying to make men everywhere see Christ! For she sensed that he had spoken of His Saviour to the stranger, and that his word had been graciously received. How was it that she had not understood how fine he was when she first met him? How was it that she had even resented his presence?

Ah, she had been looking upon him merely as another young man, judging him in the worldly sense, from her own personal interest in him. She had not realized that he was an envoy from another world who might perhaps have important messages for her own soul.

What was it that made him so different from other men she knew? Well, of course it must be this death-union with Christ he had been talking about. But how had he got that way? How was it that he alone of all the young men she knew anywhere should be like this? Had it been through his own efforts, through some special environment, through some experience? Then she remembered.

"You promised to tell me about your experience with high places," she suddenly said. "May I know now? When you were in danger once, and how you got over it."

"Yes?" he said looking at her sharply. "Are you sure it will not make you dizzy again to hear it so soon?"

She smiled.

"No, I think you have helped me over that place," she said. "My obsession came when I dreamed myself into a situation for which I could see no help when I woke up. I had to be continually going over and over it in my mind trying to find a way to save myself, and so the dream returned again and again. But you showed me a way out. You brought a strong arm and carried me down. You gave me the sense of being secure anyway, even if I was in peril, and I haven't had the dream since. I don't believe it will ever bother me again. I can't thank you enough for that."

He smiled.

"I'm glad I was there!" he said with satisfaction. "Well, I'll tell you my story. It isn't long. I was in a high place on the scaffold of my biggest job, the biggest I had ever had then, and it was nearing completion. I was very proud of the work that I had done. I knew it was good work and was going to make me a degree of fame in my profession so that I might continue to go on up and do bigger things. I was rather swelled up about it I'm afraid, *my* bridge over a great chasm, and *I* was the designer and builder!"

Marigold looked up at in surprise. He certainly had no look of conceit about him now.

He went on:

"And then, something suddenly went wrong, while I was standing up there, looking up and about at my almost completed job. A piece of machinery weighing tons crashed down beside me, carrying with it scaffold and stone work and flying masonry, and leaving me standing there on just the slender board that was left, wavering out over an abyss, nothing to hold to, no way apparently to get back to anything tangible at all. It didn't matter then whose fault it was. I found out incidentally it had been partly mine, away back in the beginning of the job. I hadn't been as careful as I should. But that didn't concern me then. All I saw was that I was standing in awful space between heaven and earth with no possible hope of my life, no way ever to get back to earth again, and only a few minutes, perhaps seconds, left before I too should crash down into the horror of debris below. All my pride, my ambition, my attainment was in ruins below me, and I dared not look down at it. I dared not look off and try to forget it, I dared not look up, and I could not plan any way to save myself! And then, a man risked his life and crept out on the tottering masonry of the arch above me, and let down a rope. He let it down carefully in front of my hands where I could grasp it. It had a loop in it that I could hold to. And I stood there holding to that little loop of rope, knowing the masonry from which it hung might presently come crashing down too and carry me with it, yet I had the rope, and how I clung to it! After what seemed eons more they made a way to get down to me, and strong arms drew me up and into safety. I won't harrow you with the details. I came out of that terrible situation knowing that one man had risked his life to save me.

"For days I lay in a dark room trying to steady my senses, knowing that I was ruined, body, mind and soul if I could not get away from the horror that possessed me. I never could go on an operation again. I would always have death staring me in the face if I climbed to any high place.

Then one night as I lay tossing, unable to sleep, the Lord came to me, across great space to that terrible pinnacle upon which I always seemed to be standing alone whenever I tried to sleep, came down, and as easily as I picked you up that day, took me in His arms. He looked me in the eyes, and He said to me:

" 'Ethan, you belong to me! Don't you know it? Don't you remember that day long ago when you told your Sunday School teacher you would accept me as your Saviour? You were only a boy then, but you meant what you said, and I accepted you. You haven't thought much about Me since. You've been wandering strange paths where I can't go, and you haven't listened for my voice when I called you. But now you've found out where they lead and that they end in ruin, those paths you thought were so bright when you started out, those paths of ambition that you thought would lead you to fame.

" 'And now you think you are done, that your career is ended. But you are mistaken. You are *mine*. You have been mine all the time, even when you wandered so far you could not hear my voice, And I never lose

197

my own. I've come after you, and I'm going to bring you back, and let you go on in your profession, but you must walk with *me!* It is the only safe way. No, you needn't be afraid of this horror any more, because you are going to remember that from now on I am with you, and wherever duty calls you I will be there and have my arm around you. I gave my life for you once, and I'm never going to let you fall. Now get up, Ethan, and go on with your work, for you and I have died together once, and we're going on to live together now, and show men what the power of the resurrection in a life can do.' "

Ethan was still a minute, and then he looked down at her and smiled.

"That's all," he said. "That's how it came about! I know He'll do that for you, too, if you will let Him!"

"Oh, I'd like Him to," breathed Marigold softly.

Just then they came within the city traffic, and there was no more opportunity to talk.

10

That very afternoon Irene Trescott had stopped in at her sister-in-law's home to talk over the party. Knowing her sister-in-law as well as she did she hadn't thought it wise to go sooner lest the reaction to the affair would not be over yet. Adele Trescott always had a lengthy season after any social affair, during which she harrowed herself with all the petty details that had, to her way of thinking, gone wrong. Irene wanted to give her time to get over this before she appeared.

But she had reckoned without knowledge. Mrs. Trescott had not yet recovered.

She was sitting up in bed attired in a costly negligee, beribboned and belaced to the utmost degree, her heavy form lolling against many pillows, a large box of sweets on the bedside stand within reach, and a couple of novels on the bed beside her.

But she was not reading. When her sister-in-law entered the room she looked up with eyes that were swollen with weeping, and dabbed futilely at her sagging cheeks and heavy lips that for once were guiltless of rouge and lipstick.

"Oh, my dear! Is it you?" she sighed heavily, her words ending in a half-sob. "I

199

wondered why you didn't come. I didn't think you would desert me in a time like this!"

Irene sat down heavily, after having helped herself to a handful of chocolates selected carefully, and settled to a siege.

"For heaven's sake, Adele! What's the matter? Haven't you recovered from the party yet? I thought you would be up and planning for another by this time," said Irene, carefully biting a fat chocolate peppermint in half and surveying the portion still in her fingers speculatively. "What's the matter now. Was the caterer's bill larger than you expected, or did Mrs. Osterman's little pet step-daughter have a more expensive dress on than some of your favorites?"

Adele gave her a withering look.

"How can you be so trivial when you were there and know perfectly well what happened. You saw how Laurie behaved. You know he was positively under the influence of drink the whole last half of the evening. It was the most mortifying thing I ever went through. You saw what he did, went out in the street and brought in that unspeakable girl and danced with her. You don't mean to tell me that you didn't see that, Irene?"

"Well, what could you expect, Adele? You furnished the liquor, didn't you? And you were down on the girls he wanted you to invite for him, weren't you?"

"Irene! Of course you would take up for him and go against me," whimpered the mother putting the lace-bordered soppy little handkerchief to her swollen eyes again. "Blaming *me!* When I did all I could. I invited the little nobody he wanted me to, — and I — tried to humor him — in every way —"

"Oh certainly, you always humor him," said Irene dryly. "You can't reproach yourself about that. You humored him — in your way. But you despised the girl he was in love with, and you probably have been so cold to her in the past that she didn't care to accept your invitation when it came."

"There you go, taking Laurie's part against me! I haven't been cold to her. I haven't had anything at all to do with her! I haven't had occasion to."

"Exactly!" said Irene licking the peppermint off her finger. "You've been cold to her. You've ignored her. You *meant* to ignore her and freeze her out. You can't blame Laurie for his attitude last night."

"My dear! You don't know what Laurie did last night. You don't know what he said to me. His own mother!" whimpered Adele, her big overfed body shaking with her sobs.

Irene got up and went and stood at the window looking out, where she wouldn't have to watch her sister-in-law weep.

"Yes, I know. I was standing right behind him. I know what he said. He told you you had fixed it so his girl wouldn't come to the party. You hadn't been friendly and she wouldn't come, and now he was going out and get a girl from the street, any girl he could find, and bring her in and dance with her."

"He was drunk, of course," sobbed Laurie's mother. "He wouldn't have said that if he had been sober. At least he wouldn't have said it *right before people!* That was what hurt so, having people hear him say that to me. To *me!*"

"Well, you got the liquor, and you never brought him up not to drink —" reminded Irene again. "I never thought it was a good thing to drink — at least not to drink too much — and Laurie always does everything just as hard as he can."

"You're hard, Irene! You're very hard! I never *taught* Laurie to drink, and I always told him a gentleman knew how to carry his liquor. That's what my good old father used to say. He was a real southern gentleman, and he always said a true gentleman knew how to carry his liquor! My father never was *drunk!*"

"Well, it's evident Laurie can't carry liquor. Perhaps your father's drinking is coming out in Laurie now, in his not being able to carry it. I wouldn't blame Laurie altogether!" said Irene contemptuously.

"I suppose it's *his* father coming out in him," said the indignant mother, "not *my* father!"

"Well, it really doesn't matter, does it? What I was thinking was that if you had let Laurie have that girl that you despised so he wouldn't have been drunk. She would have kept him from it. I happen to know she doesn't drink."

"Oh, I suppose she never had a chance, being a minister's daughter! But she would have learned quick enough. Those are the worst ones, when they've never been taught self-control."

"No, she wouldn't have touched it. She doesn't believe in it. She's that kind of a girl."

"Well, you talk as if *I* kept her away. I sent her a perfectly good invitation, didn't I? I told you about it, and I showed you her acceptance. And then she sent word she couldn't come after all — an awfully rude thing to do, *I* think, after she had once accepted. *I* think it was because she found out what kind of an affair it was going to be, and she simply knew she couldn't dress up to the occasion, and so she didn't dare come."

"You're mistaken there!" said Irene in a superior tone. "I happen to know she had her dress all ready, a gorgeous dress, all bought and paid for."

"You happen to know? How could you possibly know a thing like that?" said Laurie's mother lifting her tear-streaked face in astonishment. "Did she tell you so herself? Probably she was lying then. Of course she couldn't possibly afford the kind of dress one ought to wear to such an affair as we had Saturday night."

"No, she wasn't lying," said Irene with satisfaction. "She didn't tell me herself either. She isn't the kind of girl who would lie, or who would speak to me about such a thing. She's *refined*, I tell you, Adele. She wouldn't consider it was my affair."

"Well then, how in the world could you possibly find out whether she had a dress fit to wear? Where would she get money to buy a proper dress?"

"Well, I'm sure I don't know where she got the money, but she had it. I don't think she stole it. I've always heard she was perfectly honest. But she bought the dress and paid a hundred and fifty dollars for it! And then when she found she couldn't come she took it back and exchanged it for some other dresses just as handsome. In fact she spent *more* than the hundred and fifty!"

Irene was enjoying herself heartily as she watched her sister-in-law's face filled with incredulity.

"And you say she didn't tell that extraordinary tale to you herself?" Laurie's mother had utmost contempt in her voice.

"Oh, no, she didn't tell me. I haven't even seen her. No, I got my information from Rena Brownell. You remember Rena? I'm sure you do. She always used to head your list for parties till her father lost all his money and then died and left them penniless. She's working in François' Gown Shop, a model there. You know she had such a lovely figure."

"You don't say! Well, that explains who that model was! She tried to recognize me but I only stared at her. I thought she looked somehow familiar. But of course I wasn't expecting to see anybody I knew *serving* in François'. You see I was there last week with Robena to get a dress for Saturday night. You saw it, didn't you? That gorgeous white taffeta, with the stunning scarlet velvet sash? I thought that was the most stunning dress we had present."

"Yes, I saw it," said Irene with a sardonic

grin. "The irony of it all was that that was the very dress that Marigold Brooke bought and then took back because her mother didn't approve of the low back."

"You don't *mean* it, Irene!"

"Yes, I do. Rena Brownell told me all about it. She said Madame made Robena pay two hundred for it because she knew she wanted it so much."

"And she dared to do that to a friend of mine!"

"Good gracious, Adele, don't be so snobbish. Robena *bought* the dress, didn't she? She telephoned and asked for just such a dress, white with a crimson sash. I heard her myself when you were at the telephone with her. You were as sweet as honey to Madame yourself, said you'd do all sorts of things for her if she would try to get a dress like that for a friend of yours. You didn't expect Madame to do it for nothing, did you? And now you are making a fuss because you know Marigold didn't want it."

"Well, but — daring to pass off a second-hand dress on *us!*"

"Second-hand nothing! Marigold exchanged it. She hadn't had it out of the shop but a few hours. You were grateful as could be that Madame found the kind of dress you wanted. Don't be a silly fool, Adele. You know that dress was the sensation of the whole evening. If you don't believe it go and read the society notes over again and rub up your memory. And what's more, I can tell you it would have been a still greater sensation if it had been on Marigold Brooke, instead of that stiff awkward Robena, and you wouldn't have had half so much to regret if it had, either."

"Irene! I will not listen to any more of your rantings. You are just saying these things to make me suffer, and you know I have practically been in tears all day over this thing. My darling boy Laurie acting that way at the party, bringing in that unspeakable girl from the street and insisting on dancing with her, and letting Robena go without a partner! My darling Laurie, telling me *before people* that I had kept his girl away, and now I could take my medicine!" And the distressed mother wept into her handkerchief again, though it already had a saturate solution of tears, and only made her whole face sloppy and desolate looking.

"Where is Laurie now? Why didn't you tell him it wasn't true? Why didn't you show him the notes from Marigold, and make him understand that it wasn't your fault?"

"Oh, I did. I tried to, but he wouldn't

listen. He just went on drinking and drinking, and dancing with that one awful girl."

"Well, you've Robena to thank for that. She started him drinking. Every time I saw them together the first part of the evening she was either handing him another glass or he was handing her one. And if you ask me, I think *she* was the disgrace of the whole party, the way she carried on with that Russian-looking man that came in late. She was drunk herself! She's the one I would have been ashamed of if *I* had been in *your* place."

"Really Irene I don't think you are very kind. You've just taken a dislike to Robena because you know I like her. And the idea that that other girl should presume to buy a dress like that! It's absurd! It's not suitable for her position, a little school teacher!"

"All right, Adele! Talk that way if you want to, but if Marigold Brooke had been here wearing that sumptuous white dress with the crimson velvet girdle you would have seen something worth describing in the society columns, and you wouldn't have seen her lolling around with any foreign counts and acting crazy either. It's my opinion that she wouldn't have remained here long if she had come. She isn't used to a drunken crowd. I thought it was disgusting the way that Robena acted. You needn't be surprised at anything your precious Laurie does if he stays around that girl long. She's enough to be the downfall of a saint, and I don't mean maybe. But if Marigold had been here I suppose you would have somehow blamed it on her. Though you couldn't if you'd once see her face. Really, she's lovely, Adele, and if you had any sense at all about managing Laurie, you'd cultivate that girl and get her to use her influence with him to keep him away from drink. He can't stand it, and that's the truth! Where is he now, did you say?"

"I didn't say," said Mrs. Trescott severely. "But he's probably asleep. I'm sure I hope he is. And when he comes to himself he probably won't know what it's all about. But I feel disgraced forever, having him bring in that awful frumpy girl. Why, my dear, did you notice? I'm sure her evening gown was made of *rayon,* and her make-up was execrable."

"Well," said Irene thoughtfully, "she was pretty awful, but I don't know as you deserve any sympathy. You deliberately asked for it. I've heard Laurie myself asking you more than once to be nice to Marigold, and she really is a nice girl, even if she hasn't much money. She doesn't use any makeup at all. She doesn't need to. She has plenty of her own color, and charming taste in dress, even when she has no money and has to make her own clothes. However, as I told you, if she had been here at the party she would have worn the white and crimson, and your precious Robena would have had to seek further for something royal enough to wear."

"I really can't credit that, Irene. A little nobody wouldn't know enough to buy a frock like that white one, and wouldn't have had even a hundred and fifty dollars to say nothing of two hundred to spend on one dress. It's just some cock-and-bull story that some of those salespeople have put over on you."

"Suit yourself, Adele, I'm sorry I mentioned it. But someday you'll find out. Go down and ask Madame, if you don't believe me. She'd have to own up. I'm sick of the whole story, though I do feel sorry for you after all the trouble and time and money you spent on that party. But I must say you brought it on yourself. When you could have had a perfectly good girl for Laurie that doesn't ever drink and you *chose* to bring Robena here who drinks like a fish, I don't see that you can ask pity of anyone.

Marigold *never* drinks."

"But that's not respectable either, Irene. A girl *has* to drink to a certain extent today when everybody expects it. The difference is she ought to be trained not to drink *too much*. Not to get beyond the respectable limit."

"You don't seem to have succeeded very well in training your son," said Irene coldly.

"There you go again, Irene. You've no human kindness at all. When you see how sick and nervous I am about having that awful little street girl in here. He just *picked her up!* Somebody he *never heard of* before! And *introduced* her in *my parlor!* I am ready to *drop with shame!*"

"At that he didn't pick so badly," said Irene contemptuously. "And she *wasn't* a stranger to him. He told me so."

"What do you mean!" demanded the irate mother. "He told me he was going out to pick up the first girl he met in the street just to get it back on me. He told me that right before everybody before he went out!" She began to weep again.

"Yes, but he didn't. He went outside and saw a girl he used to know in grammar school, Lily Trevor. She used to be a cute smart little thing. And when he went outside and saw her going by with somebody else to the movies he made her come in, just to make good his word. But he knew her. She wasn't a stranger."

"What difference does it make!" sneered the outraged mother. "Everybody saw she was just a cheap little thing, beside herself with conceit because Laurie had brought her in."

"Well, if you ask me, I thought she behaved as well as the rest of them," said Irene dryly. "I think myself the gem of the whole evening was the fact that your precious Robena appeared in the frock that had been turned down by the girl you scorned. Wasn't that something you'd call, 'the irony of fate?' I haven't been able to stop laughing since I heard it."

"Well I *don't believe it!* I don't believe a *word of it!*" said the irate mother flashing her swollen eyes as well as they would flash. "I wish you would go away and leave me to my misery. *Every*thing has gone wrong since that awful Brooke girl came into the picture, and I believe in my soul *you* had something to do with my Laurie meeting her! Anyway, if you didn't introduce them I'm sure you *encouraged* the intimacy. You with your outrageous bourgeois tastes, and your strange whims and fancies! *Gold* hair, you say. Probably *bleached!* There isn't any real gold hair

212

today. An intriguing little fortune seeker! And I have to have all my plans and ambitions and hard work for nothing just because Laurie has an infatuation for her. Now, if he becomes a drunkard, I shall have *you* to thank for it," and she plunged into her damp handkerchief again in new self-pity.

Irene cast a withering glance at her.

"Some day," she said cuttingly, "you'll see that girl, and then you'll know what a fool you've made of yourself, turning her down, and then you'll have to eat your words! But you're mistaken about me! I never had anything to do with Laurie meeting her. I wish I had. She's quite the decentest girl I know, and would have done Laurie a world of good. But I'm sure if she knew what *he* was, she would never have anything to do with him again."

"What do you mean, Irene? What is the matter with my Laurie? Why should a little upstart nobody turn down Lawrence Trescott?"

"I mean just what you've been telling me. He drinks too much, and does horrible things like bringing in mortifying strangers when he gets beside himself. *Drunk,* you said he was! But you've always given him too much money, and let him have his own way. What can you expect?"

"Yes, you who have brought up so many children! Of course you know all about it," sneered the mother.

"Well, all right. You can sneer, but you try it a while. Take Laurie's money away, and don't have so many cocktails around, and see if Laurie doesn't turn out to be something worth while after all — unless perhaps it's too late. Goodbye. I'm going home till you are in a pleasanter mood." Irene took herself off angrily, a secret gleam of triumph in her eyes to think that she had been able to find out about the white dress with the scarlet sash that everybody had raved so about. What a pity Marigold Brooke hadn't stuck by her first acceptance and come in the dress, instead of Robena! It certainly would have opened Laurie's mother's eyes to a few things. Marigold Brooke in that gorgeous array would have been a winner! Irene gave a wistful sigh. She would like to see her favorite nephew paired off with a girl like Marigold instead of a vapid creature like Robena. But of course Robena had money, and that was everything in the eyes of Laurie's mother. Poor Laurie!

Then she went home and that night she sat in front of her mirror for a long time, reflecting on her own face which was beginning to age. Not that she was old yet by any means, but she could see the flesh beginning to sag, she noted the dullness of her eyes, the threads of silver that had slipped in among her well hennaed locks. It wouldn't be long before she would look as old as poor Adele, though never quite so fat she hoped. And life! What was it worth? What was the use of living anyway? Just clamor and conceit, and ambition, each trying to get ahead of the other, weary contests, and what did it all amount to? Why did anyone want to live? And yet there was nothing attractive in the thought of dying. One must go on with the race, the losing race, unsatisfied soul struggling with unsatisfied soul, and never getting anywhere!

Marigold didn't look as if she felt that way. She was young yet. Life hadn't disappointed her, and left her a piece of flotsam cast up on the edge of the stream. But it likely would. Probably Laurie would disappoint her. Some day she would find out he got drunk whenever he liked and made a fool of himself. And then where would her bright looks be? Her flame of hair would turn white, the firm pink flesh and the rounded cheek would grow fragile, and even a Marigold would begin to fade. Or would she? Irene had seen her that day, and there had been such a look about her of fadelessness and peace, as if she had a source of endless life within her that would never let the sparkle go from her lovely eyes, the prettiness from her sweet face. What was it that made Marigold look so entirely content? She wished she had the secret.

And about that time Marigold was kneeling beside her bed giving herself utterly to her Lord, that she might know the joy of a resurrection life lived by faith in Christ, in the strength of His resurrection power.

She was not even thinking of Laurie at all.

Ethan Bevan had taken her straight home to the apartment, carrying her baggage up and turning on the lights, exactly as if he belonged there. He cast one glance about him, and said with satisfaction:

"This is nice. It looks like home!" and there was wistfulness in his eyes. Then he threw off his hat and coat on a chair and went to work.

He brought in the milk that was left outside the door according to the note left in the milk bottle, and the loaf of bread that lay beside it.

Marigold hurried into the kitchen and started some coffee, got out a can of baked beans, a glass jar of tongue, and another of luscious peaches.

"It isn't a very grand meal," she said with a deprecatory look at the can-opener she was holding, "but it won't take but a jiffy to have it ready."

"It looks like a swell meal to me," he said happily, putting his hand around hers and gently but firmly possessing himself of the can-opener. "I'll do that. That's my job," he said, and attacked the cans capably.

Marigold laughed happily and surrendered the cans to his ministrations. There was butter in the refrigerator, and there were tins of cookies and sand tarts. Marigold did things to the beans with butter, molasses, salt and pepper, and a brisk bit of cooking, and they sent forth a savory odor. She whisked a clean tablecloth onto the little table in the kitchenette, set the table invitingly with her mother's lovely sprigged china and silver, then she scrambled some eggs. It was all ready in no time and they were sitting down together, just the two of them, with such a pleasant sense of cosiness upon them, that a sudden shyness came upon Marigold. As she bowed her head while Ethan asked the blessing, she felt as if peace were descending into her heart, as if the presence of God were there with them. How wonderful to have a cheery reverent strong friend like this! How nice that he had been willing to stay and eat this simple meal with her.

All too soon the minutes flew away, and he looked at his watch.

"Well, time's up!" he said with a wistful smile. "I'm glad we had this brief hour together. It's been a wonderful meal, and we've pretty well cleared the cloth and licked the platter clean, haven't we? I wish I could stay to help wash the dishes, but I guess I must go, for that fellow said the shop closed at six and I must be there to get my package."

Then he was into his overcoat, hat in hand, and standing by the door about to leave, when there came a tap on the door.

Marigold looked up in annoyance. Why did it have to come just then? Somehow that last minute seemed important. She didn't like to be interrupted. But of course that was silly.

She opened the door and Mrs. Waterman stood there, looking her slatternliest, her hair in crimpers, a soiled torn dress on.

"I forgot to give you this letter," she said apologetically. "Your young man was here about noon wanting you. I told him you'd likely be here tonight, and he wrote his letter. He said he'd be back. You must excuse my looks, I'm getting ready to go out this evening."

The color flamed into Marigold's cheeks and she stared at the woman annoyedly.

"*My* young man?" she laughed embarrassedly. "Who is *he?*"

"Why, the fellow with the swell car that comes here to take you out so much."

Marigold took the letter, her cheeks still glowing, and closed the door annoyedly after the retiring neighbor. She looked clown at the letter with troubled eyes. Then she looked up and saw the expression on Ethan's face. She didn't stop to analyze it. She wasn't just sure what it meant, but there was tenderness in it, she was sure of that. Suddenly she spoke from the impulse of her own need, looking down at the unopened letter which bore her name in Laurie's large bold handwriting.

"I'm going to need a lot of help," she said slowly. "Would — you — sometimes — pray for me?"

She lifted her lovely worried eyes with a look that went straight to Ethan's heart.

"I surely will!" he said earnestly. "Shall we begin now?" Right where he was he knelt beside the chair, flinging his hat down on the floor, grasping her hand in his and pulling her gently down beside him. Marigold knelt, her hand enfolded in that warm strong clasp, the letter lying between them

219

on the chair forgotten! Laurie's letter! She was not thinking about it. She was listening to the tender prayer. She felt she would never forget the words, they were so indelibly stamped on her heart. She felt as if she were brought into intimate touch with her Saviour, as she heard this earnest voice pleading Christ's precious promises, claiming the resurrection power in her life, not only for herself but for her friends. She felt suddenly a strength at her command that she had never dreamed existed.

When they rose the letter was left lying on the chair, and Marigold looked up with a radiant face. There were no words to express her feeling, but somehow she knew he understood.

Ethan stood for a moment looking gravely down at her. There was something so deep and tender in that look that it almost brought the tears to her eyes, but she did her best to turn them into a smile, and the answering smile she got was something she felt she would hide away in her heart to remember.

She wanted to thank him for what he had done for her, but still the words would not come. He might be going out of her life forever, now, but she felt he had taught her to know the Lord Jesus, and put her into touch with the resurrection power. Whatever came she never would forget him.

Then he reached out and took her hand in a quick clasp once more.

"Good-bye," he said quietly. "I'll be praying! And — sometime — perhaps you'll let me know how things came out."

Then, before she could answer, he was gone. She heard his footsteps outside on the stairs. Would she ever see him any more?

She went to the window, and sudden tears blinded her eyes, but she brushed them away and looked out. She could see the lights of his car down there, and now he was opening the car door. But before he swung himself into the seat he turned and looked up, waved his hand, and she waved hers back in farewell, glad that her room lights were on and that he could see her. This was perhaps the best way of saying what she could not find words to speak.

And then the car glided away from the curb, and shot down the street. The little red lights at the rear seemed to be blinking to her as it swung around a corner and into the highway.

She turned back to the room and felt all at once most desolate. What a happy hour they had had together getting supper and eating it in the little intimate kitchen. How wonderful he had been, acting just as if he belonged there. It thrilled her to go over the moments of the incident.

And then, with one more wistful look down the street where he had disappeared into the fast-gathering darkness, she turned and went over to the chair where they had knelt to pray and there lay the letter! How mortifying that Mrs. Waterman had brought it just then, and called Laurie *"her young man."* What must Ethan have thought? But how he had taken it all as a matter of course and entered into her vague anxiety about the future, promising to pray, kneeling right down and praying!

She thrilled again as she went over the prayer word by word, conning it like a lesson that she must not ever forget.

It was some minutes before she brought her mind back to the present and realized that there was a letter to be read. How that letter would have stirred her just four or five short days ago. Even the very outside of it, sealed, as she held it now. Yet now she opened it with a divided attention, treasuring the moments just past, and looking into a new kind of life to which she was committed.

11 Marigold roused to read the letter at last, with a curious aloof mind which seemed to be far removed from the writer of the letter, as if time had swept in and obliterated the little filaments of happenings that bound her interest to him.

Mara darling:

What have you been doing with yourself? I called this afternoon to make a date with you for this evening and found you away, although it is the time when you usually get home from school.

The human slat that resides across the hall informs me you will be home this evening, and that you are coming *alone!* So much the better. We shall not have your mother to spy on us and can have a real time.

I'm coming along to get you sometime after seven or a little sooner, and we'll have dinner and then do the night clubs in a regular way, see sights you've never seen before. We'll have *some evening,* Mara my beautiful!

So light up the front windows for me, and let me know you are ready. I'll know by your lights that you are waiting for me.

Yours as ever,
Laurie

Marigold, as she read, began to grow cold about her throat and to tremble. Somehow there was something strange about that letter, not like Laurie! Or, had it been there all the time and she had been blind to it?

She felt like a person whose eyes had just been opened and she was seeing "men as trees walking." She couldn't be sure of herself and her own judgment.

But when she had read the letter over again several things stood out sharply. First of all was the thought that Laurie had not mentioned the party to which she had not come, nor said a word about his long unexplained silence! All her anxiety, and uneasiness, and anxious waiting, when she first got to Washington, and he hadn't even noticed it! Far from telephoning her in trepidation and begging her to come to the party as she had expected he might, offering to drive down after her perhaps, he acted as if he had not even known she was invited. Exactly as if the party wouldn't be counted within her world.

And next there stood out the fact that

Laurie was beginning on night clubs again, and she was going to have to meet that question right away tonight before she had thought the matter out on her knees. It was then she began to tremble.

And reading the letter over the third time now like a stab in her heart there came that reference to her mother as being a spy. Laurie had never spoken of her mother's carefulness as "spying" before, and something in her rose up and resented his attitude. The whole letter didn't sound like Laurie, the Laurie she had so admired and enjoyed and loved to companion with. It was as if she were seeing a new side of him entirely.

Then it flashed upon her that she had been holding in abeyance her judgment about Laurie, that had tried to force itself upon her ever since she had seen him in the company of that other girl, looking down into her eyes with the glance that Marigold had supposed was all her own.

Yet now the whole thing seemed unreal. She seemed to have grown beyond it all since she left home last Friday.

But he was coming tonight, and was expecting to take her to a night club! What should she do?

With a quick motion she went to the

switch and turned off her lights. Laurie was going to look to her lighted windows to signal him she was at home, and there would be no lights! She was not going to any more night clubs! That was settled. She had known in her heart while she was talking with Ethan Bevan that they would never interest her again. In fact they never had of themselves. It was only Laurie's insistence that drew her a couple of times. She had never felt at home there. It was an alien world, and she had felt ashamed. She saw it plainly now. She had been half ashamed to be there.

She had always evaded her mother's questions as to what kind of places Laurie took her. That had hurt her conscience too. But now she was face to face with the whole thing, and she knew it must be settled for all time. She had told Ethan Bevan, and she had told her Lord, that she wanted to die with Him. She had felt already the joy of realizing what that was to mean to her whole life. She could not compromise.

If Laurie came anyway, even though there were no lights, she would tell him plainly that she would go to no more such places with him. But she felt somehow that she did not want to have to talk it over with him to-night. She wanted to get her feet firmly fixed, to get near to her Lord. She wanted to be alone, and to think over that wonderful prayer that had put her so far beyond these things of earth, and made her see herself as a redeemed sinner commissioned with a message to other lost sinners. Laurie would not understand that now, probably, and she must learn the best and wisest way to say it to him.

So she sat in the dark and faced her problem. Looked at Laurie, *her* Laurie as she had considered him for long pleasant thoughtless months in the past, looked him straight in the face and made herself acknowledge just where he now seemed to be lacking.

Laurie was not of her world. That was plain. Mother had said so, and her own honest self had sometimes been afraid of it. Yet she had told herself that her influence would gradually give him different ideals. Had it? Had her influence done anything for him?

Looking at the question as she sat there in the dark she had to acknowledge that far from bringing Laurie to see as she saw, *she* had been yielding little by little to *his* wishes, going here and there and breaking down standards that had been hers since childhood, until she had come to the place where she had even once or twice questioned whether those weren't outworn standards, and perhaps she wasn't doing such a dreadful thing in giving them up, if it pleased Laurie.

But now as she faced herself and her world, with that sense of God's presence in the room that had been there since Ethan's prayer, everything looked different to her, and she began to ask herself why she had wanted to please Laurie anyway?

She had had beautiful gay times with him, oh, yes, but was Laurie all that she wanted in life?

She tried to bring a vision of his handsome face, his gay smile, his adoring eyes looking into her own, and in spite of her best efforts she could only see him looking into that other girl's eyes! Was Laurie wholly false, or just gay and irresponsible? And if only irresponsible would he ever grow out of it into a strong dependable friend, such a man as Ethan Bevan?

Her thoughts grew more and more troubled, and finally she arose and went into her own room, dark but for the arc light from the street that sent long fingers of brightness across the wall. There she dropped upon her knees and began to talk to her Lord. And when, half an hour later, Laurie drew up at the corner of the street and slowed his high-powered car to a crawling gait, Marigold had forgotten that he might be passing. She was gazing into the face of her dying Lord and saying softly with closed eyes: "Oh, Jesus Christ, I want to be crucified with Thee, and though nevertheless I have to live here in this earthly body, I want it not to be myself that is living in me any longer, but Christ who lives my life for me; and the life that I now live in the flesh, I want to live henceforth by the faith of the Son of God who loved me, and gave Himself for me."

When she got up from her knees and turned on the light she was surprised to find that it was much later than she supposed. If Laurie had come that way at all, he saw no light and he must have gone on his way, thinking she was not yet at home.

She drew a breath of relief. Then she remembered that the dishes were not washed. and she had not unpacked her suitcase. She did not want to talk to Laurie tonight. She did not want to argue about night clubs. She was tired, and she felt as if such an experience would dispel some of the glory and beauty from the talk she had had with Ethan before he left. She wanted to fix that in her memory so that its joy could never be effaced. She did not want it dulled by other experiences yet. Ethan of course did not belong to her, and after he felt the need of praying for her was over he would probably never think of her again, but the touching of their lives had not been for nothing. It was a sacred experience.

So she turned on her light, changed into a little cotton house dress and went about the work of putting the kitchen to rights for the morning when she would have to hurry off to school.

The kitchen seemed to be filled with bits of pleasant memories floating about among the dishes. The bread plate she had passed to Ethan when they had almost dropped it between them, the look in his eyes when he smiled; the clean clear ring of his laughter when she told a funny little story about her childhood; the delicate sprigged china coffee cup that he had admired and drunk from. She handled them all gently as she washed and wiped them, her face vivid with happy thoughts. She was by no means trying to think how to talk to Laurie about not going to night clubs. That subject had a reprieve in her mind, while she gleaned every bright little memory from the brief time that Ethan had been there with her. Ethan, who had helped her to find peace and had lighted the perplexity of her pathway.

Then, just as she was opening her suitcase to hang up her garments and put everything to rights, the telephone rang.

It startled her. She almost contemplated not answering it, for perhaps it was Laurie. Let him think for this one night that she had not returned. But then she thought better of it and answered the second insistent ring.

It was her mother's voice, and her heart gave a glad little extra beat, for after all, the apartment was a bit lonely. She hadn't realized that it would be so without her mother, not for just a few days.

"Oh, Mother *dear!* Yes, I'm all right. Yes, we had a lovely drive, the day was perfect. Yes, Ethan came in for a few minutes and had a bite of supper. We had fun getting it together, beans and scrambled eggs and tongue and peaches, some combination! But Ethan had to hurry, you know, the office where he was to get those parts he went after closed at six. Yes, he has gone. Started back right away. Yes, I'm quite all right. No, I'm not going out anywhere. Just unpacking and then I'm going to bed. Be good and don't worry about me. I want you to stay all next week and get really rested up yourself. Besides you mustn't leave Aunt Marian until Elinor gets home."

When she hung up the receiver she looked

around her and the place seemed all at once terribly empty and lonely. More than a week yet before Mother would come back! Perhaps she would accept some of those invitations from the teachers which she had always declined before on the plea of not leaving her mother alone.

She went into the bedroom and began to hang up her dresses again, touched lightly the smooth silk of the little green dress, remembering with a thrill the evening she had worn it when Ethan had taken her to the symphony concert. What a lovely time she had had that evening! How happy she had been, and how Ethan had admired the dress! Strange for such a quiet serious young man to notice a dress! But he really did admire that. She could see it in his eyes, and her heart quickened as she remembered his look when he said it. She gave the dress a little soft pat, shook out the folds and put it on a hanger wistfully. She was glad she had that dress. It was a much better dress to have than the white one would have been, regal as that was. Suppose she had bought the white instead, and gone to the party! It would be at the cleaner's by now very likely, and never be quite as pretty and fresh again. And what further use would she ever have had for it? Oh, she was glad she had taken that white dress back!

Then the telephone rang out sharply again, and startled, she went to answer it. Had Mother forgotten to tell her something and called again? How extravagant of her!

But it was Laurie's voice this time that sounded harshly over the wire.

"Mara! Is that you at last? Well, it's high time! I've been driving back and forth, passing your place every little while, waiting to see a light, and I couldn't understand why you didn't get home. Didn't you get my note? I thought I saw a light from the back room just now, but couldn't be sure, and I didn't care to risk another conversation with that woman across the hall so I thought I'd telephone. Did you get my note or not?"

"Why, yes, I got it," said Marigold trying to think swiftly what she should say. "I — haven't been home — so long, Laurie! And — well, you see I really couldn't go out tonight anyway."

"Why not? Your mother didn't come home with you, did she? You didn't have her notions to deal with, did you?"

"Laurie! Really!" Marigold's tone was indignant. "What is the matter with you, Laurie? I never heard you talk that way before about Mother."

"Well, I'm getting about sick of having to run my affairs to suit her straight-laced ideas. I don't see why you can't break loose and do as other girls do. She's no right to tie you down this way. You don't get a chance to see anything at all of life!"

"Laurie! I don't care to talk to you if you are going to say things like that. I never heard you be rude before!"

"Oh, well, forget it, Mara. I've lost my temper, I'll admit. But I'm fed up waiting around for you. Where have you been, anyway, and what have you been doing? I tried to get you all day yesterday."

"I've been away visiting in Washington," said Marigold a bit haughtily. "You didn't suppose I had nothing else to do but sit around here till you called me, did you?" She tried to end her caustic words with a laugh to take the sting out of them. It wasn't like her to be sarcastic to Laurie, and she knew it. Neither was it the way she wanted to speak to Laurie, but it had suddenly come to her sharply that Laurie had had plenty of time to call her up before she went to Washington and he hadn't explained yet why he didn't.

"That's a nice way to talk!" snarled Laurie, speaking in a tone Marigold had never heard from him before. "I've been busy. Company at the house, and a lot of engagements. I came this way as soon as I could. But you certainly don't seem very glad to see me."

"Well, I haven't seen you yet!" she said trying to force a little laugh, and was instantly sorry, for now perhaps he would try to call this evening and she didn't want him to come, not so late. She hurried on: "But listen, Laurie, I wasn't finding fault. You have a right to arrange your coming when it is convenient. I was just joking."

"That sounds more like my Mara," said Laurie, somewhat mollified, yet his voice was still harsh to Marigold's ears. Somehow he did not sound like himself. "All right, Baby, get your togs on and meet me down at the door in five minutes. We'll go somewhere and get some food, and then we'll make a night of it. Nothing to hinder. I've been wanting to show you for a long time what night life is really like in our little old town. Put on something bright and giddy, and touch up your features a little. I'm going to take you where they know what a pretty girl is like. I never had a chance to really take you 'out among 'em' before, your mother has always kept you so close, and censored every place I wanted to go."

Something seemed suddenly to take Marigold by the throat, and a great fear and heaviness came into her heart. For a moment she didn't answer, and then she summoned a cold little threat of a voice and said, almost haughtily:

"Thank you, Laurie, but I wouldn't care to go places Mother wouldn't like, and I don't think I care to know what night life is like."

"Oh, now, look here, Baby, don't get stuffy! I'm not taking you places that are any harm. Your mother doesn't understand what up-to-date places are, and she just gets anxious, but tonight we can go without worrying her, see? Hurry up and get your things on. I don't want to waste any more time. I've hung around long enough waiting for you now."

There was kind of a snarl in the last words, and the whole thing wasn't like Laurie. He had never called her "Baby" before, either. And he had said the word in a careless, too-intimate way, not in a gentle, tender way that would have made the word a real endearment. What could have come to Laurie? Had he been drinking? She put the thought from her as impossible. She had never seen Laurie drink but two or three times, and then just a glass of what he called "light wine." It hadn't seemed to affect him. But tonight he was talking so strangely. She was half frightened. She wished she had not answered the telephone at all.

"Listen, Laurie, I'm not going to any night clubs any more, either tonight, or any other night! I've been thinking the matter over seriously and I've decided it's something I don't want to do ever again."

"But you don't really know anything about night clubs, darling," said Laurie contemptuously. "You oughtn't to decide a thing like that without knowing. I'm going to show you what a really good night club is tonight. Come on, Baby! Hurry up and meet me at the door!"

"No!" said Marigold firmly. "I'm not going to any night clubs, now or any other time. That's final!"

He was still for a full minute and then his tone changed.

"Now, Mara, you're not being kind to me! It's not like you to talk that way. Come on, Mara, be a good sport and come out with me. I'm lonely. You've been gone a long time. If you don't want to go to a night club tonight come on and we'll go to the ice palace and have a skate."

"No," said Marigold, "I'm not going anywhere tonight. It's too late and I'm tired."

Her voice trailed off almost into a sob. She felt so shocked at the change in Laurie. She felt almost afraid of him when he spoke in that voice, and utterly sick at heart at the way he talked. He must be drunk or he never would be so rude. It was not at all like Laurie as she knew him in the past. He was always courteous, always gay and laughing, never cross.

"Well, then, how about tomorrow?" Laurie asked, after an ominous pause. "We'll have a good time tomorrow night. I'll meet you at the school, and take you driving somewhere, and we'll get dinner and —" he hesitated for an instant, "and then go to the ice palace and skate!" he ended.

She finally compromised on the ice palace explaining that she had things to do at home and couldn't go till evening.

After she had hung up the receiver she turned troubled eyes across the room, wondering if she had done right to promise even for tomorrow night. Somehow she felt strangely disturbed about the whole matter. Laurie had been so different from his usual gay self. Was he just sore that she had not come to the party, and yet wouldn't say anything about it?

The party. Why, she had been home almost the whole evening and hadn't even thought to look at the papers that Johnny Masters had dutifully brought, and Mrs.

Waterman had left on the table by the door! Somehow the interest had gone out of them for her.

But she went over and took them up, settling down in a chair and turning on the lamp beside her. She turned over the pages till she reached the society columns, and there right at the head of the page was the face of that girl she had seen with Laurie before she went to Washington! She couldn't be mistaken. There was something about the haughty self-centered face, handsome though it was, that was stamped indelibly upon her memory.

"Miss Robena DeWitte of Sandringham-Heights-on-the-Hudson," the legend beneath said. And "Guest of honor at the exclusive entertainment given Saturday night in the Trescott mansion, Walnut Terrace and Gardingham Road, this city."

The article describing the affair occupied three columns, with minute descriptions of the outstanding costumes of what was exuberantly described as "this city's best dressed crowd of the season." And as she read it Marigold's face flamed scarlet to think she had been about to compete with that company of peacocks, each aiming to have the prize for the best feathers.

She glanced down the column and caught

the name of Robena DeWitte once more, and read:

"Miss DeWitte, the guest of honor, was wearing a stunning white costume of taffeta, the kind our grandmothers used to buy when silk was silk. It was closely molded to her plump form, with perfection of line such as only the great artists of the mode can attain, and girdled with a crimson sash, deep fringed, that hung to the floor. It was adorned at the shoulder with a single velvet rose of the same new crimson that is now considered so smart. One could not but see that Miss DeWitte was the center of attraction, and that her gown was greatly admired. With her dark hair that was sleek like a satin cap, and her long lashed dark eyes, she had a regal bearing that took attention from all others present whenever she moved or spoke. It was noticeable that the son of the house, young Lawrence Trescott was her constant attendant, to the obvious annoyance of most of the other men present."

Suddenly Marigold stood up and cast the paper from her, a look of utter disgust on her face.

Was that what she had made herself miserable about only a few days ago? Had she really wanted to compete for that sort of notoriety? For Laurie's sake, she had made herself believe, but had it not been for her own pride's sake, if she told the truth? Yes, she had wanted to prove to Laurie's mother and friends that she could be just as smartly gowned and just as beautiful, as any of that crowd who had millions of money! What a little fool she had been! Actually spending a hundred and fifty dollars for a dress! But — stay! Wasn't that the same dress? White with a crimson girdle!

She caught up the paper from the floor and looked carefully at the girl's picture again. Yes, that was the same dress! She could not mistake those unusual lines, the hang of the sash, the very placing of the rose! The girl had had it taken before the party just for the papers! Oh, it *must be* her dress the other girl was wearing.

She had taken her lover, and then she had gone and bought her dress and worn it to the party!

Marigold flung the paper down again, threw her head back and laughed aloud. How funny! How very very funny!

She laughed so loud that Mrs. Waterman came across the hall and tapped at the door.

"Did you call?" she asked in a curious voice. "I thought I heard you call."

"Oh, no," said Marigold, giggling again, "I was just laughing at something — a joke

— I found in the paper! I'm sorry I disturbed you."

Mrs. Waterman went back baffled. She had hoped that Marigold would tell her something about her trip, or at least something about the two young men, the one at home, and the one who had come home with her and then gone so soon again. Well, she was glad she had got that cut in, anyway, about her young man at home, to warn the poor fellow who came up with her from Washington. But why didn't he have sense enough to stay the evening when he had the chance, if he was interested in her?

Mrs. Waterman was keen for any romance, having had little of her own. She was always scenting out love stories in any young things she met.

But Marigold stopped laughing and picked up the paper again, looking long and steadily into the eyes of the girl in the picture, trying to realize that this was the girl to whom she had seen Laurie making love. Her rival! Could it be possible that Laurie really was interested in that vapid selfish-looking girl? There wasn't a hint of moral character in her face.

Of course it was only a picture, and newspaper pictures were noted for being very poor likenesses, but she had seen the girl herself. She knew!

After a long time Marigold gathered up the newspaper, went over to the fireplace and burned it. Then she went in and knelt by her bed and prayed:

"Oh, Lord Jesus, won't you teach me what to do about Laurie? I thought I loved him, but perhaps I shouldn't. I want to be crucified with you and have your resurrection life. I want to count myself dead to the things of this world, and alive only to you. Won't you please show me the way, and not let self come alive in me and make me go astray. I'm trusting you to live for me, step by step. Help me, Lord Jesus, please! I'm yours, now. Not my own any more."

12 Marigold slept late the next morning and had to hurry to school, with no breakfast except half a glass of milk swallowed in haste. It was raining, a fine thin drizzle, and somehow the gloom of the day had entered her soul. The peace of last night seemed to have been rudely broken in upon, and she had awakened with a burden upon her. There had been no time for prayer, and her heart felt strangely depressed.

As she hurried along to school in a taxi she tried to search into her depression and find out its cause, and finally traced it back to Laurie. She had an unsatisfied feeling about having promised to go with him tonight. And yet as she thought it over, she couldn't understand why. She had been plain enough about not going to night clubs. She had taken her stand about that. And if he was willing to go to the ice palace and skate for a while instead, she couldn't really in decency decline, could she? There was nothing wrong in skating. Mother hadn't ever objected to her going.

Yet again and again that vague shadow of uneasiness kept returning. All during the morning classes it came back, filling her

244

thoughts and making her distraught and inattentive to her class. And the children realized it of course and took advantage of it. Her class was a riot once or twice, and she found her temper slipping, and a dazed, sick feeling coming over her. The children were restless, too, on their own account, for the long, unexpected vacation had put an unusual spirit of mischief into them.

So it was with a sigh of relief that Marigold closed her desk at three o'clock and hurried home, puzzling over and over in her troubled mind the exact reason for her worry.

It was Laurie, of course, but what could she do about it now? She had promised to go skating with him. She couldn't call it off at this last minute. She would not know where to find him. He had never given her his telephone number. Of course she could easily find the number of his home, but she sensed that he did not want her to call there, and she was too proud to call him anyway.

After all, she had to see Laurie at least once more, even if it turned out that she was to break with him. And perhaps this engagement to skate was about as simple a way to see him as any.

So with determined lips she hurried on, and went swiftly to work when she reached the apartment, setting things to rights, even doing several things that were not necessary, because she could not bear to stop and think.

It was when she was dusting the living room that she suddenly spied a little leather book lying unobtrusively on the floor between two chairs. Wondering she stooped and picked it up, and a thrill of comfort went through her as she saw it was Ethan's pocket Testament that he carried with him everywhere. It must have fallen from his overcoat pocket. That was where he had put his hat and coat while they had been getting dinner last night. And it had fallen out when he put on his overcoat in such a hurry!

She held it between her two hands for a moment as if it were a talisman, as if its very contact could give her strength. How she wished he were here and she could talk all this troubled situation over with him.

But of course it was her own situation. In a way no one but God could help her.

She bent her head for an instant and closed her eyes, touching her forehead softly to the Testament as she sent up an inarticulate prayer. Then she went and sat dawn by the window, and opening the book read:

"Be ye not unequally yoked together with unbelievers: for what fellowship hath righteousness with unrighteousness? and what communion hath light with darkness?"

She paused and stared at the words amazed. It was as if the great God had stooped to answer her questions in person, as if He had sent down through the long ages words to that little book for her to read, that afternoon, words that would fit her very situation.

She read on through the passage.

". . . what part hath he that believeth with an infidel? . . . what agreement hath the temple of God with idols?"

She paused to think. An infidel was one who did not believe in God. But perhaps this went deeper than that. It meant an unbeliever in Jesus Christ as Saviour. She knew that Laurie was not a believer. He had often laughingly said he had no religion. He was not bothered with a conscience. He thought you had only one life and you ought to enjoy it as best you could for you were "a long time dead." Strange that hadn't bothered her before. She had never counted herself an unbeliever, although she could see now that she had never before accepted Christ in His fullness, nor really understood what salvation meant until her talk with Ethan. But she had been enough of a believer to be a little shocked at Laurie's open declaration that he had no religion, that is, the first time he had said it. She remembered she had reproved him laughingly, though, and never taken it very seriously. Laurie's fine eyes laughing into hers, Laurie's highhanded way of carrying all before him, of flattering her into thinking he was making her a kind of queen, had erased any feeling of uneasiness she had had. But now suddenly it was very clear to her. Laurie was an unbeliever, quite openly, and she now was one of the Lord's own. She had surrendered her life to Christ, had asked that she might be counted as crucified with Him. She belonged to Him in a peculiar way.

"For ye are the temple of the living God; as God hath said, I will dwell in them and walk in them."

And now she had asked what she was to do in the matter of this friendship with Laurie, and this was her answer.

She was not superstitious. She had never been one who would have lightly settled questions by picking up a book and taking her guidance from the first words her eyes met. It was not like that. No, the Lord had caused this little book to be left here and had brought it to her notice just when her heart was crying for light. And here was the light in these words. The verses were marked heavily with penciled lines, and of course had called her attention to this side of the page instead of the other. She could not but think that the Lord had intended that too. Things so startling as this did not just *happen!*

And now she noticed that there were penciled words written above the passage, and down along the margin, very fine, but clear. This must have been written by Ethan. She wondered at the comfort that thought brought. It was as if Ethan had come into the room and were helping her to solve her problems.

"To Christians!" the passage was headed. She paused to think that out. Then she glanced at the writing along the margin.

"You never know full privilege until you are a grown *son*," and a tiny line led to the last two verses of the chapter. Marigold read them eagerly:

"Wherefore come out from among them, and be ye separate, saith the Lord, and touch not the unclean thing; and I will receive you, and will be a Father unto you, and ye shall be my sons and daughters, said the Lord Almighty."

Could anything be plainer that that? Such separation was made a condition to experiencing sonship, to close walking in fellowship with God!

There was no longer any question in her mind. She had her answer, and she must break with Laurie. But strangely the thought brought no terrible sorrow as she had expected, no great wrench, only sadness for the friendship that had been so pleasant while it lasted. Could it be that she did not care for Laurie as she had shyly dreamed she did? Or was God making it easier for her by thrilling her soul with Himself, and the thought of walking with the great God?

She had turned on the light to read the little book, for the dusk had been coming down, and now as she looked up when the clock struck she saw that it was quite dark outside. Laurie would be coming soon, and she must be ready. Perhaps this was the last time she would go out with him.

She was not sure what the next step was to be, or whether the break was to come suddenly, or would be gradual. But she was definitely sure there was to be no more compromise, and that she must somehow let him know where she stood.

Hurriedly she got a hasty meal, and dressed for skating. She was barely ready when she heard his horn below. He always drew up with a flourish and plenty of horn as a greeting. And now that horn with its gay call did something to her heart. Always she had been so happy to hear it. After all, Laurie was dear! So bright and gay and handsome. Oh, was she going to be strong enough to do this thing which she had set out to do?

It was strange that there should come words out of the past few days just at that instant: "Surely He shall deliver thee!" She could vision Ethan's face as he read them last Sunday night in Washington. "He shall give His angels charge over thee, to keep thee in all thy ways!"

As she went down the stairs she had a feeling that a guard was all about her, and a new strength came to her.

But down in the car it was not the same gay Laurie she knew so well. It was a scowling, haughty Laurie, with his handsome chin held up, and his eyes cold and disapproving.

He was courteous as usual, rather elaborately so, but before they had even started on their way she was made to feel like a naughty little child who had transgressed the laws of the universe unbelievably.

"What's the idea, Mara," he said haughtily, as he stepped on the gas and they dashed down the road, "all this nonsense about you won't go here, and you won't go there? You never acted that way before. Has your mother been putting the screws on you, that you don't dare to call your soul your own?"

Something constricted Marigold's throat so that for an instant she could not voice the indignant protest that came to her lips, and Laurie went right on.

"You surely are old enough to know your own mind, and go your own way, and no parent in these days has a right to restrict a child. Such actions are a relic of the dark ages! You have a right to see life as it is, and choose for yourself what you will do and what you will not do. It is your life, not hers, and you belong to yourself!"

Suddenly Marigold spoke.

"No," she said quietly. "you are utterly mistaken. It is not my mother who has anything to do with my decision that I will not go to night clubs any more. She does not even know that I go. I have never told her. But I do not like the way you speak of my mother. You never spoke of her in that way before."

"Well, as long as she minded her business and didn't interfere with what I wanted to do I didn't mind her," said Laurie bluntly. "But when it comes to putting fool ideas into your head I'm done with her."

"I tell you my mother has nothing whatever to do with this," said Marigold, her own tone haughty now. This was not her old gay friend Laurie, this was a stranger, a rude disagreeable stranger. "My mother would never dream of my going to a night club. I am ashamed to say I have never told her that I went with you two or three times. I did not feel happy in going. I went to please you, and I feel I was wrong."

He swept aside her explanation with an impatient motion of his hand.

"If your mother didn't influence you, who did?"

Marigold spoke in a clear voice.

"God did. He made me feel that it was something not consistent with Christian living. You said just now that I belonged to myself. But that is not true. I belong to the Lord Jesus Christ who bought me with His own precious blood. I know I have not been living lately as though I believed that, but I do, and I always have, and now I have come to a place where I can't go on that way any longer."

Laurie turned his handsome steely glance toward her, searching her face as well as he could by the lights that glanced into the car from the street.

"So!" he said after his old scrutiny was over, "you have turned fanatical on me! Is that it? Well, I certainly was deceived in you. And who, may I enquire, did this to you? Some fool woman I'll bet! If it wasn't your mother, who was it?"

"I don't like the way you talk, Laurie," she said gently. "If you are going to talk that way I wish you would take me home. I can't listen to you when you say such things!"

"Oh, you can't, can't you? Well, you're going to listen and you're going to like it too, when I get done with you. I have no intention of having you spoiled. You're one of the best sports I ever went with, and I don't intend to give you up. You promised to go skating with me, and you're going! We're getting out at the ice palace and have the time of our life tonight, and when the evening's over you will have learned a thing or two, and you won't be quite so old-grannyfied in your notions, either. I'll teach you how to forget you had a conscience, and just be happy."

Marigold was silent for a moment, as they dashed on. She cast a quick glance at Laurie's face which was still cold and angry, and finally she spoke:

"Certainly, I'll go and skate. I'll keep my promise to you, and try to have a pleasant time as we have had in the past, but you'll have to promise not to speak about my mother that way, and not to cast contempt upon my God."

"Well, I don't believe in your God, see?" said Laurie contemptuously. "He's nothing in my young life. But as for the old girl, we'll leave her out of the matter for the time being, since she isn't in these parts just now. If you can be a good sport as you've always been, I'm willing to go on, but I won't have whining fanatics around me, and that's flat!"

Marigold, startled into horror, sat there and stared at him through the darkness. What had happened to Laurie? She had never seen him angry like this. She didn't know he had a temper. He was always so gay and breezy. It is true she had never crossed him before in what he wanted to do, but — something more than that must be the matter.

She did not speak until he stopped the car and gave it into the hands of an attendant at the ice palace. It seemed there was nothing she could say that would not provoke him more. Perhaps he was ashamed of himself already and would presently apologize.

Silently she walked beside him into the ice palace. Strains of blithe jazz music floated out to greet them, and the tang of cigarette smoke, the chatter of gay voices and laughter was in the air. But Marigold no longer felt the cheery anticipation of the evening. She was full of trouble. She looked at Laurie and saw that his eyes were over-bright and there was a feverish color in his face. There were heavy shadows under his eyes, too, and his whole manner was unnatural. She did not know what to make of it.

She let him fasten her skates as usual, but there was no gay banter, no lifted eyes full of admiration, no gentle almost fond lifting of her foot as he laced the skateshoes. Instead he drew the laces almost roughly, till she had to tell him he was making them too tight, and then he flung away from her and told her to fix it to suit herself.

Sudden tears sprang to her eyes at that, and her heart was hot with shame and wonder. What had happened to Laurie?

He lighted a cigarette and swung away on his own skates while she slowly unlaced and relaced her own shoes. He returned just as she was ready and stood sullenly before her. Then, when she stood up he caught her hands and swung away into rhythm, but it was not like his usual long graceful swing. He kept changing his motion, and tripping her up. Once she almost fell, and he caught her close to him and swung her along, so that she had no choice but to let her feet follow where he led. But he was holding her close in a way he had never done before, a way he knew she despised, when occasional bold skaters had done it, a way he had been wont to criticize himself. She struggled to get loose, but he held her fast, and bent his face over, almost as if he were going to kiss her, murmuring with white set lips:

"You little devil, you, I'll teach you to go religious on me!"

It was then she caught that strong whiff of his breath and knew that he had been drinking.

"Let me go!" she cried, struggling frantically against his vise-like grip. Then, suddenly she slumped, relaxing and becoming a dead weight on his hands. Her feet slid out from under her and she went down in a pitiful little heap on the ice. Laurie had to execute a number of frantic gestures to keep his own balance, while other skaters came on and piled up in a heap upon Marigold.

The spill partly sobered Laurie, and looking half ashamed he picked her up and helped her over to the bench.

"Now," he said half savagely, "what did you do that for? You know you did it on purpose. Why did you do it?"

"Because I did not like the way you were holding me, the way you were skating. It — wasn't — respectable!" She was almost in tears. "I — didn't know you ever acted that way, Laurie! You never did before!"

"No?" he said, lowering his heavy unhappy eyes, "perhaps not! I was trying to teach you a few things. Trying to open your eyes to life!"

She stared at him in unspeakable horror.

"Laurie!" she said. "You *did it on purpose?* You knew how it would look to those about us, and yet you did it? I thought you were my friend!" The look in her eyes scorched him deeply, but he suddenly tottered to his feet.

"Oh, Heck!" he said. "Have we got to be tied down by little antiquated ideas of propriety? You've just spoiled this whole evening for me! I'll get a real skate who knows how to take things! Just sit here and watch us and see what you think the world cares!"

He flung away from her in a long sweeping curve, grace and skill in every movement, and darting in among the skaters he came to a little flashily-dressed girl who was executing some startling tricks, and bore her off in his arms, holding her close, and looking down into her impudent little face surrounded by bleached hair. A face with a tiptilted nose, and a painted mouth. He caught her about the waist with a daring leap, and swung her off with him, drawing her closer and closer until she lay with her face almost against his as they glided crazily on. Everybody was watching them, and they knew it. Marigold's cheeks burned as she turned her eyes away and began hastily to unlace her boots. This sort of thing was not supposed to go on here. As she lifted her eyes after putting on her street shoes she saw that an attendant on skates was approaching the two! Laurie could see him coming, too, but he went right on. Laurie doing a thing like this! Oh, it was unspeakably awful. Laurie who had always been the pink of propriety. Laurie was *drunk!*

She fastened the buckles of her shoes with fingers that were numb with sorrow and shame, and then with her heart beating wildly she slipped behind the crowd of watchers and got away out of the building while Laurie and the girl he had picked up were skating off with their backs to her.

She did not realize until she was in the trolley that she had left her shoes with the skates on them lying on the bench with the bag she always carried them in. They were a gift from Laurie and heretofore greatly cherished. But now they did not matter. Nothing mattered but to get away, not to have to talk to him again with that awful frown upon his face, that thickness of speech so foreign to him, that roughness upon him. Actually swearing at her once! Laurie had never sworn in her presence before.

She felt cold as if she had a chill, as she rode along, watching the streets anxiously, only in haste to get home. She wanted to hide her face in the pillow and ask God to forgive her for having let Laurie lead her so far into the world that this thing could have been possible tonight. She felt as if she could never get over the shame and the humiliation of it. Laurie, gay bright Laurie, so devoted heretofore! And he had scarcely spoken a friendly word to her tonight. Oh, how long had he been drinking? Was it a habit with him? How was it that she had never seen him under the influence of drink before? Could it be that because he was angry with her about the party he had deliberately taken a drink or two to show her she had no right to frustrate his plans? Oh, surely he wouldn't be so mean as that! Did liquor change men and make them into fiends like that? She had supposed that one had to be a seasoned drinker to have it make such a difference. The men she had always known would never think of drinking. Never until Laurie had taken her for the first time to a night club had she been among people who were drinking, and never before had she been offered liquor. Of course hers had been a guarded life. She had always known there was a world in which habitual drinking, social drinking, hard drinking went on, but it was not her world. And she had been shocked when she saw Laurie once toss off a glass of what he told her was "only a light wine." But she never knew he drank enough to get under its influence, and she felt almost stunned with the idea.

When she reached her corner and got out of the trolley she looked about her fearfully. Laurie would likely follow her as soon as he found she was gone. She couldn't conceive of Laurie letting her go, not the Laurie she knew, and doing nothing about it. Even a little drunk he would surely follow her to be sure she had got safely home.

But there was no Laurie in sight, and with relief she went up to her apartment, and locked herself in. She did not turn on her light at first, but flinging off her wraps threw herself on her bed and wept. The old time happy companionship with Laurie that had been so beautiful a thing in her life was spoiled, ruined. She could never think of Laurie again, no matter what happened, without a heartache. The things he had said that night, even though he was not himself, had seared their way into her heart, and disillusioned her.

The tears came at first, a deluge of them, until she was worn out. And gradually her thoughts grew steadier, and she could look things in the face.

She had gone forth to face her problems, and the problems had become more than just the simple matter of firmly refusing to go to night clubs. They had come swiftly to be the giving up of a lot of things that she had thought were dearest of all in life to her. And as she lay there facing facts, one by one many pleasant things of the past were torn away!

Then, suddenly as if someone had spoken the words she heard Ethan's voice reading that psalm:

"Because He hath set his love upon me, therefore will I deliver him . . . I will be with him in trouble."

Was that a promise for *her?* Could she rest quietly upon it? She had handed over herself to her Lord, as crucified and risen with Him, could she not trust herself utterly to Him?

And so she fell asleep.

An hour later her mother called up again

to know if she was all right, and she wakened, surprised to find herself on the outside of the bed. After she had hung up the receiver she undressed quickly and slipped back into bed, too sleepy to think about anything.

In the morning when she woke she was startled to find it was very late. She had forgotten to wind her alarm clock and had overslept. And there was the whole thing spread out before her, all that had happened the night before!

However, she had no time to think. She would be late to school unless she hurried.

She sprang out of bed, dressed as rapidly as possible, and was about to get herself a brief breakfast when there came a tap at the door.

She opened the door quickly thinking it was the milkman for his money. Here would be another hindrance.

But when she opened the door there stood Laurie Trescott, looking at her with stormy miserable eyes of reproach!

Laurie! And she hadn't a possible minute in which to talk to him!

13 Laurie's eyes were giving quick hinted glances about the room to see if she was alone. Then they fastened on her face with heart-breaking reproach.

"So! You were here all the time!" he said hoarsely, "and I've spent the night hunting for you. Nice way to do when I take you out, run away and leave me! And I didn't know what had become of you. Had to go out and hunt for you all night!"

"You knew where to find me," said Marigold coldly. "You knew I would come straight home. I have been here all night and you didn't attempt to see if I was here. You didn't telephone."

He dropped his haggard eyes and didn't answer for a minute and then he said:

"Why did you go off and leave me like that, Mara?" There was the old imperious tone again, finding fault with her instead of asking her pardon. Her indignation rose.

"Don't you remember what you did to me, Laurie, made me ashamed of you before everybody? Held me as no gentleman holds a lady in skating!"

"I had no trouble in getting other girls to

264

skate that way with me," he argued. "You're getting prudish!"

"No!" said Marigold sharply, "I'm not getting prudish. You didn't used to think such ways were nice yourself. I can't talk about it, Laurie. I've got to go to school at once. I'm going to be late as it is."

"But we've *got* to talk about it, Mara!" His voice was thin and high and full of anguish. Laurie was always dramatic, whatever he did. He stepped inside and shut the door sharply after him, leaning against it. As he stood there with the morning sunlight streaming across his face he looked like the wreck of something beautiful, and it was as if a rude hand suddenly jarred across the girl's heartstrings. Then his voice changed and grew pitiful, reproachful again. "Mara, I came here to make everything right with you. I came here to tell you I'm going to marry you!"

Marigold gave a startled look at him, a look which took in his worn haggard face, his bloodshot eyes, his disordered hair, his soiled expensive linen, and rumpled garments, and suddenly saw him in contrast to the Laurie she used to know. Only a few short days before, so immaculate, so gay and handsome, so assured and splendidly overbearing! A pang shot through her heart. All

the torture and revulsion of her disillusion-
ment were in her voice, as she covered her
face with her hands and shuddered.

"Oh, *Laurie!*" she cried out with almost a
sob in the end of her words.

He came toward her quickly, recognizing
the compassion in her voice, and tried to put
his arms about her, but she stepped back
out of his grasp.

"No! No!" she cried. "I could *never* marry
you, now, Laurie!"

"Why not!" He glared at her, and she
could see he was not himself yet. "I'll apologize!" he went on imperiously. "But I did it
for your good, you know. I wanted to teach
you what life was like, but I'll apologize
again if that's what you want." He lifted his
bloodshot eyes and gave her one of those
pleading looks, the kind that always used to
reach her heart. But Marigold steeled herself against it.

"You had been drinking, Laurie!" she said
furiously. "Why don't you tell the truth?"

"Yes, I'll admit I had had a glass or two
too much. It was your fault, though, you
know. You went away and I didn't have anything else. You kept me waiting the night
you got home, and all into the next night. I
had to do something. But I'm sober now.
I've come over to ask you to marry me."

"This is no time to ask me to marry you. Besides, I would *never* marry a man who drinks! I wouldn't go through last night again for anything in the world." There was scorn in her glance.

"Now, Mara, you're exaggerating. You mustn't make too much of a small thing. I'll admit I must have been half stewed last night. I'd had a heck of a week, and was all in. I took a little more than usual to carry me through. But I'm not often like that. Oh I get lit up now and then of course, but nothing like last night! If you'll marry me I'll quit drinking. I swear I will!"

Marigold looked at him aghast.

"No!" she said gravely. "People do not reform after they are married. I would never marry a man to reform him!"

"Now, Mara, that's not like you! You were never hard like that. You always did what I asked."

"Yes?" said Marigold with almost a sob, "I was that kind of a fool. I thought you were fine and grand and wonderful. And I thought I could respect you, and that you honored me!"

"Now, Mara, all that fuss just because I got lit up a few hours —"

"Don't!" said Marigold putting her hands over her face and shuddering again.

Again Laurie came near to her and tried to take her hands down from her face.

"There, now, Mara, don't you feel bad. You love me, don't you, Baby? We'll get married and then I'll quit, and everything will be all right."

Marigold jerked her hands away from him.

"Don't you *dare* to touch me!" she cried. "And don't you ever call me *Baby* again! I hate it! *No,* I don't love you."

"Oh, but you do love me, Mara! I've seen it in your eyes!"

"No!" said Marigold in a hard young voice. "You are not what I thought you were. I hadn't got around to think about marrying yet, but if I ever do get married it will have to be to someone I can trust and respect. I couldn't marry anybody who might go off and get drunk. Never! It wouldn't be *right!*"

Laurie's face darkened.

"There you go, talking fanatical stuff. What's *right?* Who's got any right to say one thing is wrong, another right?"

"God has!" said the girl, lifting a firm young chin and looking him straight in the eyes. "And if I'd known you didn't believe in right and wrong, and hadn't any use for God and mothers, I never would have gone anywhere with you. I'm sorry I ever did!"

"Now, Mara!" the boy pleaded, coming toward her again, "Mara, you don't realize what you are saying. Don't you remember what good times we've had? Can't you forget this and go on from here? Come, Mara, let's go and get married and then everything will be all right!"

"No! Never!"

"Now, Mara darling, don't get that way! Don't you know you'll drive me to desperation? Wouldn't you marry me to save me? I swear I'll stop drinking when we are married. Can't you believe me? I'm sober now, and I tell you it's the only way I can quit drinking."

Marigold's face hardened.

"Laurie, if you can't get sober without me, it wouldn't be long before you'd be at it again. *No!*"

"But I swear I'll drink myself to death if you don't marry me!"

"Look here, Laurie," said Marigold suddenly turning upon him, "that's ridiculous! Anybody who could say a thing like that isn't fit to get married! And I can't talk any more about this. I've got to get to school. I'm late already."

Laurie muttered a curse at the school, but Marigold darted about the room frantically, putting on her hat, gathering up her purse and coat and gloves, while he stood with angry eyes watching her. Then as she came toward the door with the evident intention of leaving he stood before her and tried to prevent her.

"Mara, my Mara, *darling!* Say you'll marry me, and I'll be all different. Everything will be as it used to be!"

"Will you please go out, Laurie? I've got to lock this door!" She said in a voice that was trembling from excitement, "Please don't talk any more either. It's useless!"

She stepped into the hall and he perforce followed. Then she locked the door and darted away.

"But wait!" he shouted after her. "I'll take you to school!"

But Marigold had gained the street and signaled a taxi that happened to be passing, and when he reached the street she was getting into it. She did not look up nor wave to him, just drove away, and he stood there gazing angrily after her, his brow drawn in a heavy scowl.

And back behind her curtain Mrs. Waterman was watching, feasting her eyes and her imagination on what had happened, getting ready a story to spread out for the delectation of her friends who lived in the neighborhood.

But Laurie climbed slowly into his car, a look of defeat on his weakly handsome face. He drove off like a madman, whirling around the next corner so that Mrs. Waterman held her breath expecting to see the car overturn, or smash into the oncoming bus. But Laurie was off to a place where he knew he could get another drink to carry him past this unpleasant memory. Marigold, the only girl he had ever really loved *almost* as much as himself, had scorned him, and he could not understand it. Scorned him though he had gone so far as to offer to marry her! That was really farther than he had intended to go when he went after her. He had only meant to hunt her up and smooth down her temper a little, he told himself. His mother would make a terrible fuss if he should marry Marigold, a girl without a cent of money. She might even go so far as to stop his allowance for a while, as she had several times threatened to do. She had been terribly tiresome ever since he brought that little girl in out of the street and danced with her at her old party. Why did old people have to be so terribly stuffy? Well, he would be twenty-one in seven months now, and then he would come into some money of his own, a mere matter of two hundred and fifty thousand of course, but it would tide him over until his father's money should come to him. And in case he married Marigold he wouldn't have to tell anybody until he was of age. That would be just as well for Marigold too. Her mother couldn't kick then either. And when they got their money they could clear out and let the old folks whistle.

By the time Laurie had had a couple of good stiff drinks he felt better, and started out to try and find his impromptu friend of the night before, the little girl he had brought into his mother's party. He was quite well pleased with himself and his plans. He would take Lily Trevor out to lunch and maybe a spin in the park, then when Marigold's school was out he would go and get her and thrash this thing out once for all. Marigold had to be made to understand just how far she could go. He wasn't going to have things all haywire. She'd got to cut out this fanatical stuff, and learn to do as other girls did, and if one lesson didn't teach her he'd give her plenty.

But Lily Trevor was working in a factory, running a silk machine, and the rules of the factory were stiff. He couldn't even get speech of her. So he went back to one of his haunts and got several more drinks to prepare him for the afternoon. He still had a haunting memory of the look in Marigold's eyes when she had scorned him, and he needed to be reinforced.

Marigold had a hard day. The children were still unusually restless because of their long holiday the first of the week, and seemed unable to settle down to serious work. The tired, troubled little teacher longed to get home and think her problems through, but there seemed no chance for that. When three o'clock came the principal approached her apologetically with a request.

"Miss Brooke, would you mind looking after some recalcitrant ones in my room? They are not through the work which I told them positively must be handed in tonight or they will not be eligible for basketball next term. I've just got word that the parents of a boarding pupil who is quite ill have arrived. I must meet them and take them to the child's bedside. I really don't see what I can do but ask you kindly to stay for a little while. Would you mind coming into my office in my place? I hope they'll be through soon, but I can't give you a definite time. I'll be glad to return the favor sometime when there's something you want."

The principal smiled. She had a winning way with her. And of course there was nothing for Marigold to do but assent as pleasantly as she could.

So Marigold took a great bundle of papers she had to correct and went to the principal's room.

But it was after five o'clock when the last dallier had finished his work and she could dismiss him and feel free to go herself.

Wearily she closed her desk, put on her wraps and hurried out to the street, deciding that she would walk home. She needed the exercise.

But what was her annoyance when she reached the pavement to find Laurie's car parked in front of the building, and Laurie himself tall and formidable standing on the sidewalk waiting as if he were a stern parent come to punish her.

"Oh, Laurie!" she said with a troubled note in her voice, "why did you come here now? I told you I had nothing more to say. Please go away. I cannot go anywhere today. I have things to do at home."

"So that's the way you greet me, is it, when I've taken the trouble to come after you? You think you can turn me down just like that! Well, you can't! I'm not one to take a slap like that and do nothing about it! I'm having it out. You've got to go home, have you? Well, I'm taking you home, see? Get in! I'm taking you home when I get good and ready."

Never had she seen Laurie in this mood before. She looked at him in astonishment, and started to back away from him, but suddenly he seized her wrist and with an iron grip pushed her toward the car. She could not free herself from him without making an outcry and drawing the attention of others to herself. And to make the matter worse three of the teachers and several scholars who had been holding a school club meeting were just coming down the steps behind her, and she was painfully conscious of their nearness.

"Laurie, *please!*" she said in a low tone. "This isn't a joke. I really don't want to ride now. I have an errand. I want to speak to one of those teachers."

She tried to stand her ground and resist him, but he held her arm like a vise, and forced her about.

"I'm not joking!" he said grimly. "I came here to get you, and I'm taking you with me. Get in!" and he pushed her to the car so that she must needs get in or stumble headlong. Moreover it was the driver's seat into which she was shoved roughly, and she had to struggle under the wheel to the other side, as he forced her over, springing in after her, and starting his car almost before the door was closed.

Her face flamed scarlet with anger, and then turned white and she began to tremble. What did he mean, treating her that way? Then as the car shot out into the road, and he turned sternly to face her, she got his breath, and it was heavy with liquor. Laurie had been drinking again!

**14** A new kind of fear possessed Marigold now. She had had very little experience with drinkers and so the situation was all the more startling. What was he going to do? Where was he taking her?

She tried to steady herself, casting furtive glances at his stern face as he threaded his way recklessly through traffic, dashing through lights, disregarding a possible whistle of the traffic cop, whirling around a corner and back into the highway again, without reducing his speed.

Oh, what was going to happen? He could not keep this up! They would both be killed! There would be sure to be an accident before many minutes. She must do something to stop him. Wasn't there any way to calm him? He sat there without looking at her and driving like a mad man. If she only knew how to drive! She had had a few lessons back in the days before her father died, but there had been no car after he was gone, and she did not dare trust herself even to try to stop this one, not with Laurie's hand upon the wheel, and Laurie looking like a crazy man, his face white with anger, his eyes wild and bloodshot. What could she do? Oh, Father in Heaven, help!

Like an answer to her cry there came the words to her memory, words from that last morning in Washington when Ethan had read the psalm: "Surely He shall deliver thee —" and "Thou shalt not be afraid —" Those were all the words she could remember, but they calmed her frightened heart.

They were out of the city now, and on the broad highway, but it was little better here. The traffic was thick, and Laurie, not satisfied with traveling along at a reasonable speed, was dashing in between cars, and thundering past at a mad pace, rocking from side to side, and barely escaping collisions on every hand.

"Laurie, please," Marigold managed to whisper with white lips, "*please* go a little slower. You frighten me!"

Laurie looked down at her with bright strange eyes in which triumph sat like a demon.

"Frighten you? Ha, ha! Nothing to be 'fraid of!" His speech was thick and unnatural, and suddenly he reached out an arm and thrust it about her, drawing her close to him and forcing her head down on his shoulder.

"Needn't be afraid. I'll take care of you! Nothing ever happens to me! Just lie down there and go to sleep."

Trembling with fear she slid out from that embracing arm with loathing. She had never been so near a drunken man in her life.

"No!" she said as quietly as she could manage her voice, "I'd rather sit up! It makes me a little sick, this going so fast! Couldn't you go just a little slower, Laurie?"

But he only gave an evil grin.

"Sorry, can't 'commodate you, Mara," he said thickly, "got a date, and have to get there! But you'll feel better pretty soon, Baby! Do you good, riding fast. Good for the lungs. Blows the cobwebs away!"

"But you said you were taking me home, Laurie," she pleaded, "and this isn't the way home. I'm feeling quite sick, Laurie, and I'd like to go home."

"Yes, after while," he said indifferently. "Gotta go shumwheres else first. Didn't I tell you where we're going? My mishtake! You shee we're on our way to get married! Some wedding trip, Baby! Like it now?"

Horror froze her throat. She could not speak. She could not think. Was God going to let this awful ride go on? Was He going to let them come to some terrible end? A crash, terrible injuries, or death? Was a tragedy like this coming to her dear mother to bear, all because she had been so silly and thoughtless, and self-willed, and determined to have a good time with Laurie?

"Because He hath set his love upon me, therefore will I deliver him —" the words came to her like a voice from far away, out of that quiet happy Sunday night when Ethan had been reading God's word. She had been longing then for something deep and sweet in her own life that would calm fears and doubts and questionings and help her to anchor her soul, as the soul of the young man who was reading seemed anchored.

"Like that, Baby?" demanded Laurie suddenly. "Like to get married?"

Her soul was one great cry for help and strength and guidance. What should she say? She loathed his calling her Baby, but what was that in the midst of such danger? Not worth mentioning. The ravings of a maniac who must be calmed, not excited. She roused her frightened soul to self-control and tried to speak quietly.

"Have you told your mother what you are planning to do, Laurie?" she asked as steadily as she could.

"Told the mater? I should say not, Baby! She'd fall into a rage and stop my allowance, and that would never do at this shtage of the game, shee? I've got eight bucks left in my pocket and my 'lowance is due day after tomorrow. Never do to tell the old lady I'm getting married. No, we'll keep it quiet awhile, Baby. Bimeby when I get my money, come of age, you know, then we'll shpring it on 'em. That ish, if we make it a go. If we don't, nobody's the wisher, and what no body knowsh won't hurt anybody. Shee, baby?"

He cast a devilish grin at her, and she wondered with a sharp thrust of condemnation, how she had ever thought him handsome. Oh, could just a few drinks make a man into a devil like this? Or had he been at it a long time, and she had been such an ignoramus that she hadn't suspected it?

She shrank farther away from him into her corner.

"I'm — feeling pretty — sick," she gasped out. "Do — you — mind — if I — don't talk — much?"

"Shick! Tough luck, Baby! Thatsh a nish way to act on your wedding trip!"

She barely suppressed a shudder at that, and putting her head down on her hand closed her eyes.

"Oh, God!" she prayed. "I'm trusting You to see me through this somehow. Keep me quiet, and control this situation. You are stronger than the devil. You are stronger than a drunken man. *Help!*"

It seemed a miracle that they were still on the road. The car tore on amidst traffic, and barely escaped again and again. She began to hope and pray for a traffic cop, but none seemed to be in evidence. Once there were two on motor cycles, but there was an accident ahead, and when Laurie dashed by they were engaged in trying to control the cars involved, and did not seem to notice them until they were well past. Once Marigold heard a shrill whistle ring out far behind them, and hoped they had been sighted and followed, but Laurie pressed on, almost overturning the car once as he rounded a corner at high speed. Often he sent them up in the air and bumping down again with terrific force. But Laurie only rushed on.

It was growing dark now, and beginning to snow, and Marigold's heart grew heavier. She sat silent in her corner and almost she hoped that Laurie had forgotten she was there. If the only could contrive some way to make him stop at a service station she would try to make her escape! Just run around behind some building and disappear. Would that be possible? But she dared not ask Laurie to stop. Perhaps the car would run out of gas or something pretty soon. Perhaps there would be help somewhere.

But suddenly Laurie burst forth again.

"We musht be almosht there! Down in Mar'land shomewhere — ! You've heard of the plashe! Get married shlick and quick. Everybody doesh it. Don't cosht mush either. Guess we c'n get by on eight bucks. If we get shtuck I'll call up the old lady and tell her I'm bushted!"

Marigold tried to control the shudder that passed over her involuntarily, visioning such a life as he was planning for her. "God! Oh, God! I'm Yours! I can't do anything for myself! You sent a strong one to help me down from the high place. Please come Yourself now and help me!"

It was snowing hard now, a blinding snow. The windshield-wiper was tripping back and forth on the glass, but the snow in great flakes clogged its movements, and placed large soft curtains of snow quickly and neatly over the spot they had cleared. The visibility was poor. Marigold closed her eyes. She had no longer strength left to watch the near escapes, the oncoming lights of cars that seemed about to crash into them.

And now they were coming into a town. Marigold knew it even without opening her eyes, because the light through her eyelids was more continuous. Laurie was still going at a breakneck speed. It was a wonder that he did not get arrested.

Suddenly she felt the speed slowing, and then the brakes were jammed on with a shudder and the car screamed to a slower pace.

"Thish musht be the plashe," she heard Laurie say. "Nish little town. Marriage lishenshes on every shtreet. Shee there!"

Marigold opened her eyes enough to see a great sign lighted with a row of electric bulbs above it, under a small sheltering roof. She could read the lettering through the fringes of her lashes.

MARRIAGE LICENSES
Minister!

it read, and a great fear took possession of her, more dreadful than anything she had experienced before. Was there going to be no way of escape? Would it be possible for an unprincipled man to go through with a ceremony and make it legal? Oh, God! What should she do?

"Nish place," said Laurie thickly. "Like to live here myself. Look, Baby! *Minishter!* How 'bout that? You're so religious, I shupooshe you'll be tickled pink about that!"

Marigold continued to keep her eyes

closed as if she were asleep. It seemed her only defense. If he thought she was asleep perhaps he would let her alone a minute. Perhaps he would get out and go into the house without her. If she could only drive a car she could get away from him. The car was standing by the curb, now, and Laurie was still for the instant. Would it be possible that he might fall asleep and give her a chance to slip out the door and away?

There was not any possibility that she had not conceived of during that awful ride.

But no, he was not asleep. He was reaching down into the pocket on the door of the car and getting that awful flask. Twice before he had taken a swallow, the car lurching crazily as he did it. She dared not turn her head and look, but a second later she smelled the strong odor of the liquor again. And now that the car was standing still he was drinking deeply.

Then suddenly he reached the bottle toward her.

"Take a drink," he said foolishly. "Got plenty left for you. Shusht a drop, Baby! Do you good! Take away your shicknesh! Better take a brasher. Then we'll go in and get tied."

But she steadily kept her head turned toward the corner of the car, and presently he desisted.

"Shtubborn! Thash what you are! Have a heckuva time breaking your will, but ish gotta be done! Awright, Baby, you shtay here a minute and I'll go tip off the parshun!"

Slowly and laboriously, Laurie opened the car door and got himself onto the sidewalk, slipping and sliding drunkenly about in the snow as he made his way across the pavement and in at a little white gate.

"Oh God! Oh, Jesus Christ! Send me help. Send a strong One."

Marigold's heart seemed to be praying of itself, while her mind suddenly came alert.

She sat without stirring while Laurie half skated up the little path to the white house, stumbled up the two steps to the veranda, and reached out an uncertain hand to a doorbell, adding a knock on the door itself, just to make sure.

Now! Now was the time!

She cast a quick glance about to get her bearings, and reached a cold trembling hand out to the door handle. Was there a place to hide? There were lights ahead, cars coming — trucks perhaps — she must get across before they came. It was her only chance. The headlights would show her up as she ran, but she must keep well behind Laurie's car so he could not see her. Once out she would scream for help before she would ever let him put her back there. But — would he tell some tale, make them believe he had the right? Oh, she must not think of such things now. She must go at once. God, my God, Jesus, my Saviour, are You there? "Surely he shall deliver thee —"

The cold steel handle in her hand yielded and the door swung silently away letting in a rush of cold air. She could feel great snowflakes in her face.

She cast one quick glance at Laurie. The door was opening and a man in a black coat was standing inside. He would see her go if she waited an instant longer. She swung herself out into the road in the snow, struggling to keep her footing, and immediately the sharp light from an approaching car picked her out, and startled her to action. She sprang across into the darkness beyond that path of light.

She was dazed from the long hard ride, her senses were almost stupefied, but the snow stung her sharply in the face as she hurtled across to the shadows on the opposite side of the street and huddled there for an instant. Should she just crouch there somewhere and wait till the cars were past? No, for Laurie would raise an outcry as soon as he discovered her escape. She must be out of sight entirely before he found out. She darted a look toward the road and suddenly she saw that the colored lights coming were on a bus! A bus! Oh, if she could get into a bus! It didn't matter where it was going, if she could only get away *some*where. It was coming on swiftly, but she dared not try to signal it here in front of this house where Laurie stood. She cast a glance ahead and saw that the road curved around a slanting corner. Perhaps she could get past that and manage to signal the bus, somehow.

She started ahead, slipping and stumbling as she went, but hurrying on. The snow blinded her, the sidewalk was slippery, the paving beneath the snow in places rough and uneven. Once just as she had almost made the corner, daring not to look back, she stumbled and almost went down, but a passing man reached out a hand and steadied her. She thanked him breathlessly and flew on, around the corner, past several stores whose bright lights made her shrink, and on to another corner. Now, was she safe?

The bus was rounding the corner now, and coming slowly on. It was halting, it was going to stop in front of the drug store. Would she dare run out and get in while it stood there in that bright light, or should she wait until just before it started again, and make a dash for it?

She was standing in a little alleyway between two stores in the shadow, just for the moment hidden in the darkness. But there was snow on the ground behind her, and the whole world seemed too bright because of the snow. Her dark coat would show up dearly against the white background.

There were not many people in the bus, and they seemed to be asleep, their heads thrown back comfortably against the seats. The bus stopped just a little past the drug store, the shadow of a great willow tree trunk half hiding the entrance from the sidewalk. The driver sprang out and dashed into the drug store. He was carrying a long envelope in his hand. One passenger roused and followed him, digging in his pocket for a coin, Marigold peered out cautiously from her hiding place into the store window. The driver handed the envelope to a clerk, threw a coin down on the counter, and now he was tossing down a glass of something. The passenger had just received a pack of cigarettes and was in the act of lighting one.

Marigold gave a quick glance back to the corner from which she had come. Laurie was not in sight yet. Could she make it? Oh, if he should appear just as she came out into the light she felt that her trembling limbs would let her down in an unconscious heap on the snowy pavement. But she took a long breath and dashed across into the open door of the bus, sinking into a seat far back in the shadow, scarcely able to get her breath again, though she had run not more than five steps. Was she really out of danger yet?

Then she heard a car come thundering up the street behind the bus. Had Laurie discovered she was gone and come after her?

She shrank lower and lower into the seat and closed her eyes, turning her face into the shadow.

It seemed ages before that driver came out, and the passenger who was smoking his cigarette. She dared not open her eyes and look at them. Not until she was far away from this town. Would the driver notice that he had another passenger? She prayed fervently that he would not, at least until she was too far from the town to be put off.

At last the engine started, the bus lurched forward, made a wide circle, and turned back on its tracks down the street out of which she had just fled! Her heart stopped still. To her horror she saw the big sign "MARRIAGE LICENSES" loom into view. Was she caught? She couldn't jump out of that bus and run back. It was well under way now.

Marigold shrank into the cushions, putting her arm on the window seat for a pillow, and turning her face so that it was entirely hidden from view, thankful that in her hasty choosing she had lighted on a seat on the opposite side of the white house where Laurie had gone to arrange for their marriage.

Her heart almost stood still as the bus rumbled on down the street, expecting every minute that it would be held up and Laurie would come staggering in in search of her. What a fool she had been to get into a bus without knowing which way it was going!

She shut her eyes and did not dare look out until she was sure they had passed the place where Laurie's car had stood.

Then suddenly she was seized with anxiety to look back.

The snow was coming down so thickly that she could not be sure of anything but the two blurred points of Laurie's car lights. But there seemed to be a group of dark figures standing on the sidewalk near the car. She could not tell whether one was Laurie or not, but as she looked she was sure she saw one of them jump into the car, and a moment later those two bright lights came wallowing on toward her. Was Laurie's brain clear enough to have figured out her way of escape? Certain it was that a car was following the bus in wavering uncertain lines! Was it Laurie?

15 And while all this had been going on, down in Washington Marigold's mother was having a time of her own.

Some seventh sense vouchsafed to mothers only, had told her that there was need for worry.

Three times during the evening, quite casually, she had tried to call her daughter on the telephone, and had got no answer. She could not understand it. She was unable to think out a situation that would explain Marigold's not being in at any of her calls. And surely all three could not be blunders of a sleepy operator, because she had started calling quite early in the evening, to ask Marigold for the address of a secondhand book firm that was famous for being able to ferret out old books, even out-of-print books, and produce them in short order.

But when the third call failed she could not control her nervousness and she said she guessed she would go to bed. Her sister watched her speculatively. She was older than Mrs. Brooke, had practically brought her up, and had learned through the years to read her face easily. She knew that her sister was worried about something.

Marigold's mother had been very surreptitious with her telephone calls. She had gone quite openly the first time, and coming back said she guessed Marigold was out to supper with some of the other teachers, but when at nine o'clock she thought to try again, she waited until Sarah, the house servant, was talking to Mrs. Bevan about the next day's ordering. The third time she had professed to go and get a clean handkerchief, but it took longer than was necessary and Marian Bevan studied her face when she returned. She was pretty sure what the trouble was, but couldn't quite think how to speak about it and so held her peace. She had a rare talent for holding her peace when many other women would have plunged in and torn away reticences and demanded an explanation. So she let her sister profess to be weary and retire to her room without asking what was the matter.

However, she did not drop the matter from her own mind, but took it to her usual refuge and began to pray about it.

About two o'clock Marigold's mother could not stand it any longer, and sure that her sister was long asleep, she stole from her room, velvet shod, and went stealthily downstairs to the telephone booth. Having closed all the doors possible to the upper floor, and shut herself into the telephone booth she made a prolonged effort once more to reach her child, becoming insistent, declaring that she *knew* someone was there, perhaps asleep, and *please* to keep on ringing till she got her. But all to no purpose. The operator finally grew irate and said very crossly, "Madam, they do not answer! Your number does not answer!" and at last she desisted, and stole silently back upstairs, with slow worried tears trickling down her cheeks. She was almost sick with worry.

She had reached the upper hall, and was cautiously moving past her sister's open door, confident that she could not possibly be heard when her sister's voice spoke out clearly:

"Mary, what is the matter? Why are you worried?"

She paused for an instant and caught her breath. Then she stepped to the dark doorway.

"Oh, my dear!" she said penitently. "Did I waken you? I'm so sorry! I just thought I would try again for Marigold. I was awake, and thought I might be asleep in the morning and miss her before she goes out early to school. But I wouldn't for the world have wakened you."

"You didn't wake me, dear! I haven't been asleep yet. But Mary, why are you worried?

295

Don't you trust Marigold? Come here and sit beside me. I've been wondering about it all evening. I saw you were worried, and I couldn't quite understand. Your dear girl seems so dependable. I thought you trusted her fully."

"Oh, I do, entirely," Marigold's mother hastened to say. "I trust *her* fully. But, Marian, I do not trust all those with whom she companions. You see I have called her up three times before this, and always the report is that the number does not answer. I have tried to put it out of my mind, but to save me I cannot help imagining all sorts of things."

"Yes? Such as — ?"

"Well, I don't know exactly. Weird things that probably wouldn't be at all likely to happen, but they happen like a flash in my mind and then I cannot get rid of the thought."

"But you know, dear, the phone might be out of order."

"Yes, of course," said Mrs. Brooke crisply. "I've told myself that again and again. But it wasn't out of order last night."

"Oh, but there may have been a storm that tore the wires down."

"Of course!" still briskly.

"But you still fear — ?"

"Yes, I still think of all sorts of wild things."

"Well, suppose you get them off your mind by telling them to me. What's first and greatest?"

"Well, Laurie Trescott!" said Mrs. Brooke sharply. "I don't trust him. He may have inveigled her into doing something, going somewhere — oh, I don't know where nor what, only I'm afraid. He isn't a bit discreet."

"Oh, well, if that's all, don't fret. A little mess of gossip isn't pleasant, but it can't really harm her. Her friends know what she is, and perhaps it may serve to open her eyes a little. You don't think the young man would do her any real harm, do you? He's a gentleman, isn't he?"

"Y-e-s!" said Marigold's mother uncertainly. "I suppose he is. I've always thought he was. He has lovely manners, he is courteous and quite charming. I sometimes think that is what has fascinated Marigold."

There was silence in the dark house. Nothing could be heard but the soft plashing of snowflakes on the window panes.

"It's snowing again," said Mary Brooke anxiously, looking toward the window where even the street lights wore a shroud of snow. "It may be a terrible storm up at home. It's colder there than here, you know, and I think the storm is coming from the north. I've been thinking, if she's out in it, it would be so easy to have an accident. A crash! And they lying dead somewhere, and we not knowing — !"

"Mary, dear, you don't trust your Heavenly Father very much, do you?"

"Oh, yes, I do, Marian, but when I hear those great sleek snowflakes thud against the window panes, a little demon gets up on my shoulder and mocks me, and then I get to thinking how wild and reckless Laurie Trescott sometimes seems to me, and I forget I don't have to run the universe."

She tried to laugh but the anxiety was still there beneath her smile.

"Yes, I know, dear. And He understands. 'He knoweth our frame, He remembereth that we are dust.'"

"Yes, I know. Thank you, dear!" sighed the mother. "But oh, I can't help thinking, if Laurie were only more like your Ethan, how happy I would be. Ethan is wonderful! I felt fairly envious of you when he was here. He is a charming young fellow, and seems so responsible and mature for his years. But then of course, he's a Christian, and Laurie isn't!" She sighed deeply.

"Yes, he's a rather wonderful young

Christian," said his aunt warmly. "And he's a dear boy! There is none better! Yes, I could fervently wish that your dear little girl might find a friend as strong and fine as he is. But now, my dear, you must just trust this with the Lord. You must get some sleep, and in the morning you will be shown. You and I will pray, and then sleep and trust! Good night, dear!"

"I'm sorry I've kept you awake," said Mary Brooke as she stooped to kiss her sister, "but you've been a wonderful comfort, as you always were."

And then she slipped away to her room to pray for her child.

16 Marigold lay in her dim little corner of the bus while the agony of the moments dragged by. Car after car came dashing by, a long bright stream of light that shot past and left only the dim whiteness of the snow-filled air again. The snow was dense now. She watched beneath her lashes as the windshield wipers played a mad dance together on the glass. The driver's outlook was like a half circle cut in a white blanket. Slower and slower lumbered the bus. Marigold could sense that the road was slippery. It seemed that nothing had ever gone so slowly before. A deadly contrast to the mad ride she had taken down from her home. But oh, if she was followed, what chance had she at this snail's pace to get away? And how much liquor did Laurie have with him? Would he keep on drinking until it was all gone?

An hour dragged by. She stole a glance at her wrist watch but it was too dark to tell the time accurately. She was thankful for the darkness, and for the curtains of snow hung deeply at all the windows. It would not be easy through that for a driver outside to spot a traveler inside.

Marigold's sense of direction had deserted her for the moment, but after a little she had a feeling that she was not on her way to Philadelphia, and then she tried to reason it out. Of course, since they had passed by Laurie's car, going in the same direction that his car had been pointed, they were going *away* from, not *toward* Philadelphia. But *where* were they going? How could she find out? Not by questioning the driver, or any one of her fellow travelers, she resolved. She must not come into the public attention at all. She must act as if she were a perfectly normal traveler out for a chosen destination, not one who had merely taken refuge here and knew not whither she was being taken.

So she lifted her eyes to the dim walls to see if there was any sign of destination anywhere posted. There at the front, above the driver's head was a sign in colored glass, backwards of course, for the benefit of the outside world. They who traveled inside were supposed to know where they were going. What a fool she had been not to read it as she stood in the alley waiting for the bus to be ready to start. But it was so clogged with snow it was impossible to be sure what it said. Was it Baltimore? She measured the space with her tired eyes, counting the letters. Yes, it must be Baltimore. Her heart leaped up. So near to Washington! How she longed to go on to her mother, fling herself down with her head in her mother's lap and sob out the whole dreadful story! For an instant she was tempted.

But she couldn't do that of course. She had to be in school in the morning. It would be impossible to get back in time. And it would only alarm her mother beyond anything. She would never feel safe about her again. Besides, she was no longer a child. She must keep this terrible experience to herself, at least for the present. She must think what was the best thing to be done and do it.

She was thankful that she had enough money with her to cover all necessities. She had debated that morning when dressing whether to leave in the apartment all but the change she usually carried in her purse, and had decided against it. There would be no trouble about paying her fare. But if she were on her way to Baltimore, was it going to be necessary for her to go all the way? Wouldn't it be possible for her to change to another bus at some halfway stop?

Oh, but that would be to return on the same route, to go again through that awful town where she had left Laurie, where Laurie, by this time might have raised a posse to hunt her. No, she mustn't go back that way. Better to go on and take a train from Baltimore. There were always fast trains from Baltimore to Philadelphia, weren't there? Every hour or so? She thought she remembered that. And a train would get there much quicker than a bus, especially in this storm.

She tried to calculate what time it was, and came to the conclusion that it must be somewhere around eight o'clock. She had come out of the schoolhouse a little after five, and they certainly must have been nearly two hours on the way. She had no means of knowing just where they had gone, nor how far she was from Baltimore now. She could only guess. It seemed ages since she had come out into the winter dusk to find Laurie waiting for her grimly beside his car. He had been out there all afternoon, perhaps, waiting, drinking at intervals while he waited, and growing more and more frenzied with impatience. She turned away from the memory with a shiver. Could she ever forget that awful afternoon? But she must get back to her planning and forget everything else. Yes, if they should reach Baltimore at, say, nine o'clock could she make a train at nine-thirty, or ten? Surely by ten. That would bring her home by midnight or a little after. She could take a taxi home, and get a reasonable amount of sleep for her next day's work. She could doze on the train, too, and get a little rested.

But presently another passenger made his way up to the front of the bus and asked questions of the driver.

"What time you calculatin' ta get ta Baltimore?"

"Can't say," said the driver amusedly. "Due there at nine-thirty, but at this rate it might be ten-thirty 'fore we get in. Can't make any headway at all with this here snow cloggin' the atmosphere. It's as bad as a fog. And this here slippery road is just one glare. I don't dare go beyont a crawl. If you fellers was to lean hard on the side o' this here bus she might skid inta the middle o' next week. I ain't sayin' when we'll get ta Baltimore. We'll git there sometime tanight, likely, ef we have good luck, but I ain't sayin' when. Not 'nless this here snow quits, which she don't seem likely ta do at present."

Thereafter Marigold looked helplessly out the window, studying those great slow-moving lazy flakes as they came down, each one of mammoth size and thickness, and reflected how mighty were little flakes, if there were enough of them. Was it even thinkable that she might not be able to get back in time for school in the morning? And if so how was she to explain her delay? She couldn't tell that she had been kidnaped and driven away to be married. She couldn't have them all know her private affairs. What kind of an explanation was she to give when she got home, if she was going to be later than midnight? There was Mrs. Waterman, too, always poking into her affairs and having remarks to make afterward. Well, she would just have to let that go and deal with it when the time came. Perhaps God would take care of that with all her other troubles.

So she put her head back and before she knew was asleep. In the face of all that trouble and excitement she had gone to sleep!

When she awoke with a start it was to realize that the bus had come to a halt and people were brushing by her getting out. Everybody was getting out. They were yawning, and talking with a dreary sleepy accent.

Marigold didn't realize where she was at first, till sitting up staring around her it suddenly all came back.

This must be Baltimore! Would there be a train soon? Oh, to be at home in her own bed asleep.

She paid her fare as she got out, handing out a ten dollar bill. The driver seemed to understand where she got on, though she hadn't known the name of the town herself, but he told her how much it was.

When she got out she gave a quick furtive look about lest somehow Laurie would have followed and be waiting to take possession of her again. Would she ever get over the feeling that evening's experience had given her? Was it going to be like that awful dream?

Then she remembered. The dream had utterly gone. Strong arms had carried her away from that dream. She had a strong One with her always now, living in her, she had His power to carry her through.

With a steady step she went to the ticket window and enquired about trains. She had just missed one. There would not be another until twelve-twenty-seven! That would bring her to Philadelphia around half past three in the morning! A taxi couldn't get her to her apartment before four o'clock. What would Mrs. Waterman think? Could she possibly get in without being heard?

Her ticket bought, she stole into an obscure corner of the station restaurant where she could watch the door, and ordered a bowl of soup. She was chilled and faint, and it tasted good, but she ate it hurriedly. It was not beyond possibility that Laurie might have followed down here somewhere, or, having sighted her in that bus might have been cunning enough to telephone the police to watch for her. She felt he would stop at nothing in his present state of mind, and she must run no risks. She must get home as soon as possible.

It seemed a long time to wait, and she dared not sleep. She was too nervous. She took refuge in the ladies' waiting room in a sheltered corner, scanning alertly everyone who passed through the outer waiting room, and watching the clock. When at last the train was called she hurried out and got into a day coach, taking a seat at the rear of the car where she would not be seen, and where she could keep her own watch.

Now and then she would cast a glance at the window, but the world outside was but a whirl of white, and the windows were plastered with snow so thickly that they were perfectly opaque. She drew a long breath of relief. She was on the last lap of her journey now. She could count herself to have escaped. But she felt such an utter weariness that it seemed as if she would like to die. Why had God let all this dreadful thing happen to her? Especially just now when she was beginning to know Him in a new way. She couldn't understand it. She had asked to be shown — but stay! Wasn't that just what this had been for, that she might be shown? Quickly and definitely shown just what to do about Laurie? Well, she had the answer to her prayer. Not for anything in life would she want further fellowship with Laurie. Oh, there might be excuses for him. It might not be all his fault. Doubtless others had influenced him, and his home surroundings had not given him the background to resist drinking, but after all had been said for him, Laurie was himself to blame of course. And even if he tried to reform she could never trust him. She had been well taught concerning the hold that drinking has on its victims. She wanted no dealings with men who drank. She had had her lesson. She could forgive, and perhaps — she *hoped* — she could forget sometime, but she could never marry a man who thought there was no harm in taking a drink.

The experience had done something more for her also. It had shown Laurie apart from the gay life he led, the pleasant nothings he was doing, the vista of pleasure that his companionship always opened for her. She had seen what it would be to be bound to Laurie for life, to be in his power. She had seen him to be weak, selfish, hard, unprincipled. Of course some of that was due to the effect of the liquor. But, Laurie would never more in her eyes be the perfect creature that she had imagined.

And more than that, Laurie was not a child of God!

She had known that. She had felt when she came home that she was going to have to give him up. But she had expected sore heartbreak. And now God had shown her what he was in such a way that the heartbreak was gone!

Oh, it had been a shock when the illusions were torn away, but it had left her astonishingly whole, uninjured. There would doubtless be times when she would feel lonely and wish for a gay comrade to while away an idle hour with her, but just tonight she was glad to be lonely. To have that fearful ride ended, and to be safe and quiet and alone. With no wild red eyes glaring into hers, no hoarse thick words flung at her, no madman trying to embrace her as they rode along at breakneck speed knowing not but the next moment would be the last. Oh, it was good, *good,* to have escaped, and God *had* answered her prayer and shown her without the shadow of a doubt what she ought to do — or rather what she ought *not* to do.

When they were almost to Philadelphia she dropped off to sleep for a few minutes, but started awake as the train drew into the station.

It was still snowing hard when she got into a taxi and they drove out the familiar way. She looked at the old landmarks with welcome. Even the ugly houses that she had always disliked, looked good to her. Oh, it was wonderful to be home and safe!

There was no sign of Laurie anywhere about. And now the snow would hide her footprints and perhaps Mrs. Waterman would not know how late she came in.

She stole into the house and up the stairs with great caution, and at last was safe in her own room, with her door locked.

She did not turn on the light. She had a feeling that its radiance might somehow shine beneath the crack of the door and advertise her presence to Mrs. Waterman, advertise to the neighborhood that she was but just home.

Then first she knelt and thanked God for saving her.

She undressed rapidly in the dark and was soon sound asleep, her little alarm clock set and ticking away beside her like a faithful watchdog on guard.

**17** Marigold awoke startled in the morning to the tune of her prompt little clock screaming at her over and over again. She didn't waken quickly enough to turn it off at its first sound as she usually did.

And then, suddenly, as she came fully awake the whole awful night was spread before her, and she had a quick sick feeling that all her world had gone wrong, and her troubles were by no means over.

When she had tumbled into her bed at four o'clock she could only be thankful that she was safely at home and her troubles were past. But now in the light of the morning it came over her that she was by no means so safe and out of danger. For if Laurie were alive and not too drunk to remember he would certainly be raving somewhere and trying to find her, perhaps still angry enough, and still under the influence of liquor to be determined to pay her back for having run away from him. She recalled how angry he had been the morning after she had gone from the ice palace and left him. But this offense was still greater. She had deserted him on what he was pleased to consider the eve of her marriage with him.

She shuddered even here in her warm bed to think of the things he had said. And now as she lay for a minute trying to get her full senses, she realized that there was no telling what he might undertake to do that day. And if he was still in the mood he had been when she left him it was conceivable that he might take some drastic method to punish her. Kidnap her, perhaps!

She stared across at the wall in the morning light, and grim fear came and mocked her.

Suddenly she remembered.

"Surely He shall deliver thee —" And he had delivered! He had brought her home safely. Could she not trust Him for the rest? "Because he hath set His love upon me, therefore will I deliver him!" There was nothing she could do but go through her duty for the day, and perhaps be unusually alert to keep out of Laurie's way for the future. She must trust the Lord who had brought her thus far!

She slipped out of bed to her knees. A quick cry for help! Then her next act was to fling a warm bathrobe about her and call up her mother.

"Mother, dear! I was afraid you would be worrying."

How her mother's heart thrilled when

she heard her voice!

"Did you call? Oh, I'm so sorry! I didn't go right home from school. I went in another direction. I expected to call you but there was no opportunity, and when I got home it was quite late and I was afraid of waking Aunt Marian. Yes, I was out last night. I haven't time to tell you about it now for I'm going to be late to school I'm afraid. What? Did I have a good time? Well, no, not exactly, but I guess it was rather good for me. Anyway I'll tell you about it later. Oh yes, indeed, I'm all right. Are you? No, don't you think of coming home until Elinor and her husband get back. No, I won't hear of it. You needn't worry about me. I'll get along beautifully. Bye bye and I'll call you tonight again."

She gave a little shiver as she hung up. That had been hard, to talk lightly of that awful experience and not have Mother suspect. She felt she had done very well. Of course she mustn't ever let Mother know what an awful time she had been though — at least not now. Not till it was so far in the past that there would never be any more worry about it for her precious mother anyway.

As she turned from the telephone she had a sick longing to crawl back into bed and sleep, just stay there all day and sleep. But she knew she could not do that. She had a job and must get to it. She was not a child to lie in bed when she was weary.

A quick shower while the coffee prepared itself, toast made while she dressed, breakfast eaten a bite at a time as she prepared for the day.

The dress she had worn yesterday was mussed and dejected-looking after the ride in the train. A glance in the mirror showed her face looking gray and weary. She must keep up her appearance and not have everybody asking if she was sick. She slipped into a little knitted dress of bright cherry color edged narrowly with black. It was her one cherished afternoon dress, and very becoming, but one must do something to brighten up a day after the night she had spent.

She hunted up her galoshes, put on her old fur coat, and a gray felt hat that matched the squirrel of her coat and started out.

Mrs. Waterman poked her head out of her door across the hall as Marigold came out.

"Well, upon my word! Are you here? I didn't hear you come in last night at all. Weren't you awful late? I didn't see you come home from school at all."

Marigold smiled engagingly.

"Yes, I was pretty late," she admitted brightly. "You see, I didn't come right home from school. I had to go somewhere else. And then when I started home I got on the wrong bus and went out of my way and had a tiresome time getting back again. It was snowing very hard or I probably would have seen my mistake sooner. But I got home all right. I'm glad I didn't disturb you coming in. Isn't it grand that it has cleared off this morning? I didn't think last night it would. I thought we were in for a blizzard."

"Yes, it is clear again. But I guess the walks are pretty bad. People haven't had time to get them shoveled yet. You better be awful careful not to get flu while your mother's away. Have you got your galoshes on? I guess at that you'll have to be careful. The snow's pretty deep."

"Well, I have a taxi coming for me, and there it comes now, I guess. Didn't he ring? I must go."

She hurried away, glad to escape further questioning, almost gleeful that she had got by the house gossip so easily. She put her head back and closed her eyes for a brief respite before she reached the school. How she longed to go to sleep. How was she going to get through the day, after such a night?

But the day rushed by with its round of inevitable duties and Marigold had no time to indulge her desire to close her eyes for just a little minute. The children were filled with a fine frenzy of glee over the snow, and to control them was like trying to rein in a lot of little wild hyenas. Marigold in desperation finally finished the afternoon by reading them a story about a wolf hound in the far northland, until at last the relief bell rang and they all rushed out to pelt one another with snow, and fill the air with the melodious glee of young voices.

Then quickly sudden fear descended upon her, the fear of what might be coming next. Just twenty-four hours ago she had started on that terrible compulsory ride. Was Laurie even now preparing some new torture to repay her for having escaped from him?

It was the first time she had let herself think of Laurie all day, and now it came to her all at once to wonder what had become of him. It scarcely seemed possible that he could be alive if he kept on with his wild riding, drunk as he was. Yet they said that drunken men were somehow protected. She shuddered as she glanced out of an upper window furtively, from behind a curtain, and searched the street all about the school. There was no sign of Laurie's car.

She called a taxi, giving instructions for it to come to the back steps at the school house, and she did not go out until she saw it arrive, and had scanned the neighborhood carefully. All the way back home she watched most carefully. Now, in a few short minutes she would be at home, and she would lock herself in and let no one enter. She would get herself some hot soup and then she would go to sleep and sleep all night. What luxury! And yet, somehow there seemed to be a thought of terror in it all because she couldn't seem to believe that Laurie might not turn up again.

But God had protected her so far. He would see her through.

As the taxi drew up in front of the house she noticed an elegant limousine standing near, with a sedate chauffeur in livery. The limousine was flashy with much chromium, and there was an air of ostentation about it as if this car were well cared for, like an overfed pet dog. Marigold eyed it carefully as she prepared to get out. But this was not Laurie's car. He never came with a chauffeur. She drew a breath of relief and hurried into the house, wondering who in the neighborhood had such stylish visitors.

But once inside the door she encountered Mrs. Waterman, lying in wait, and speaking in a penetrative confidential whisper.

"You've got a caller!" she declared speaking into Marigold's shrinking face, and gesticulating energetically with a long bony finger. "She's a real lady!" she apostrophized. "She came in that big car out there with a chauffeur to ring the bell for her and help her out, and she's got a real chinchilla coat! What do you think of that? It's real, I know, for I had a muff of it once when I was young, my great-aunt gave to me. She was wealthy and had all sorts of nice things and was real generous, so I know good things when I see them."

"Who is she?" Marigold managed to insert the question in a very low murmur.

"I don't know," said Mrs. Waterman. "She didn't give her name, but just said she'd wait. She asked for you, and I said you'd soon be in, I guessed. So she said she'd wait and I was real embarrassed not to have your key to let her into your apartment. I couldn't take her into mine because I'm getting ready for the paper hanger. So I just brought out my great grandmother's rosewood chair for her to sit in and she's up there in the hall. I thought I'd come down and let you know she was there, so you wouldn't have to go up unprepared. But I've been kind of worried about my chair. She's a very heavy lady, and sort of flowed all over the sides of it when she sat down. I've been wondering if she'll be able to get out of it when she gets up. Chinchilla coat and all. It's a deep fur, you know, and fills in a lot. I wonder a wide lady like her would wear that fur, especially a woman with as fine a car as that. But I've been more worried because I mistrust she's smoking cigarettes up there, and if she should burn a hole in that sweet old plush I'd never forgive myself for not getting her a chair from my kitchenette!"

Something cold and dreadfully foreboding gripped Marigold by the throat, but she flung away from this avalanche of words and went up to interview the interloper.

The caller did indeed overflow the Waterman ancestral furniture but she seemed entirely comfortable. She had drawn the chair over by the window, and she was puffing away on a cigarette in a long ivory holder.

Marigold had rushed up the stairs breathlessly, her eyes bright with worried excitement, her cheeks suddenly grown pink. The old squirrel coat she was wearing was unfastened and showed her gay knitted dress. The jaunty old gray felt was perched like a bird of passage on her bright hair. She flashed before the astonished vision of her caller with startling unexpectedness amid the drab surroundings. She drew herself up with her best schoolma'am manner, and the afternoon sun which had a concession of only about five minutes a day shining into that hall window, suddenly crept in and blazed forth, lighting up Marigold's face and figure, throwing her into relief against the bareness of the desolate hall.

The caller put up a platinum lorgnette and surveyed Marigold as if she had been an article offered for sale in some out-of-the-way shop that the great lady had ferreted out and descended upon.

"I am Miss Brooke," said Marigold lifting her chin a trifle, and eyeing her caller unfavorably, "did you want to see me?"

"Why, yes," said the lady, "could we go somewhere and talk? I'm Mrs. Trescott. You are acquainted with my son. Lawrence Trescott."

"Yes?" said Marigold lifting her chin still higher. There was an icy little edge to her voice, and her heart was full of flight. What now was this? Had Laurie sent his mother to upbraid her? Or had he been injured somehow and was his mother here to charge her with murder?

Marigold gave her caller one steady look, noticing that there was a mean stubborn little twist to her chin that reminded her of

Laurie, yesterday, when he was putting her into his car.

"We'll go in here," said Marigold frigidly, whirling to unlock her door, and hoping that she had not left things in too wild confusion when she hurried away so early in the morning. She felt she needed the moral support of a perfect setting. She was conscious of Mrs. Waterman listening avidly at the foot of the stairs. They could not talk in the hall.

She opened the door and escorted the lady in.

"Will you take this seat, Mrs. Trescott," she said quietly, pointing to a substantial armed chair by the window.

Mrs. Trescott however was not quite ready to sit down. She was surveying the room in detail through her lorgnette, stooping to examine a few really lovely ornaments on the table, lifting her head to a fine old picture on the wall, and then giving minute attention to a framed photograph of Marigold's father.

It was quite evident that she was bristling with questions when Marigold came back from removing her hat and coat, but the girl faced her caller almost sternly.

"Now, Mrs. Trescott?" she said, with a really impressive manner for so young a person.

Mrs. Trescott whirled about and eased herself into the great chair, staring at Marigold, who took a straight chair opposite her.

"You have really stunning hair, you know," she remarked irrelevantly. "I *heard* that you had."

Marigold looked at her coldly, almost sternly.

"You wanted to see me about something?" she asked again.

"Yes," said Adele Trescott, shifting her fur coat a little lower on her shoulders. "I came, you know, to say that I withdraw my opposition!"

"Opposition?" said Marigold with a perplexed air. "I was not aware that you had opposition to anything. To what were you opposed? I don't understand."

"Why, to your marrying Lawrence, my son."

Marigold's eyes suddenly flashed angrily.

"But I have never had any idea of marrying Laurie, Mrs. Trescott."

"No, I suppose not," said the mother complacently. "Of course you would scarcely expect a young man out of your class to stoop to marrying you. But as I say, I have removed my opposition, and I'm not sure but in some ways it might be a good thing. You seem to be quite presentable.

And of course Laurie — Lawrence I mean — has always had his own way, and I always try to humor him if I can. He has such a delicate sensitive organism, you know."

Marigold recalled the silly angry look on the face of the delicate sensitive organism yesterday as he whirled her through the storm to an undesired wedding, and her expression froze into sternness.

"Mrs. Trescott, you are evidently under a misapprehension." She spoke icily. "Your son is not a *very special* friend of mine, and there is no question whatever of my marrying him, and *never will be!*"

"Ah, but there is where you are mistaken, my dear! You see *I* am managing this affair for you now, and I have come to say that I will be very glad to have you marry Laurie! He seems fond of you and I feel that you may be a good influence in his life."

"Mrs. Trescott, that is quite impossible! I have been out sometimes with your son in the evening, and we were friends, but recently I have come to see the matter in an entirely different light and our friendship is definitely at an end."

"Ah! But my dear, you would not let a little lover's quarrel stand in the way of a good marriage."

Marigold was growing angry and frightened. She wished her mother would walk in. Perhaps she would. It was Friday, and she had threatened this morning in their telephone conversation to come back today. But oh, she would not like to have her walk into this awful conversation, either. This was another thing that her mother must never know. This humiliation! This awful woman! Oh, she didn't need this visit of his mother's now to show her how utterly of another world was Laurie, the Laurie that she used to call a prince!

Marigold rose and came a step toward her caller.

"Mrs. Trescott, you are utterly mistaken. Laurie and I were never lovers, and never will be. Laurie is not the kind of man I would wish to marry!"

"Indeed!" said the mother haughtily. "What do you mean by that? Are you casting aspersions on my son?"

"I mean that your son does not believe in the God to whom I belong, and he also thinks it is quite all right to drink. He belongs to another world than mine. I would not want to marry him."

"Oh — *God!*" laughed the mother. "Why, that is a small matter! I'm quite sure Laurie would be entirely willing to go to church sometimes with you. What more could you ask? And as for the drinking, that's the very thing I came about. Laurie is at this very minute in the hospital being treated for alcoholism. At least I *hope* he stayed. I had him sent there. He came home quite under the influence of liquor, which I much regret of course. A young man should know how to carry his liquor. My father always did. But Laurie had been out in a terrible storm, had a wild ride somewhere, and a collision! He broke his arm, and injured his ankle, and is quite under the weather. He got a bad bruise on his forehead. I feel that he narrowly escaped death. He was somewhat under the influence of liquor of course when it happened. So I thought it over and decided to come to you. I had heard that you had very good ideas, and that your influence might be good, and I came right over to ask if you won't go over to the hospital with me now and see Laurie. Try to influence him to give up drink, at least for a little while, won't you, till he learns self-control? I felt that if you would promise to marry him just as soon as he got out of the hospital and would go and visit him every day while he has to be there, that it might have quite an effect on him."

Marigold was aghast but she took thought with thanksgiving that evidently this woman did not know that she had been out with Laurie last night.

"No!" she said sharply. "I cannot do that. I do not love Laurie, and I know that even if I did, it would do no good for me to try to stop his drinking. A man does not stop drinking just for a girl! He needs some deeper urge than that. He needs God, and Laurie does not believe in God. He said so."

Marigold was holding her young head high and speaking earnestly. There was mingled pity and disgust in her eyes that gave her a look of wisdom beyond her years.

"Ah, but my dear, I haven't told you my proposition yet. You don't realize that I would make it fully worth your while. I would settle an ample allowance on you, *ir*regardless of how my son behaved, so that you would be practically independent."

"Stop!" said Marigold suddenly. "I don't want to hear you say another word! Mrs. Trescott, I am not for sale!"

"Now, don't flare up and be a foolish child! You know you will regret it by and by when you come to think it over. You don't realize that it will mean a small fortune. I would be willing to give you —"

But Marigold marched over to her.

"I wish you would please go away!" she said, her eyes flashing fire. "I don't ever want to hear another word about this. It is *disgusting!* You fill me with such shame and horror. If my father were alive he would demand an apology for what you have said. Now go, or I shall have to call someone to escort you out."

There was a tremble of almost rage in Marigold's young voice, and Mrs. Trescott looked up astonished.

"Why *dear me!*" she said lifting up her lorgnette and watching the girl fascinated. "They didn't tell me you had a temper! But it's really quite becoming! I'm sure you would be a social success if you would make up your mind to try it. You know we are immensely wealthy and you could have almost anything you want."

For answer Marigold whirled about and marched into her bedroom, locking the door audibly, dropping down on her knees beside her bed and sobbing silently.

The older woman thus left to herself, waited a minute or two, walked over and tried the door, called good-bye, then hesitating, added: "If you change your mind, just call me up. The offer still holds. Or even if you didn't want to consider marriage, if you would just come over to the hospital and try to influence him to give up drinking for a while, I would be willing to pay you well! You see Laurie blames me for being opposed to you, and I can't endure it! My dear angel child!"

She delivered this to the door panel, with a sob in the end of her words. It was always her last appeal, that sob. But when after duly waiting she got no reply, she turned and made her heavy way out of the room and down the stairs. Marigold, holding her breath to listen, could hear Mrs. Waterman's quick steps downstairs scuttling out of the way, and then could hear the front door close, and the limousine roll away from the street.

Suddenly the ridiculous side of it all came over her and she burst into mingled laughter and sobs, her tired nerves giving way in a healthy minute or two of hysterics.

But after that was passed she continued to kneel.

"Oh, God, my Father," she cried at last, "was I so headstrong and self-willed that You had to send me a terrible lesson like this to show me how far from Home I was getting? I see that I was. I know now that I have sinned, and I'm not worthy of all the care You have had to bring me back. Forgive and help me, dear Lord, and teach me not to seek my own way any more. Let my life be ordered as Thou wilt."

**18** After her telephone conversation with Marigold that morning Mrs. Brooke seemed more satisfied, though her sister noticed that she was more than usually quiet and thoughtful. Finally she spoke.

"You aren't quite at rest about Marigold, are you, dear?" she said at last.

Mrs. Brooke looked up thoughtfully.

"Yes, I'm at rest about her," she said slowly, "but somehow I keep on feeling that she needs me. I don't know why I should. I reason it away, and then the idea returns. If Elinor were back I think I should go home this morning, or perhaps not till this afternoon. I just feel as if I didn't want Marigold to be there another night alone. There! Now that's silly I know, but I'm telling you the truth."

Her sister smiled.

"Yes, I understand. Well, dear heart, you mustn't stay for me if you feel you ought to go! But make it this afternoon, anyway, Mary. You can get there before night if you go late this afternoon. Get there in time to take her out to dinner. Surprise her."

Mrs. Brooke pondered that.

"But I don't like to leave you alone. You

don't think perhaps Elinor and her husband might come tonight?"

"They might. They said they would telegraph as soon as they knew. But you needn't worry about a night or two more or less for me. I've my nurse here, and the servants. And it isn't as though we lived in the wilds. There are neighbors close at hand, and lots of friends. I'll be quite all right if you think you ought to go."

"Well, perhaps I am foolish. I don't *want* to go, Marian, you know that, for there will be no certainty when I can get back again once my vacation is over. But yet I can't settle down to feel right about leaving Marigold alone any longer. Perhaps, though, I could wait till noon and telephone her at the school. You see this is Friday and she might be planning something. I'd like to know just how things are with her."

Mrs. Brooke's brow was troubled, and her sister wore a sweetly concerned look also.

"What are you two ladies worrying about?" suddenly spoke Ethan Bevan appearing from the stairs.

"Oh, Ethan! Are you here?" they both exclaimed eagerly. "How did you get in without making any noise?"

"Stealth is my middle name," said Ethan solemnly. "It's the best thing I do. I make my living at it. I just ran away from my job for a few minutes to see how my family were getting along."

"Well, I was just wishing you would come in," said Mrs. Brooke. "In fact I had some thought of trying to call you up if I could find out your number without rousing my vigilant sister. Ethan, if I should go home this afternoon, could you come and stay with your aunt till Elinor gets home?"

Ethan studied her thoughtfully a minute.

"What's the idea, going home so soon?" he said. "I just felt it in my bones you were trying to slip away from us, and that's one of the reasons I ran over, to prevent it. I guess I could arrange to stay with Aunt Marian, if you *had* to go, but I'm here to try and persuade you differently. I just know Elinor and her husband will be disappointed to have you gone when they get back, and besides, there is your job. You'll be so much fresher for it if you stay a few more days and get a little rested. What's the idea, anyway?"

"She feels Marigold needs her," explained Aunt Marian. An instant gravity came over Ethan's face, and a reserve in his voice.

"That's different," he said gravely. "But *does* she? What makes you think so, Aunt Mary?"

"I don't know," confessed Mrs. Brooke. "I just feel so!"

"Well, then, something ought to be done about it," said Ethan determinedly. "But see here, why do *you* go? I have a better plan. Why don't *I* go up and get her? She wouldn't resent it, would she? She doesn't have any school till Monday, does she? I'd promise on my honor to bring her back with me, or die in the attempt, and there's always the telephone in case she balks. Besides, there are later trains on which you could go home if you had to."

"Oh, Ethan, that would be wonderful! But I couldn't think of making you all that trouble, and taking you away from your job," said Mrs. Brooke.

"*Could* you, Ethan?" beamed Aunt Marian.

"I *could* and I *will*," said Ethan. "You see, Aunt Mary, it's Friday with my job, too. That is, Saturday is only a half day, and I could make up a lost Friday easily on Saturday. Besides, I have to go up to Philadelphia again soon anyway. I would have to go next week at the latest and personally I'd prefer to go today, provided I could have good company back. That's a great inducement, you know."

"Well, I know Marigold would enjoy it, too," said Mrs. Brooke gratefully, and hoped in her heart that she was speaking the truth.

If Marigold didn't enjoy the company of a wonderful young man like this she ought to be spanked, she thought. "But I don't think we ought to let you do it," she added wistfully.

"But if he *has* to go anyway, Mary?" put in Mrs. Bevan.

"All I want to know is," said Ethan, "would it solve the situation? Or would you still feel uneasy, and as if you ought to have gone? Because in that case I'll stay with Aunt Marian and let you go."

"Yes, I think it would solve the situation," said Mrs. Brooke slowly. "I'd far rather have Marigold here this week than at home, and I don't see why she wouldn't jump at the chance. It would be wonderful for her and all of us."

"Wonderful for *me!*" said Aunt Marian softly.

"Then I'll go!" said Ethan getting up with determination. "I'll have to run back to the job for a while, but I'm free at noon or a little after. I'll stop at the house and see if you've any errands you want done at home, a clean apron or anything you want to send for."

"I could get Marigold on the telephone," said Mary Brooke meditatively. "Would you like me to, so she won't plan anything else?"

He considered that an instant and then shook his head.

"No, I think I'd rather appear on the scene unannounced. She wouldn't have so much chance to think up excuses. I'll go armed with authority and tell her I have orders to bring her back. Just let it go at that. I'll get in touch with you by phone if any situation arises in which I need backing."

Then with a grin he hurried away, and the two sisters settled back to enjoy the morning. Mary Brooke kept praying that her girl wouldn't have gone and got up some precious engagement with that Laurie that would make her refuse to come to Washington. What silly unwise creatures girls were sometimes; the Lord arranged nice plans for them, and they already had others of their own.

Then toward noon there came a telegram from Elinor. "Arrive home late Saturday night. Make Aunt Mary and Marigold stay over till next week. We want to see them."

"Now that makes it just perfect!" said Mrs. Bevan. "My girl and her husband will be here too before you leave, and I can't imagine anything nearer to heaven on this earth." There came a lilt in her voice that had not been there before. So the two went placidly to knitting and talking about old times. Ethan came back for a minute and went again, and the smiles on the two mothers' faces grew more radiant as the hours went slowly by, full of eager anticipation.

Even out in the kitchen there was a flutter of expectation. Delectable things were being manufactured for the next day's menu because Miss Marigold was coming back.

But secretly, as the evening drew on, Marigold's mother kept wondering, would Marigold elect to come? And supposing she didn't, how would Ethan feel about it? How could she ever apologize for her daughter's rudeness?

Oh, but she wouldn't let herself think that Marigold wouldn't come. She put the thought of the gay Laurie, and the plans he might have made to absorb Marigold, right out of her mind, and tried to trust it all to the Lord.

She had, however, secretly folded her garments, and got things pretty well packed in her suitcase, in case Ethan should telephone that he couldn't find Marigold and he was going to have to return without her.

Suddenly her sister spoke.

"He wouldn't!" she said, right out of a silence.

"What?" asked Mary Brooke, looking up astonished from counting stitches.

"He wouldn't come home without Marigold," said Marian Bevan, knitting away hard on the coat that she was making for Elinor. "Isn't that what you were thinking, dear?"

"Why, yes, something like that," faltered the other, "but how in the world did you know?"

"Oh, you had it written right out plainly across your forehead. You were thinking what if Ethan should come home without her. You were wondering what you would think next. But he won't. I know Ethan."

"Well, but suppose she isn't there? Suppose she's gone home with one of the teachers to supper, and hasn't left any word? I should have reminded her always to leave word with Mrs. Waterman. Ethan wouldn't find her if she hadn't left any word."

"Ethan *would* find her," said Mrs. Bevan calmly. "He's uncanny. He would find her or he wouldn't come back till he did. And what's more he would telephone before it was late enough for you to be anxious."

"Oh, of course," said Marigold's mother relaxing into a smile.

"I'll tell you what we will do, Mary," said her sister. "There's nobody near enough to hear. Let's sing! The servants are down in the kitchen, and the nurse is out. It can't hurt anybody, and there's nobody to laugh at us either. Let's sing all the old songs we used to sing when we were little girls washing the dishes. You take the alto as you always did, and I'll take the soprano. Let's begin on "When you and I were young, Maggie," and go on to "Silver threads among the gold," and "Juanita" and "Bide A 'Wee," and a lot of others.

Mary's eyes sparkled.

"Oh, and 'Little Brown Church in the Vale' too, and 'Where is now the merry party, I remember long ago?' I haven't thought of them in years. Yes, let's sing!"

So the two sweet old sisters began to sing. Their voices were still good, though higher and thinner, and with a quaver here and there, but they blended out in the dear old songs they had both loved, and in between each there were old memories to be trotted out.

"Do you remember, Marian, how Randall Silver came in that day while we were singing that, and asked for a piece of the chocolate cake Mother had just baked for the church supper that night? The new minister was to be installed, you know — and you *gave it to him?*"

"Yes, and how Betty Hemstead was

jealous and baked a cocoanut cake for him the very next day, and *left the baking powder out!*"

"Yes, and Ran said it reminded him of a pancake it was so thin," contributed Mary. "How long has Ran been dead, Marian? Almost thirty years, isn't it? Seems strange we never knew his wife. They said she was sweet. But Marian, what did Mother say when she found you'd cut her cake before she had a chance to send it down to the church? I don't remember."

"Why, she just went and made another," smiled Marian. "That was the deadliest punishment she could have given me. Mother, working away patiently, and frantically, to get that cake done, when I knew she was so tired she was ready to drop. I never did that again. Mother was sweet, you know."

And then there was a space of silence during which both sisters counted stitches assiduously, brushing away surreptitious tears now and again.

Presently they drifted into more songs. Sweet old hymns now, "Softly now the light of day," "Abide with me, fast falls the eventide," "How firm a foundation, ye saints of the Lord," and others, each bringing its set of memories, sweet and sad.

As they sang they glanced from time to time at the clock ticking away on the mantel, and smiled remembering that it was Ethan Bevan, and not Laurie Trescott, who had gone after Marigold, and that God was with Ethan Bevan. At least that was what Marigold's mother thought.

Though sometimes, again, she would go over quickly in her mind just how many things had to be put in her suitcase, and where she had placed her gloves and coat and hat and purse, in case it became suddenly necessary for her to take the train home that night.

Then Marian Bevan, watching her quietly, would start another song:

Children of the heavenly King,
As ye journey, sweetly sing;

It was a song their father used to love, and it brought back the picture of the family gathered at evening for family worship. They sang on through the well-remembered verses:

We are traveling home to God
In the way our fathers trod;
They are happy now, and we
Soon their happiness shall see.

How many years it had been since they had all sung that together, those two girls and their brothers and parents, all now gone on before them to the heavenly home, except one brother in the far west whom they hadn't seen for years. Their voices choked as they went on with the other verses:

Fear not, brethren; joyful stand
On the borders of your land;
Jesus Christ, your Father's Son,
Bids you undismayed go on.

"And now, Mary, I think you might go and turn on the porch light, don't you? They ought to be here in about fifteen minutes if they come on the same train you did."

19

In a quiet, sparsely settled, somewhat obscure suburb of Philadelphia, in a great massive stone building entirely surrounded by dense foliage, which was now heavily draped in snow, Laurie Trescott thrashed about on a luxurious bed and cursed his man nurse who was really his jailor.

He had tried all the arts and cajoleries he knew, and these were many, for this was not the first time he had been confined within stone walls for a brief period. No period of confinement however brief was to be tolerated, Laurie felt. He had offered bribes, varying in value according as his keeper grew stubborn, regardless of the fact that he was not at present in a position to pay even the smallest. But when it became evident that his parents' bribe was greater than he could exceed, he had gone on to promises, and cunning.

The man, however, into whose charge he had been put was a knowing man, and twice as big and strong as Laurie. He paid no more attention to all this than if Laurie had been a rabbit trying to cajole him.

Laurie had wearied himself by coaxing for liquor, and he was now in torment, as the effects of the liquor taken the last twenty-four hours began to wear off. He was desperate and frantic.

As he lay there thinking back over all he could remember of the time previous to his installment in this bed gradually a grudge evolved from the vagueness, a grudge against Marigold Brooke. He wasn't just sure how she became connected with it all, but little by little some of it came back. He had offered to marry Marigold and she had declined. She had deserted him at the altar, as it were. There was a little white house in the snow, and a minister. That was it. There had been a sign which said so. He was smoking a long black cigar, and he needed a haircut, but he had opened the door cordially and put out a flabby hand. Laurie had told him he wanted to get married, and had called to Marigold to come, and she didn't answer. He went out to get her, and she wasn't there. He didn't exactly remember what came next, only there was some snow connected with it, down his neck, and he couldn't find Marigold. Then he had jumped in his car and somebody ran into him and smashed things up. All Marigold's fault, and he'd like to get even with her. He thought hard about that, drawing his brows in a frown. He might get married to someone else. That was it. Show her she wasn't the only girl there was. That would teach her a good lesson. Next time she'd do as he said. Yes, that was it. He'd marry someone else. Now he knew where that minister lived he could go back. Minister wouldn't know whether he had the same girl or not. He would go and get Lily. Lily was a good sport. He remembered when she had lied once in school to keep the teacher from finding out who it was that put chewing gum all around the inside of her hat. Lily would go through with anything if she agreed to. Not that Mara had agreed. She never did any more. She was getting stubborn. But Lily always agreed to anything he asked. Lily would marry him quick enough. He would marry Lily and afterward he would call up Mara and tell her he was married and she had lost her chance to be a lady. *Then* she would be sorry.

The excitement of his plan kept him quiet for a few minutes and the attendant came near with medicine. That was dope to put him to sleep and he didn't mean to go to sleep, but he opened his mouth and took in the spoonful, keeping it carefully in his cheek as he turned over to his pillow and closed his eyes as if for slumber. It was an old trick he used to do when he was a child and they gave him medicine. He simply let it run softly out of the corner of his mouth into the pillow, and that was the end of it.

He lay very still after he had pretended to swallow the medicine. He knew it was almost time for the attendant's supper downstairs, and that he was anxious to have him go to sleep, so he breathed steadily, and tried to snore a little. He was coming into his own rapidly now. He began to think how he was to get out. He knew all the tricks of the place. This was the old side of the building and the windows were wooden frames, not steel sash. His room was in the end of the building, a large room on the second floor. There were no bars to the windows. It was the policy of the place to put the patients on their honor, but also to reinforce that honor by plenty of alert attendants. If one played good-boy and got trusted, it was possible to slip over a trick now and then. Laurie was good at tricks. Even when he was drunk he was canny. He had practised tricks on his mother long years now.

But there would be the matter of clothes! His clothes were locked up. He was sure of that. And they never left keys around, no chance of that. He was now in pajamas, pink and blue flannelette. They hadn't let him have his silk ones. In fact he hadn't been himself when they brought him here, so the attendants had had their way with him. Well, he would have to scout around and see what was available, but he would go, even if he had to go in pink and blue plaid pajamas.

He remembered he had a suit down at the tailor's being pressed. Maybe more than one, he couldn't be sure. He could get an overcoat at Neddie the tailor's too. And there were several places he could borrow money if he once got out. He cocked one eye open toward the window and measured possibilities by the trees. That would be the window that faced toward the garages. There might be a car, or cars, out there. Once in a car he could make it to the tailor's without detection, and after that all would be clear sailing.

The attendant was sitting very still over by the other window reading the paper. He held it so that it didn't even crackle. He was very anxious for Laurie to go to sleep.

Laurie attacked the problem of getting out, his mind getting more and more keen.

Those windows over there. He could take several layers of blanket and press hard and they would break without much noise, supposing they were screwed in and immovable. Then he could surely break out the mullions with his whole strength, leaning against a mullion at a time. But stay! Why not the hall, openly? His experience had been that if one were bold enough he could usually get away with anything. If only that fellow would go to his supper. There! There was the signal bell!

He lay very still and when the attendant tiptoed over to look at him he was apparently sleeping, sodden, dead, the kind of sleep the drunkard sleeps when he is coming out of a spree. Laurie knew perfectly how to simulate it.

At last the man opened the door softly and went out. Laurie listened intently. He heard the rubber footsteps going down the hall, heard the man speak to another attendant. Then silence. There seemed to be no one along the hall. There were footsteps in the hall below, going toward the nurses' dining room. There was a faint tinkle of glass and silver. Now. He must work fast!

He flung the bedclothes from him and peered about the room carefully, discovering his shoes in the corner over near the closet door. He stepped into them. No socks. That was immaterial.

A search of the closet brought only a long brown flannel bath-robe to view. That would do nicely in lieu of his own garments. He stepped to the door and opened it cautiously. There did not seem to be anybody about. They were a trusting lot, after all, these jailors of his. But nobody would think anything if they saw him in such informal array walking in the hall.

He closed the door silently, and stalked boldly down the hall. From the bathroom window he reconnoitered. Yes, there was a car parked right down at the foot of the fire escape. If he could but get to it he was safe.

If he had stopped to consider he might have been too late, but he usually acted quickly. Besides, he was crazed and desperate for a drink, and this was the only way to get it.

A moment more and he was out on the fire escape, backing down rapidly, crouching, so that he would not be noticeable. His arm in its sling hurt, but he did not stop. This was going to be hard on his ankle too, but what was a little thing like an ankle when one was going to get a drink?

The last length of the fire escape was strung up from the ground, and he had to swing by his good arm and drop. The pain in his ankle was fierce for a minute and turned him sick, but he rose from the snow bank where he had fallen, and with a stealthy look around crept over to the little roadster that was parked so near, and crawled within. He closed the door so quietly that it could not be heard in the house.

Yes, the key was in the car, and there was gas.

Boldly he backed the car out and sent it leaping down the road. Now, a minute more and he was safe!

The cold air cleared his brain, and the excitement brought the color to his pale cheeks. He did not know what a sight he was, but the car hid him well from view. He must go to the tailor's first. He threaded his way through the city which he knew so well, avoiding traffic lights and well known traffic cops who might take him in.

Neddie the tailor was a kindly obsequious little man who had pulled Laurie out of more than one scrape. Presently Laurie drew up in front of his modest establishment and blew his horn furiously. Neddie hastened out, recognizing the call that Laurie gave, and the wave of his hand. Laurie hadn't any idea what a grotesque figure he presented, but Neddie didn't bat an eye. Laurie always paid well, and eccentric young gentlemen were not to be questioned. If they chose to travel the avenue in pink and blue pajamas with brown frog-fastened bathrobes and their hair standing on end, it was none of his business. He hastened out.

"Yes, Mr. Trescott, what can I do for you?"

"Why, you see Neddie, I'm in a jam! Had an accident and lost my clothes. Got any o' my suits here?"

"Yes sir. I think so. A brown suit."

"That's it. Got an overcoat you can sell me? Something somewhere near my size? No, I don't care what color. Okay! Well, just let me come in and change, will you?"

The accommodating Neddie opened the door for the startling customer, and the pink and blue legs hurtled across the pavement into his shop. But it was in the neighborhood of the university dormitories. Any queer thing might happen around there and be only a bit of harmless hazing, today's freak orders to the freshmen.

Laurie vanished into a convenient cubby where he had often changed his garments in the past, and presently came forth arrayed in his own suit.

"Better comb your hair," suggested Neddie, presenting him with a comb.

"Oh, that's all right," said Laurie indifferently, but he ran the comb through his crisp waves. Then Neddie helped him arrange the cheap shoddy overcoat over his arm that was in a sling, loaned him ten dollars he demanded, and he marched forth, a free man. Neddie knew he would lose nothing in the long run.

Laurie abandoned his appropriated car, and hailed a taxi. He knew he could find Lily in half an hour at the factory when the day shift came out from work. But he must have a drink first. He stopped at one of his haunts, and after a few drinks he came out and took another taxi. It was awkward not having his own car. He wondered what had become of it.

He had no trouble in locating Lily who hopped into the taxi proudly and rode away with him.

"We're going ta get married, Lily, see?" he said, with uncertain eyes looking sleepily into hers.

"Oh yeah?" said the girl with a grin.

"Tha's right, Lily. We're going ta get married right away. Got any money, Lily? Because I'm in a jam. Had an accident and got my car smashed up."

"Where we going ta get married?" asked Lily sharply sitting up and looking at him keenly.

"Oh, down in M'ryland, a place where it's easy. But we'll havta go in a train. My car's gone somewhere for repairsh."

Laurie's speech was getting thick and his eyes dreamier every minute.

"Oh, I know something better than that," said Lily with a cunning look in her impish eyes. "I gotta friend'll take us down an' we can pay him afterwards. He'd do for a witness too! He's real accommodatin'."

"Okay! Thash so! We havta have a witnesh! Didn't think of that before."

Laurie stood uncertainly outside Lily's house while she arranged with the friend to take them down in a rattly old Ford. He shivered as he waited. The cheap overcoat was thin, and he had no socks on. But what did that matter? He was getting married in a little while to Lily. Lily was a good scout. She always did what you wanted her to. And then he was going to call up Mara and get it back on her for running off. He was going to tell her what a "mishtake" she had made. His thoughts were getting very much muddled now.

Lily put him in the back seat of the old car, and let him sleep. She sat in front with the driver and conversed with him affably. He was an old man and seemed to be somewhat related to her. Laurie found out afterward that he was her uncle. Laurie told him indefinitely where to go. But he said he knew, he'd been there before, and after a very bumpy monotonous drive they finally arrived at the white house from which Marigold had fled only about twenty-four hours before.

When they came out, less than a half hour later, Laurie looked at her dazed.

"What we going to do now, Lily?" he said drunkenly. "Lesh go shomewhere and get a drink!"

"No!" said Lily sharply. "You're married now and you aren't going to drink any more. I'm not going to have a drunken husband. I'm going to be a *lady!*"

"Shure!" said Laurie, appreciatively. "You're going to be a lady! But every lady drinksh a little. We'll go get a drink ta shelebrate!"

"No!" said Lily, "we're going home!"

"You don't shay!" said Laurie looking at her stupidly. "Going ta your house? I've never been there."

"No," said Lily calmly, "we're going to yours. I've been there once, but I'm going now to stay!"

"You're going ta my housh?" said Laurie tottering on his uncertain feet, and looking at her as if it were something he couldn't quite comprehend. "But they won't let you in. They won't like it."

"Well, I'm going there all righty, and they're going ta like it this time, too. Get in, Laurie."

"But aren't we going ta get a drink?"

"No, you've had enough drinks. I want a sober husband. Here, I'll get in the back seat with you and you can put your head down on my shoulder and go to sleep. You gotta get sober before we get home."

"Okay!" said Laurie, settling down with a sigh against the convenient shoulder. "I guesh mebbe you're right."

20 Marigold had washed her face and removed the traces of tears, and she was quietly, soberly putting the kitchen in order that her hurried breakfast had left in wild confusion, when she heard the knock at her door. Her heart contracted sickly and for an instant she contemplated not answering it. Then she reflected that it was probably the paper boy come for his money, and she hurriedly picked up her purse, and went to answer the knock.

But it was not the paper boy.

An elegantly attired, carefully groomed woman of uncertain age stood before her. The very shoes she wore showed that she gave great attention to her appearance.

She was dressed in a smart suit of wool in a flattering shade of wine color, a close hat and a trim coat of the same color as her gown. It was trimmed heavily with what Marigold at once recognized as an expensive grade of Persian lamb. There was a flash of some bright jewels at her throat.

Marigold had never seen her before. She gave a startled glance at her face and noticed her expression of deep discontent. Yet there was something wistful, too, about her.

"You are Marigold Brooke, aren't you?"

said the visitor, and her voice marked her at once as belonging to a social class of wealth and culture.

"Why, yes," said Marigold, astonished, for she thought the woman had surely made a mistake in the address.

"Well, may I come in just a minute? I won't keep you long. There is something I feel I ought to tell you."

Of course she must ask her in. She could not have Mrs. Waterman listening to everything that was said. Marigold could hear the door across the hall slam as she closed her own door. Mrs. Waterman was having a hard time satisfying her curiosity this afternoon.

"I am Miss Trescott, Laurie's aunt," said the caller sitting down on the edge of the couch as if she didn't mean to stay but a minute.

Marigold gave her another startled look.

"I came to tell you that you mustn't marry Laurie on any account! He's my own nephew and of course I love him, but he's nothing but a trifler, and he drinks like a fish. Three times this last year he's been in a sanitarium to get cured, and every time he comes out he goes right back to it. There wouldn't be anything but sorrow if you married Laurie."

"But I have no intention of marrying Laurie!" said Marigold, her face deadly white and her eyes wide with honor. "Oh, why did *any*body think I was going to marry him, when we just went out occasionally together? But I've found out he drinks, and I'm done going out with him. I — we — I don't want ever to see him again!"

"Oh, I'm so relieved!" said Irene Trescott, sinking back on the couch. "You haven't any idea how I hated to come and tell you this. But I just couldn't bear to see you hurt, you're so — so — kind of lovely and sweet, and so different from most girls nowadays. You're much too good for Laurie. He would break your heart and spoil your life. I had to warn you."

"Oh," said Marigold humbly, "I'm just a silly girl. I wasn't thinking about getting married. Laurie was nice and pleasant. I never realized that he drank. I might have tried to stop him if I had known. I don't think I've ever been very helpful to him or anyone else. You see, I was just having a good time. I wasn't considering getting married. I really wasn't!"

"You're rather wonderful," said the older woman. "I've been watching you for some time!"

"Why, I don't think I ever saw you before!" said Marigold, wide-eyed.

"No, I don't suppose you did. But I saw you, out of windows, and once in a while in a shop. Eva Petrie has spoken of you too, and once I saw you in the other room with Betty Lou when you didn't even know I was there. I was interested because I knew Laurie knew you. I wish Laurie had been the kind of boy who could have had you for his best friend. For a while I hoped that knowing you would make a difference in him, and maybe he would turn out to be worthy of a girl like you after all. But lately he's been simply awful, and I thought I had to come and warn you. I couldn't have you hurt. But now since you know, I won't trouble you any more. I know young people hate to have older people nosing into their affairs. But I'm glad you aren't heartbroken. Laurie is fatally attractive, of course."

"Yes, he is," said Marigold sadly.

"You're sure he hasn't broken your heart? You're sure he won't be coming around and persuading you to try him again? Because you mustn't trust him! You really can't! He's undependable, and irresponsible. He'll love you today, and another girl tomorrow, and he'll promise not to drink, and go at it again the next minute. I'm grieved over it, but it's true."

"I know!" said Marigold quietly, calmness coming to her now like a mantle, "I've seen him with other girls. I've seen him — recently — when he had been drinking."

She lifted brave eyes and looked at her caller.

"And that's why you've given him up?"

"Why, I don't know that I ever actually counted him mine before that to give up. But after that I knew he never *could* be mine."

"And you're not going around long-faced and heartbroken? You're not feeling terribly bad about it?"

"Yes, I feel badly. I feel shocked and sorrowful that Laurie was like that, and not the delightful friend I had counted him, but — well — lately — just lately, I've come to know the Lord Jesus better, and He's given me something deeper in my life. It's made all other things quite pale beside Him."

Marigold gave her testimony slowly, deliberately, with a hint of triumph in the lifting of her head, and a radiance in her face. Irene Trescott looked at her with a great yearning in her own eyes.

"There!" she said suddenly. "You *have* got something that other people don't have! I've thought that for some time. I wish Laurie could have it. He might have been worthy of you. I wish *I* could have it!"

"Oh, you *can!*" said Marigold, with sudden yearning to help this other soul. "I wish I had known more about it when I was seeing Laurie often. I wish I had told him about it. But I don't think I'll be seeing him any more. You see, I haven't known all this so very long myself, not in this beautiful, personal way."

"Well, I wish you'd tell me about it sometime. I need something, goodness knows! I'm terribly unhappy, and I haven't even the consolation of drink. I've seen too much of the effects of it in other lives to take that way to drown my sorrows. But I'm bored to death, and I want something. If I come to you again sometime will you tell me about what you have? Not now, for I've a dinner engagement tonight and I must be going. And next week I'm going south for a while, but when I get back, may I come and have a talk with you?"

"Oh, yes," said Marigold, suddenly shy, "I'll be so glad if I can help you."

Irene Trescott looked at her earnestly for a moment, and then suddenly stooped over and kissed her.

"You're sweet!" she said. "Good-bye. I'll come and see you when I get back."

As she turned to go to the door Marigold put out her hand.

"But you don't have to wait till you get back," she said. "You can go to Him tonight, and tell Him all about it, and He'll take you. He's the Son of God, and He died to take your place, shed His blood to pay the penalty of your sins, and it only takes believing that to make you His. If you just kneel down tonight and tell Him you will, it can all be settled."

Irene Trescott studied the earnest face of the girl for a moment, and then she said: "Well, I'll see! Perhaps I will."

Then she was gone.

21 Marigold stood there stirred, wondering, thrilled to think she had been able to tell another soul how to be saved, filled with awe at the joy it gave her.

Presently she went slowly back to the kitchen and began to put away the dishes she had washed, pondering on the strange happenings that had come to her during this week, though it seemed far more than a week, when she thought of all that had happened. It almost seemed as if she had lived a lifetime in those few short days. She gave a little shiver as she remembered where she was last night at this time. Weary, she was now, so weary and heartsick over all that experience! And yet in just one day she seemed to have come so far away from it! Laurie was put out of her life as definitely and finally as if she had never known him!

Then it came over her how very tired and sleepy she was, how much she wanted to rest, and not think any more about it. As soon as she had eaten something she would go right to bed and get rested. She would not think at all about *anything*, just ask God to take care of her, and go to sleep.

But while she was getting a piece of toast

and a cup of tea made, it suddenly came over her how strange it was that she should have had these two callers in one afternoon. Both relatives of Laurie's, and one asking her, *begging* her to marry Laurie, and the other warning her not to. She put back her head and laughed at the irony of it all. And then she put down her head on her arms and shed a tear or two! Till the toast began to burn, and then she put aside her thoughts and tried to eat something.

She had only taken one bite, however, when there came another knock on the door, and this time a heavier one, not a woman's knock.

She laid down the toast and gave a frightened look out into the living room. Who had come now? Not any more of Laurie's relatives surely. Not his father! "Oh God! Help me! I'm so tired, and I'm *all alone!*"

For an instant she meditated on keeping still and not going to the door. She just could not stand any more that night. Then the knock was repeated, a little more insistently, and it occurred to her that maybe it was somebody from the library come to ask after her mother.

She went wearily over to the door, hoping it might be just the milkman for his money. She was so tired, and hungry.

She took a deep breath of a sigh, braced herself for whatever might be waiting for her, and putting out her hand opened the door.

For an instant she couldn't believe her eyes, for there stood Ethan Bevan! Then the joy came sweeping down upon her, and she put out her hands, both hands, and her eyes gave him welcome, even more than she knew.

"Ethan!" she said gladly. "Oh, Ethan! I've needed you so much!"

Suddenly, without the slightest warning, Ethan's arms went round her, and he gathered her close to his breast.

"I love you, my little dear love," murmured Ethan, bending down to lay his face on hers.

And Marigold came into his arms like a homing bird and rested, feeling such joy as she never knew was on earth.

Suddenly the bliss of the moment was rudely broken by the sound of eager footsteps hastening toward the door of the room across the hall.

"Oh, quick! Shut the door!" giggled Marigold, lifting her rosy face from Ethan's nice tweed overcoat. "She thinks she has to oversee everything."

But Ethan had already reached out one

hand and closed the door behind him, and now gathered Marigold into his arms again, and laid his lips upon hers.

"My darling!" he murmured. "My darling Marigold!" and Marigold felt that there could be no sweeter words on earth than those.

Now Ethan Bevan had by no means come to Philadelphia with any such denouement in view. All the way up as he sat in the train he had been calling himself a fool for having come. Marigold might not want him, might put on her aloofness that she had worn that first day in Washington when she obviously resented his presence, might have some engagement, and he might be bringing about a very embarrassing situation.

Who was he, anyway, but a stranger? They had had a few pleasant talks, and he had been able to help her to understand some truths from the Bible, for which he was thankful, but he must not presume upon that!

He remembered the letter that had lain between them on the chair as they knelt to pray. That letter had troubled him a lot, ever since he went back to Washington, till he had to pray about it and ask the Lord to take it out of his mind. Marigold had a friend, whether wisely or not, a person who had been something to her, more or less, presumably more, and he, Ethan, should play no part in her life.

There might have been a break between them, it was true, but he had promised to pray for him — that had been rather understood between them he was sure, though the man had not been mentioned openly. Still, the woman across the hall had called him "your young man," and she had said that he took Marigold out often in his car. Ethan had been trying all the week to teach his heart not to give that sick thud whenever he thought of that remark. He had been trying to pray for the unknown young man as one whom Christ loved, and who might also be beloved by this girl. Yet all the while Marigold's face had come dancing before his vision with the wistful look in her eyes, or with the gay happy look when she had been enjoying something with him in Washington. And now and again, fight against it as he would, he kept remembering the thrill of her in his arms as he carried her down those stairs in the Capitol, and felt her frightened face against his shoulder. He remembered the touch of her tears on his hand as he wiped them away at the foot of the stairs.

He had prided himself on keeping away from all women, on concentrating on his job and letting the world go by, on taking his joy in giving the gospel here and there where souls seemed to need it. And now here, after all his resolutions, he had fallen for a girl who belonged to someone else — or so it seemed — and he was just going to make a fool of himself like any other fool. Traipsing off to get her! Making an excuse to spend a few hours with her on the train, just because his soul had been hungering for a sight of her all this week!

So he had reasoned with himself, told himself that he must be very distant and reserved with her. Treat her like a younger sister, help her as a Christian brother! And not for anything in the world, not under *any* circumstances, let her suspect for an instant that he had the slightest interest in herself, apart from her salvation and her Christian growth.

Having read himself a set of very severe rules for a young man calling upon a girl who was practically engaged to somebody else, and having trembled in his soul as he drew nearer to her home, and braced himself with commands like the laws of the Medes and Persians, to guard his soul, he had marched up those stairs, and — taken her right in his arms before even the door was closed! A fine gentleman he was! And he didn't *care!* He was happier than he had ever been in his life. And before he said anything about it, or even questioned his soul, he bent above his dear Marigold and kissed her long and sweetly, and thrilled to her lips as he had thrilled to the thought of her dear self all day, whenever he couldn't keep himself from thinking of her.

But after a little she drooped from the weariness of her joy, drooped in his arms, and looked up with such a beatific smile, that his heart was strengthened to speak plainly.

"I didn't know," he said, "whether you belonged to someone else or not. I told myself that I must wait and see, that I must not let you know my heart till I found out. And here I have walked in and taken you by storm! Can you forgive me? For oh, I do love you!"

Marigold looked up and forgot all the weariness and perplexity of the hours that had gone before, and smiled her joy into his face and heart.

"And I love you!" she said softly. "I think," said Marigold — and thought she spoke the sacred truth — "I think that I have loved you ever since I looked into your eyes!"

"You certainly didn't look it!" said Ethan suddenly, and kissed her again. "I'm afraid you are a dear little liar, with it all, for I could swear you did anything but love me that first day you spent in Washington."

"Well, maybe I didn't know it yet," twinkled Marigold, "but in my heart I'm sure I did, because I feel as if I had been at home with you always."

"You dear!"

Then startlingly the little clock on the mantel chimed six, and simultaneously the two absorbed lovers realized that the room was full of the odor of burnt toast, and had been for sometime, only they hadn't noticed it till now.

Marigold switched off the toaster, and Ethan suddenly remembered why he had come up to Philadelphia.

"Is that all the dinner you were getting for yourself?" he asked. "Is that why your cheeks looked pale and thin when I came in? They don't look so now, I'll admit, but I'm afraid you haven't been taking very good care of yourself. Do you know what I came up here for, young lady?"

"I thought perhaps you came to tell me that you loved me," said Marigold in a very small shy voice.

"Well, yes, that's why I *wanted* to come, but ostensibly I came to take you back to Washington, and we're starting in half an hour. Can you get ready that soon, or shall I have to take you without being ready?"

"Oh, Ethan! Really! How wonderful! But — why, I'll have to get supper for us first."

"We'll eat on the train. That's what I'd planned, only I didn't take into account how you were going to come and take me right into your heart with a look, you precious! Swallow that tea, and then go and get your hat on. Because I don't want to keep the two mothers waiting too long. They're expecting us. What do you have to take along? Can't I pack it? Just a toothbrush and that green dress perhaps. I like that."

"Oh!" said Marigold laughing breathlessly, and then rushed into action.

"Oh, you don't need to wash the dishes," said Ethan, "I'll fix this kitchen to leave. You go get ready. Don't you know I've cooked at camp?"

He held the cup and plate under the spigot, and mopped them with a towel that hung on the rack. He disconnected the toaster, turned out the gas stove, put the bread into the bread box, and fastened the windows.

"There," he called to Marigold who was wildly flinging a few necessaries into her suitcase, and folding the green dress and the brown ensemble in a scandalous hurry,

"I've fixed everything to leave! We'll let the lady across the hall do the rest."

Gloves, purse, hairbrush — Marigold was thinking over the absolute necessities, too happy to care whether she had them all or not.

Ethan telephoned for a taxi, while Marigold rushed over to tap at Mrs. Waterman's door.

"Oh, Mrs. Waterman," she said eagerly, "Mother has sent a friend to bring me down to Washington again for the week end. I'm leaving right away. Would you mind telling the milkman and the bread man I shan't need any till Monday? And — what's that? The telephone? Oh, no, you needn't bother to answer it. There won't be anything important, I'm sure. Just let it ring!"

Then suddenly the telephone rang out as if it would protest.

Marigold rushed back to answer it.

"Hello! Who? Oh, Miss Trescott! Yes?"

"I just thought I ought to tell you before you read it in the papers," said Irene Trescott earnestly, "Laurie escaped from the sanitarium this afternoon and went out and got married to that girl, that Lily Trevor, and he's bringing her home. Or rather she's bringing him home. She just telephoned and said he was pretty drunk, but they were married, and she'd see he was all right in a few days if they would just be patient till she got him in hand. I thought you ought to know. Good-bye. And, oh, Marigold! I hope your God will *bless you!*"

"The taxi is here, Marigold," called Ethan from down in the hall.

"Coming!" said Marigold happily, her voice like a sweet song as she hastily locked the door and flew down the stairs.

**22** Oh the bliss of that brief ride to the station in the quiet darkness of the taxi. Ethan's arm stealing about her and drawing her a little closer to him; her hand in Ethan's while the lights of the city flashed by, leaving no terror in her heart; Ethan's love about her like a garment. She felt almost crowned. They sat in sweet silence and let their gladness have its way in their hearts.

In the train at last, Ethan caring for her.

"We're going right into the diner," he said as he surrendered his coat to the porter of the Pullman, and tossed his hat into the rack above their chairs. "You ought to have some dinner right away. I seem to feel that you're all in." He smiled tenderly down at her.

"Not any more!" said Marigold giving him a bright glance.

People were coming into the car now, chattering about which chairs were theirs. Marigold felt proud of her escort. It seemed so wonderful that this was to be her lot now, a companion like this for her lifetime, and not just for a single hour or two. Oh, God had been good to her!

"I like that hat!" said Ethan as he sat opposite her in the diner presently, and looked across the table admiringly. "And that pretty red dress. And the fur coat. They all suit you wonderfully."

"It's a very old coat, and quite shabby," said Marigold looking down at it ruefully. "But I didn't dare come without it, this cold weather."

"It doesn't look shabby. It looks homey, as if it belonged. When it wears out I shall get you another just like it. It is wonderful on you, makes you look like a princess. It's going to be great to have someone to buy pretty things for."

"Oh!" said Marigold, pink-cheeked and shining-eyed at the preciousness of his words.

"Tomorrow," he said irrelevantly, "we're going to get the prettiest ring they have in Washington!" and then grinned at the sweet confusion of her face.

Such a happy meal, Ethan ordering almost everything on the menu, and insisting on her eating. Such joy! And only last night — !

Ethan saw the shadow cross her eyes.

"You're not sorry?" he asked anxiously.

"Oh, no!" she said fervently with such a look in her eyes that he was satisfied. "I was only thinking of some dreadful things that I've escaped," and she gave a little shiver at the thought. "There are a great many things I have to tell you. I've been having a pretty hard time since I went home — !"

"Well, we'll talk them over tomorrow and get them out of the way. But don't let's spoil tonight with any shadow. You are tired. Just forget all the hard things and be happy. We'll work everything out together, after this, shall we?"

"That will be wonderful!" said Marigold. "Oh, God has been so good to me! You don't realize — !"

"Don't I? Well, perhaps you'd better let me tell you how good I think He has been to me. You don't know how hard I worked on the way up here, trying to get you out of my thoughts, because I thought there was someone else ahead of me."

"I'd better tel you all about it right away," said Marigold with sudden resolve. "Then you'll know there's nothing to worry about."

"All right, if you feel you'd like to get it out of the way. But personally, since you've told me you love me, I'm trusting you all the way, and I'm not worrying about it any more. If any other poor fish tries to barge in I'll take him out and whale him. But eat your supper first."

So when they went back to the Pullman

Ethan turned their chairs so they could talk together quietly without being overheard, and Marigold told the story of her acquaintance with Laurie Trescott. But she found it to be astonishingly short after all, for the things she had thought important seemed all too trivial to waste many words upon when Ethan was so near, looking so strong and dependable. So when she reached the account of her last night and her terrible ride, she found it did not take long. Ethan watching her quietly, caught more of the picture from the little shudder she gave as she described her terror, and from the sudden darkening of her eyes, than from the words she used. He had no trouble in filling in where she left description unfinished. He could see just what kind of a weak attractive selfish creature Laurie was.

"Now I *know* I will whale that fellow sometime!" he ejaculated as she finished. "*Really* whale him, I mean!" he vehemently.

"I don't believe you need to," said Marigold thoughtfully. "He's married a terrible little creature. Married while he was drunk! I expect life will give him all the whaling he needs now. That was what that telephone message was about just as we left the apartment. Didn't I tell you? That's why I was so long coming down. Miss Trescott phoned me. She thought I ought to know before it came out in the papers."

"Who is Miss Trescott, and what did she know about it?"

"Oh," said Marigold laughing, "that is another story. I haven't told you about my two callers yet, and why I was so long opening the door for you. I was afraid you would be another member of the family come to plead with me."

Then she told him the whole story, and he listened, a big grin growing slowly on his nice understanding face.

"So that's what I walked in on, is it?" he said when she had finished. And then he threw his head back and laughed so heartily that some of the bored passengers at the other end of the car looked over the tops of their evening papers and wondered what those two good-looking young people had found to laugh at that was so funny; looked enviously at them when they saw the joy in their faces, and thought of their own youth, and bright spots that had relieved the tedium of the way.

"Well, now that's out of the way," said Ethan, when they had laughed together over the two callers. "I still think I'll whale him sometime, though I might try to help him get saved, too. He certainly needs saving, and I guess you've got a commission toward that aunt of his too, sometime. I'm glad you got in a word about the Way before she left. You might not get another chance, you know, and she was ready for it then. You may never know the result in this life, but perhaps she'll meet you over There! And now, I guess we're getting into the city. Shall I help you on with your coat?"

And there was the dome of the dear old Capitol looming on the night sky. But now it was no longer simply the seat of her country's government, but it stood also for the memory of a great love that had come to her there!

Marigold watched it for a minute with shining eyes. Then Ethan put her into her old fur coat and buttoned it up to her chin, giving her a loving smile and a little surreptitious pat on her shoulder, utterly unaware of the eyes at the other end of the car watching the pretty romance in their two faces.

"I think I hear a taxi," said Aunt Marian suddenly. "Did you turn the porch light on?"

"Yes. It's on."

"Shall I go down and open the door?" asked Marigold's mother eagerly.

"No, Ethan has a key."

So they sat quite still knitting and dropping stitches irresponsibly, as if nothing out of the ordinary was about to happen, and it seemed that the next three minutes were unconscionably long.

Then came Ethan's glad voice booming up the stairs: "I brought her, folks! I told you I would!"

Something in his voice perhaps, kept them very quiet, waiting for them to come.

They came slowly up the stairs, his arm about her, and their hands clasped, and came into the room that way, standing in the doorway, looking from one to the other.

"Well, Mothers, we've discovered that we love one another," said Ethan with exultant voice. "Do you mind?"

The anti-climax came the next week when Maggie arrived one day for work lugging a big pasteboard box.

"My girl, Viola May is gonta be mah'ied next week," she announced with radiant face, "an' I done brang her weddin' dress along ta show you-all."

"It's sompin' grand," she said as she untied the box. "We couldn't 'a bought it ourselves noways. One o' their comp'ny up ta the Trescott house, gib it to me fer takin' home her laundry ta wash. She was a mighty

378

hateful piece herself, awful high-an'-mighty, but I gotta gib her credit fer bein' real generous oncet. She said this dress was wuth a heap mor'n the wuk I done fer huh, but she didn't want the dress no more nohow. You see she'd spilled some kinda wine all down the front brength. But I tuk yella soap an' a piece of an ole' turkey towel, and I jes' nat'chally washed it out. Ain't nuthin' like yella soap an' water ta get stains outen things, an' it don't show no more, only hes' a dear lil bit, but I'se figgerin' ta take a stitch ur two on them red floaters on the girdle an' ketch 'em down over the spot, so Viola May can get mah'ied in it. An' den it 'curred ta me, Miss Mar'gole, you-all cud do dem stitches so much better'n I cud! Wud you mind? I'd stay an hour extra an' clean that there bookcase in the livin' room if you wud. See! Ain't it purty? Jes' like some heab'nly robe! I neveh did see such a purty dress. Nebber thought my chile wud be mah'ied in a dress like dat!"

Maggie unfolded the dress and shook it out. Marigold's grand white dress with the scarlet sash! Poor crumpled dress, its velvet streamers limp and dejected, its grandeur draggled and stained and dingy with one night's gaiety!

As Marigold bent over it to put in the few

stitches Maggie asked, her heart was murmuring:

"Father, I thank You that You didn't let me keep this dress!"